The boss wanted to see her.

Rachel scrutinized the message slip. As far as she knew, she'd done nothing to deserve a pat on the back or a blistering tongue-lashing, but she wouldn't be sure until she'd seen Russell Powell.

She looked through the open door. Her boss—tall, gray-haired and elegant—stood near a massive desk. Another man stood nearby, also tall, also elegant. As Rachel watched, he swept his unbuttoned jacket back and rested his hand on one lean hip, exposing a shoulder holster. Guns were nothing new to Rachel; most of the people who worked for Powell Investigations carried them. Her gaze skipped over it and moved upward.

She stared for a moment; then her breathing quickened, and she took an involuntary step forward. The man's head was turned away from her, and all she could see was thick black hair, but he reminded her . . .

Then the man turned, presenting Rachel with a perfect profile. She gasped and swiftly, without thought, moved away from the door.

Gabriel. After all these years.

Dear Reader,

When two people fall in love, the world is suddenly new and exciting, and it's that same excitement we bring to you in Silhouette Intimate Moments. These are stories with scope and grandeur. The characters lead lives we all dream of, and everything they do reflects the wonder of being in love.

Longer and more sensuous than most romances, Silhouette Intimate Moments novels take you away from everyday life and let you share the magic of love. Adventure, glamour, drama, even suspense—these are the passwords that let you into a world where love has a power beyond the ordinary, where the best authors in the field today create stories of love and commitment that will stay with you always.

In coming months look for novels by your favorite authors: Kathleen Creighton, Heather Graham Pozzessere, Nora Roberts and Marilyn Pappano, to name just a few. And whenever you buy books, look for all the Silhouette Intimate Moments, love stories *for* today's woman *by* today's woman.

Leslie J. Wainger
Senior Editor
Silhouette Books

Marilyn Pappano
Something of Heaven

Silhouette Intimate Moments

Published by Silhouette Books New York

America's Publisher of Contemporary Romance

SILHOUETTE BOOKS
300 East 42nd St., New York, N.Y. 10017

Copyright © 1989 by Marilyn Pappano

ISBN: 0-373-07294-5

First Silhouette Books printing July 1989

Printed in the U.S.A.

Books by Marilyn Pappano

Silhouette Intimate Moments

Within Reach #182
The Lights of Home #214
Guilt by Association #233
Cody Daniels' Return #258
Room at the Inn #268
Something of Heaven #294

MARILYN PAPPANO

has been writing as long as she can remember, just for the fun of it, but recently she decided to take her life-long hobby seriously. She was encouraging a friend to write a romance novel and ended up writing one herself. It was accepted, and she plans to continue as an author for a long time. When she's not involved in writing, she enjoys camping, quilting, sewing and, most of all, reading. Not surprisingly, her favorite books are romance novels.

Her husband is in the Navy, and in the course of her marriage she has moved all over the U.S. Currently she lives in South Carolina with her husband and son.

For Barbara, Cathy, Laura and Vee.

For their encouragement,
their support and, most of all,
their friendship.

Prologue

Jack Thomas was dead.

Gabriel stared out the glass door into the quiet night, but instead of the city lights, he saw his friend's body, motionless on the cold pavement. Lifeless. Dead.

He shuddered, and his fingers tightened around the bottle he held. A glass wasn't enough. He intended to get stinking drunk tonight and to stay that way until the images went away. Drunk enough to forget what he had seen. Drunk enough to forget the rage and the grief and the sickness inside him. He had been a cop for six years, and he had seen plenty of dead bodies, but none of them, not even the first, had affected him this way. None of them had made him feel so desperately ill. But none of them had been Jack.

He took a long drink of whiskey and shuddered again. His apartment was dark, quiet and cold. So cold. He huddled deeper into his leather jacket and took another drink, but he didn't turn the heat on. The only warmth he wanted would come from the bottle, liquid and golden and powerful. It would make him forget if he drank enough of it. For just a little while it would let him forget.

When the doorbell rang, he ignored it and drank again. He knew who it was, knew when he didn't answer that she would let herself in with the key he'd given her, knew she had come to ask for...what? Support? Warmth? Forgiveness? He gave a shake of his head. It didn't matter. She wouldn't find any of that here.

The bell echoed through the apartment again; then, as he had known she would, she used the spare key to unlock the door. The feeble rays from the porch light that he'd left burning reached into the dark room, showing her the light switch inside the door. As she was reaching for it, he spoke without turning around. "Don't."

His voice was hard and raspy. Hers was soft and quavery. "All right." She closed the door behind her and waited until her eyes adjusted to the darkness; then she crossed the room to stand at the opposite side of the sliding glass door.

She didn't take off her coat, he noticed as he lifted the bottle to his lips once more. Because she felt the cold? Or because she knew she wasn't welcome to stay?

"I—" Rachel cleared her throat and took a deep breath, but it didn't steady her voice any. "I'm sorry, Gabriel."

After another long, burning swallow, he lifted the bottle and critically studied it. It was half-empty, a good start. Its warmth was starting to spread through his body, but it wasn't making him warm.

Once he had thought *she* could do that. He had thought she could make him happy, could make him forget all the unpleasantness in his life. For the first time in seven years, since Jenna had left him, he had believed he could love again. He had thought he loved *her*. Now she had ruined any chance of that. She had killed his love, as surely as she had killed Jack.

Rachel hugged her arms to her chest. Her uniform jacket was stained with blood—Jack's blood, she thought, or maybe her own. She had been cut by the shattering windshield—nothing serious, but there had been a lot of blood. Jack had bled a lot, too, a dark, sticky pool that had drained out with his life.

A sob caught in her throat when she breathed in deeply. She shouldn't have come here, but she had thought Gabriel might not want to be alone. Jack had been his training officer seven years ago and his friend ever since, the closest thing to a father he'd ever known. He had been a good man, a good cop, but one careless moment had cost him his life. Now others were paying—his wife, his children and their families, and Gabriel.

She took a tentative step forward, then another. When he didn't react, she raised one trembling hand to his face, but before she touched him, his free hand shot up, catching hers in a brutal grip, twisting it down and back until her wrist threatened to snap.

"Why'd you let them do it?" he asked, his voice growing stronger and more violent with each word. "Why didn't you help him? They didn't assign you a partner to keep you from getting bored on your shift! You were supposed to help him, to cover him! *Why the hell did you let them kill him?*"

She could have freed her hand, but his ugly accusations left her too numb to feel the pain. He couldn't mean what he was saying, she reasoned. He was drunk. He was grieving. He had to blame somebody, and the men who had killed Jack were dead. Only she lived. But reason didn't stop the emptiness spreading through her, and it wouldn't stop the pain that would soon follow. "Gabriel..."

He tensed at the sound of her whisper; then, disgusted by the contact with her, he released her with a shove. He drained the bottle with one deep, eye-watering swallow and let it fall to the floor with an empty thud. Once more he stared outside. The image of Jack was still there, but it was fuzzier this time, making it harder to see that he was dead. "You shouldn't be here."

"I—I'll go...."

He shook his head slowly. She didn't understand. "You should be with Jack. You have no right to live when you let them kill him. You should be dead, too."

Pain, sharp-edged and vicious, started in her belly and spread outward, erasing the numbness, filling the empti-

ness. He meant it. He wanted her dead. Last night he had
held her and made love to her through the night, and now
he despised her. He wished she had died, too. Slowly, stiffly,
she backed away from him. "I came here because I thought
you might need me. Because I needed you." Her voice broke
then with the first tears, and he turned to look at her.

He was empty inside, and still frozen cold, but he could
see her anguish, could hear it in her voice. But it couldn't
touch him. Thanks to the whiskey, even the horror and the
grief were fading a little.

"My partner was killed tonight, Gabriel. *I* killed two men
tonight."

"Three."

Rachel didn't feel her tears even when the salt burned the
cuts on her cheek. "You bastard," she whispered. "You told
me I could count on you. You told me you would be here if
I ever needed you. You told me—" So many things. About
dreams, about hopes, about happiness and a future and
love. "You lied, Gabriel. Damn you, you lied!"

He heard the spare key hit the coffee table; then the front
door slammed. The room echoed with the sudden silence.
He stood motionless for a moment, then sighed softly. There
was another bottle of whiskey on the table, one he had
picked up on his last trip to Tijuana. By the time he finished it, he'd be in fine shape. He wouldn't be feeling any
pain, or anything else, and that was exactly what he wanted.

Chapter 1

I'm going to have a baby.

His hands jammed into the pockets of his jacket, Gabriel Rodriguez stared at the night sky. He'd heard those words before, a long time ago. Same words, different circumstances. Then the child had been his. This time his best friend was the father. His best friend was the lucky one.

He sighed softly, wistfully. How long had it been since he'd thought about his baby, about Jenna and the child they had created together? Once he had managed to shut them out of his mind completely, by giving his love and his heart to someone else, but when he'd lost her on that awful night five years ago, the other losses had come back, too. But for the last year, he had been free. He had forced the memories away, all of them. And now they were back, in his mind and in his heart, because Shelley Morgan was going to have a baby.

Christopher sat down in the closest chair and watched Gabriel watch the sky. "Does it bother you?" he asked at last.

Gabriel tried to focus on one dim, distant star while he considered his answer. Did it bother him that Christopher was going to be a father, while *he* would never know *his* child? Did it bother him that Christopher would see his baby's life begin, would know his love, would watch him grow and learn and live, while Gabriel had been denied those things? He wished he could deny it and mean it, but it would be a lie, and he had never lied to Christopher. Yes, it bothered him. For the first time in his life he was jealous of Christopher—incredibly, intensely jealous. It was an ugly, destructive emotion, and he hated it, but it was there all the same.

He didn't mind the money. Christopher had always been rich, while Gabriel had always just gotten by. He didn't mind Christopher's highly respected reputation as a businessman with the Midas touch, either. Gabriel loved his job with the San Diego Police Department, even if the hours were long and the pay could be better.

No, he only envied the important things in Christopher's life. His wife. Their love. And now their baby. Those were the things he wanted. A woman to love—one who loved him—and a child. The precious things.

"I was going to tell you alone," Christopher said, "so you could get used to the idea but Shelley wanted to tell you herself. She doesn't know about..."

About Jenna. About the baby. Had it been a boy or a girl? Gabriel didn't know. In fact, he didn't know if the child even existed, or if Jenna had ended the pregnancy the way she wanted to. He didn't know anything except that the ache was back. The need to know. The longing. It had taken years to put it to rest, and now one simple announcement had brought it back.

I'm going to have a baby.

He looked at Christopher and smiled, knowing his friend would understand if he wasn't wholly convincing. "I'm happy for you—really. This kid couldn't ask for better parents." And he meant it. In spite of the sorrow, the loss, the envy, he really meant it.

"I wish things had worked out differently for you." Christopher's words came softly, hesitantly. This was still a private part of Gabriel's life, one he'd kept secret even from his best friend until eighteen months ago. He didn't want to offend him or cause any unnecessary pain.

Gabriel put a lot of effort into a casual shrug. "It was a long time ago. I'm over Jenna, and I've accepted that I'll never know about the baby."

"Why?"

Satisfied that he'd given the appropriate responses, Gabriel had looked away, but now his head jerked back around. Had he heard Christopher's response correctly? "What?"

Christopher met his friend's dark, angry gaze without flinching. "Remember when Gary died and I hid away up here?"

Gabriel didn't need anything to jog his memory. When Christopher's brother had died in jail after being arrested for espionage, it had almost destroyed Christopher's life. He had taken refuge in this house, never seeing or talking to anyone except Gabriel—until Shelley.

"You encouraged me to do something about it—to find the man who had gotten Gary to spy for him, to prove that I was innocent. You showed me how. Without you I never could have done it, and I never could have married Shelley with that hanging over my head." Christopher shrugged. "You helped me find Charles Miller. Why don't you try to find your child?"

Gabriel's protest was automatic, his reason one he knew well. "It's been twelve years."

"So?"

"She could have gone anywhere. She could have changed her name. She could even be dead." Those excuses were familiar, too. He had repeated them to himself on the occasions when the longing had grown too strong, when the need to know if he had a son or a daughter or any child at all had threatened to overwhelm him.

"Or she could be living somewhere nearby, raising your child. The point is, Gabriel, you won't know until you try." Christopher paused, and his voice softened. "Has it gotten any easier?"

Gabriel raised his head to stare up at the heavens again. The distant city lights cloaked the night sky with a silvery-white glow, hiding all but the brightest stars. Yes, it had gotten easier, but only because he ignored the past, because he shut Jenna and their baby out of his mind and pretended that they didn't exist. But when he thought of them, when he acknowledged that he was a *father*... "No," he admitted sullenly. It hurt as much right now to know that he had a child out there—a child he had never seen, had never held—as it had twelve years ago. "Look, I don't have the time to conduct the kind of search you're talking about."

"So hire someone to do it for you."

The irony of the other man's suggestion brought a brief grin to Gabriel's face—a lieutenant in the Detective Division of the San Diego Police Department hiring a private detective to find someone he couldn't find himself. His friends in the department would get a good laugh if they found out....

He shook his head. He wasn't seriously considering this, was he? He, better than anyone else, knew all the reasons why such a search was out of the question. No, he was just humoring Christopher until his friend decided to drop the subject. "Do you have any idea how much something like that would cost?"

Christopher shrugged carelessly. "I'll help you with it." He knew he could offer his best friend money without offending him. He also knew that Gabriel wouldn't accept it.

"What if I found her and she admitted that she'd had an abortion?" Tension made his tone defensive. Apprehension made it edgy.

"Wouldn't that be better than not knowing?" Christopher asked gently. "Than spending the rest of your life wondering?"

Gabriel made an impatient gesture. "The odds of finding someone who disappeared twelve years ago are one in a million."

"There are birth records, driver's licenses, school records, credit records, employment records. You simply cannot disappear without a trace in this country. Shelley proved that by finding me."

As if on cue, Shelley came out of the house, stopping near both men. She looked from her husband to Gabriel, both solemn and silent, then said with only the hint of an Alabama drawl in her voice, "If I'm interrupting something here, I can go back inside."

Gabriel caught her hand and tugged her gently into his embrace. "Congratulations, sweetheart," he murmured, hugging her close. "When is the baby due?"

She laid her hand on her flat belly and smiled the happiest smile he'd ever seen. "Seven more months."

"Do you want a boy or a girl?"

"A boy," she replied thoughtfully. "As handsome as Christopher." Then the smile returned. "Then a girl as smart as me." She left his arms and went to her husband, snuggling against him on the chaise.

"Shelley's doing a series of articles for the *Chronicle* on private detectives," Christopher announced, gliding his fingers over her hair.

Wearing a grim expression, Gabriel sat down on the nearest chair. "How convenient." He should have known Christopher wouldn't enter any discussion unprepared.

"Private investigators," she said with a grin. "Ever since that TV show, most of them want to be called that."

"Met anyone interesting?"

She ignored his faintly mocking tone. "You know, it's nothing at all like they show on television. Most of them just do routine things—background checks, divorce cases, finding people. No shoot-outs, no life-or-death rescues."

"You sound disappointed." It was easy to tease Shelley with her small-town, Southern upbringing, but his teasing was always heavily laced with affection, even love. "If you want action and adventure, you ought to do an article on cops."

"And how many shoot-outs have *you* been involved in?"

Gabriel's grin faded. He'd drawn his gun before, but he'd never had to shoot anyone. He didn't know too many cops who had . . . except Rachel.

For just an instant he let pictures of her fill his mind—in the khaki department uniform, in vividly colored street clothes . . . in nothing at all. Then he squeezed his eyes shut and rubbed them with the heels of his hands. It seemed that this was his night for bad memories, for heartaches better left forgotten. For sorrow and sadness and guilt.

When he opened his eyes again, both Shelley and Christopher were watching him. She was bewildered by his behavior, he could see, although, without knowing why, Christopher seemed to understand. "None," he answered at last. "I've never shot anyone, or even been shot at. I've been lucky." But Rachel hadn't been so lucky. She'd had to go through the trauma of seeing her partner die, of facing death herself, of killing those two men, and she had gone through it alone, because *he* had been too selfish, too angry and hurt, to help her.

He pushed her out of his mind, back into the dark, seldom-visited corner that allowed him to live with himself . . . that allowed him to live without *her*. She was his past. Jenna and the baby were also part of the past. He'd be a fool to try to bring any of them into the present. Still, he asked the question. "If you were going to hire someone, who would it be?"

"A woman," Shelley answered without hesitation.

"That figures." She was a champion of every woman's right to do any job she was capable of doing. Although he shared her sentiments, he often liked to argue the point with her for the simple pleasure of arguing. Tonight there was no pleasure. "Any woman in particular?"

She rose from the chair with a pleased smile. "I'll get you a list of my personal favorites."

When she was gone, Gabriel looked sourly at Christopher. "This doesn't mean I've changed my mind."

His friend merely smiled and didn't say a word.

Shelley returned with a worn manila folder and drew out a single sheet of paper. "These are the ones I liked best. I'm going to try to talk my editor into a separate story on them—you know, women making it in a male-dominated field."

Gabriel accepted the paper, skimming the list in the dim light coming through the door. He'd heard of the agencies, but none of the names meant anything to him—until he got to the last one: Rachel Martinez.

He didn't know if the slight breeze caused the paper to flutter, or if it was the trembling of his hands. Quickly he laid the paper on his lap and locked his fingers together to hide their involuntary movement.

It was logical. When a good cop left the department, he often stayed in enforcement or investigations—another local department, a federal agency, private security or private investigations. And Rachel had been a damned good cop—too good to take any job that didn't fully utilize her talents. He should have considered it before.

But he had been beyond considering anything when it came to Rachel. There had been only the pain, the sorrow, the regret, the loss. If he had allowed himself to consider what had become of her since her leaving San Diego five years ago, the guilt would have destroyed him.

"Tell me about Rachel Martinez." It wasn't an easy request to make. It was the first time he'd spoken her name aloud in years, the first time he'd allowed himself to ask about her.

Shelley checked her notes first. "She works for Powell Investigations, one of the biggest firms in Southern California. She moved here from Los Angeles a little over three months ago, where she had worked for another firm. She's very bright, very cautious, very precise in her work. Powell thinks a lot of her. So do I."

So did he, Gabriel thought ruefully. He'd thought a hell of a lot of her five years ago...but that hadn't stopped him from losing her. It hadn't stopped him from trying to destroy her.

Shelley scanned the typed notes again. "It says here that she was once a San Diego cop. Did you know her then?"

His response was guarded and blunt. "Yeah." Like Jenna, Rachel was another of his secrets. An affair, a relationship—a love, his subconscious whispered—that not even Christopher had known about.

"Is this just curiosity, or are you thinking about hiring a private investigator?" she asked cautiously. Gabriel's job with the police department had made him adept at asking questions, but she knew from experience, when she had been trying to locate Christopher almost two years ago, that he didn't at all like answering them.

He looked at Christopher, his gaze as steady and unyielding as his friend's, then back at Shelley, and shrugged. "I don't know." It sounded like a brush-off, but it was the truth. He honestly didn't know what he was going to do about anything—Jenna, their child and, least of all, Rachel.

Brushing her black hair over her shoulder, Rachel Martinez scrutinized the slip of paper the secretary had handed her only moments earlier. The message was clear, telling her everything and nothing. The boss wanted to see her.

She exhaled softly, aware of Elaine's eyes on her. The secretary knew as well as Rachel did that a summons to Russell Powell's office meant one of only two things: a pat on the back for a job done extraordinarily well, or a blistering tongue-lashing that could very well result in the loss of a job. As far as she knew, she'd done nothing to deserve either, but she wouldn't know for sure until she'd seen Powell.

"When did this come in?"

Elaine glanced at the log she kept next to the phone. "A few minutes ago. Three-thirteen, to be precise."

Rachel smiled vaguely at the inside joke. Russell Powell demanded two things of his employees: that they show results, and that they be *precise*. Nothing less would do. "If they call again, tell them that I'm on my way up."

Elaine offered a reassuring smile. "You're doing a fine job, Rachel. Don't worry."

She chose the stairs instead of the elevator—for the exercise, she told herself. To delay seeing her boss, honesty admitted. She had worked for Russell Powell for three months now and had never been called to his office—had never even actually met the man. She had been hired by Quint Masters, Powell's right-hand man, and received her assignments from and reported her progress to another of the senior investigators.

At the door leading to the fifth floor, she paused and touched a hand to her hair. Briefly she regretted wearing it down today. Usually it was confined to a severe and very businesslike chignon, but just once she had wanted to appear a little more feminine. There was nothing wrong with that, she consoled herself. She had simply chosen the wrong day.

The door opened onto a broad corridor. The first offices belonged to the older investigators, the ones with seniority. At the end was a large reception area and, beyond that, Powell's office. The receptionist, a pretty young woman named Susan, greeted her with a smile. "He'll be ready for you in a minute, Miss Martinez. Have a seat."

Rachel returned the smile, but shook her head at the invitation to sit down. How could she sit and relax when her job might be on the line? Instead she wandered around the room, studying the paintings on the wall, touching her finger to a leaf on an ivy so healthy that it looked fake, absorbing the richness of the furnishings around her.

When the door of Powell's private office opened, Rachel turned, expecting to be called. No command came, though. It was just Mrs. Shandley, Powell's personal secretary. She had been with him from the beginning and guarded him as fiercely as a mother lion guarded her cubs. Balancing a silver tray that held an antique coffee service, she stood in the open doorway for a moment, listening to her boss.

Rachel's glance flickered over the woman and into the office behind. Russell Powell, tall, gray-haired, as elegant as his surroundings, stood near a massive Chippendale desk. Another man stood nearby, also tall, also elegant. As Rachel watched, he swept his unbuttoned jacket back and rested his hand on one lean hip, exposing the leather of a shoulder holster. Guns were nothing new to Rachel; most of the people who worked for Powell Investigations, including herself, carried one. Her gaze disinterestedly skipped over it and moved upward.

She stared for a moment; then her breathing quickened and she took an involuntary step forward. The man's head was turned away from her, and all she could see was thick, black hair, but he reminded her...

There came the sound of laughter, and the man with Powell turned, presenting Rachel with a perfect profile. She gasped and, swiftly, without thought, moved away from the door.

"Are you all right?" Susan asked in concern.

Rachel shook her head, unable to form words. Mrs. Shandley closed the office door and walked past, sending a disapproving look at her obvious loss of control. "I—I'll be right back, okay?" she whispered. Before the woman could answer, Rachel was on her way down the hall.

Don't run. It took all her effort to make her legs obey when an equally strong part of her mind was warning her to run like hell. She reached the ladies' room near the elevator, closed the door behind her with a click and leaned against it. It took a moment to control her breathing, another to still the trembling that had made her legs weak.

When the initial shock had lessened, she moved from the door to the mirror across the room. No wonder the receptionist had questioned her, she thought. Her darkly tanned skin was pale, drained of blood, and her eyes were wide. She looked as if she had seen a ghost—and felt worse.

What was he doing here? Why had he come? How was he connected to this unexpected command for her presence?

The frightened face in the mirror had no answers for her. Only Gabriel could tell her.

The pain came swiftly, slicing through her, and she hugged her arms to her belly to contain it. Dear God, she had prayed that she would never see him again! Hadn't she paid enough? Hadn't she suffered enough? She had lost her partner, her job, her lover. Wasn't that enough?

A soft knock sounded; then the door swung open. It was Susan, young, sweet, concerned. "Miss Martinez? Are you all right? Can I get you anything?"

A new life, she thought miserably. Or, better yet, a new past. One with better memories, less pain. But that was impossible. No one could give her that. She herself had already tried.

Slowly she straightened. "No, thanks. I'm all right."

The girl came closer, letting the door swing shut. "I told Mr. Powell that you'd been called back to your office for an important call, that you would be back as soon as you finished."

"Thank you. I appreciate it." She managed a smile for the girl to support the words.

"It's that man, isn't it?"

"What man?"

"The one in Mr. Powell's office. The policeman." Susan looked even more worried. "Are you in trouble, Miss Martinez?" she asked in a startled whisper.

Rachel's laughter, edged with nervousness, sounded almost normal. "No, Susan, I don't think so. At least, not *that* kind of trouble." She looked in the mirror again, brushing her fingers through her hair. It didn't do any good. The heavy black waves settled in the same careless, abandoned way. "Well . . . do I look normal enough to face the boss?"

"You look fine," Susan assured her. "I'll go back and tell him you're here."

"Thanks." Rachel took one last glance before following the younger woman out. She moved naturally, with a confidence she didn't feel, pausing only briefly outside Powell's door before she knocked, then stepped inside. "You wanted to see me, sir?"

Gabriel was standing near the wall, a tall blur in her peripheral vision. He was watching her, had wanted to see her before she saw him. She smiled faintly. He didn't know that she had already seen him, that she'd had a few minutes to prepare. He had lost the element of surprise.

"Yes, Rachel, come in," Powell invited. Taking her arm, he guided her toward the center of the office. The man had no qualms about using her first name or touching her, even though they were virtual strangers, she noticed with well-hidden distaste. If they'd been alone, she would have politely moved away. But they weren't alone. Gabriel was here.

He remained where he was for a moment, letting his dark eyes move over her. God, she was beautiful, with wild, blue-black hair and big, solemn brown eyes and a full mouth that couldn't stop being sensuous even when held, like now, in a grim straight line. She had once had a smile that could melt the coldest heart, but there was no evidence of it now. She looked as if she'd forgotten how to smile.

The questions rushed in. How did she feel about seeing him? How had she handled the last five years? Had she come to terms with Jack's death, with his own betrayal, and gotten on with her life? Had she dated, made any friends, taken a lover, done any of the normal things that people did? Had she quit hating him? He didn't find any answers in the blank expression that she wore so naturally.

There were other answers, though, truths that Gabriel found within himself. For five years he had refused to think about her, to remember her. He had ignored the emptiness that losing her had created, had ignored the cold, dark, aching place that she had once filled. He had pretended that he no longer wanted her, no longer needed her, that he no longer cared for her. And they were all lies. He knew that now as he looked at her. All lies.

Ignoring the tension in the room, Powell gestured for Gabriel to come closer. "Lieutenant, this is the woman we talked about, Rachel Martinez. Rachel, this is Lieutenant Gabriel Rodriguez, of the San Diego Police Department."

Gabriel wouldn't have offered his hand if Powell hadn't expected it. Rachel wouldn't have accepted it except for the same reason. The contact was minimal, lasting only seconds, but it was too long for her, not nearly long enough for him. She slid her fingers across his, then stepped back, away from him *and* Powell.

"Lieutenant Rodriguez has a case for us, and he's asked to work with you," Powell said, sounding as if she'd been paid a great compliment. "Now, I have a meeting in fifteen minutes, so I'm going to turn this completely over to you, Rachel. The lieutenant will give you the information you need to get started. Of course you'll give this your fullest attention."

She heard the subtle warning in her boss's voice. Gabriel was a cop, and cops could make business difficult for a detective agency, so treat him well. Make him happy. She almost smiled at the thought. *Almost.* "Of course, Mr. Powell," she replied, her voice unnaturally calm. "Would you like to come to my office with me, Lieutenant?" To her private office, where she could tell him to go to hell. Where she could convince him that the last thing in the world he wanted was *her* working for him.

Gabriel started to agree. He wanted to see the room where she worked, where she spent her days and, according to her boss, a good deal of her evenings, too. But before he could speak, Powell answered for him.

"Nonsense, Rachel. You can conduct the interview right here." Circling the desk, he picked up his briefcase. "If you need anything, don't hesitate to call Mary. Lieutenant, glad to meet you. If I can do anything . . ."

Gabriel shook his head. "Thanks, Russell. I'll keep that in mind."

When the door closed behind Powell, Rachel moved to sit in his big leather chair behind the desk. She leaned back, her fingers laced loosely together, and waited for Gabriel to speak.

He pushed his hands into his pockets as he turned to face her. "Is Mary the drill sergeant with the coffee?"

Rachel nodded.

"She keeps things under tight control, doesn't she?"

She nodded again.

He raised one hand to tug at the black tie he wore, an obvious sign of discomfort. He *should* be uncomfortable, she thought with satisfaction. He deserved it for thinking he could use her boss to walk so easily back into her life.

There was a rich leather chair in front of the desk. He decided to sit in it; otherwise, he'd spend the entire interview pacing. When he was settled, he opened his conversation with a compliment. "Your boss thinks a great deal of you."

She countered it calmly, unemotionally. "My boss has never laid eyes on me before today."

"Just because he doesn't often get involved, don't think that he doesn't know what goes on downstairs. Russell Powell is a very shrewd man."

"Is that why you chose his agency?"

For the first time since she'd entered the room, Gabriel smiled. She was acting so cool and unaffected, but the question gave her away. She wanted to know, wanted to hear him say, that he was here because of her. He denied her that small ego boost. "Powell Investigations has a very good reputation. That's what I need." *One* of the things he needed. Rachel was another.

She reached for the lined yellow pad and the pen that Powell had left on the desk. "What do you want us to do for you, Lieutenant?"

She was using his title deliberately, to distance herself from him. He knew that because he knew her. First names carried with them an intimacy, and she didn't want any sort of intimacy between them. She was overlooking the fact that they had once shared the greatest intimacy of all, and, for now, he let her.

"You could start by using my name."

"I don't think Mr. Powell would approve," she said stiffly.

His smile was lazy, arrogant and confident, his voice soft, seductive, dangerous. "Mr. Powell wants you to be nice to me. It's not hard, Rachel. You used to say it. Gabriel. Like the angel."

The angel with the devil's smile. The angel who had showed her heaven, then condemned her to hell. She put the pen down and folded her hands over the pad. "What do you want, Lieutenant?"

He knew how to fight, both fair and dirty. He knew when to push and when to back off. Now was the time to retreat. "I want you to find someone."

"Isn't that one of the Department's specialties—missing persons?"

"This isn't Department business. It's personal."

"What's her name?"

He smiled again, that wicked smile, and made her shiver. "What makes you think it's a woman?"

"Isn't it?" She'd met him nine years ago, her first week on the job, and his reputation with women—his sheer affection for them—had already been legend in the Department. He *liked* women, all women, and they liked him. She seemed to be the only exception to that. He had used her, but he had never cared for her, and she despised him too much to ever like him again.

"Yes. Her name is Jenna White."

She wrote that down, telling herself that it meant nothing to her. She didn't care that the man she had once loved more than life itself had come to her to find another woman. Her love for Gabriel was dead, had died as painfully and violently as Jack Thomas had. She could never love him, never trust him, never need him, never forgive him. But, if she had to, she could work for him. "Who is she?"

Gabriel grew serious. This was the part of his plan that he hadn't been able to work out in his mind. How could he explain one former lover to another? How could he tell one woman he'd loved about the other woman he'd loved? "She was…a girlfriend." It was an awkward word for a man his age, too immature to describe the relationship he and Jenna had shared, but it would do. It would, regrettably, tell Rachel what she needed to know.

Her expression was grim, her mouth bracketed with tiny tension lines. She understood, all right. "And why do you want to find her?" Because he loved her? Because he wanted her? Because he felt all the things for her that he'd never felt for Rachel?

It didn't matter, she silently chanted. Gabriel didn't matter. Nothing mattered except the present. Today. Right now.

He looked away from her. If telling her about Jenna had been difficult, telling her about the baby was going to be near impossible. It somehow seemed wrong—a betrayal of a relationship that had ended five years ago, a relationship that hadn't even begun until long after the affair with Jenna had ended.

But it was his reason for being here. She needed to know. She had a right to know.

"When Jenna left San Diego, she was four months pregnant," he said flatly. "I want to know what happened to my baby."

Rachel sat silent for a long time. Gabriel was a father. It wasn't an easy piece of information to accept. There was something so stable about fatherhood. So settled. Gabriel was a charmer who would never settle down. One woman would never be enough for him.

She had known another man who had never settled down, another man for whom one woman had never been enough. Another man who had fathered a child and taken a belated interest in it. The results of that situation prompted her next question. "What else do you want to know?"

He raised his head, unflinchingly meeting her eyes. "I want to know if I have a son or a daughter. I want to know what the child's name is. If he's healthy. If he's happy. If he needs anything."

"Do you intend to be a part of his life? To come in, at this late date, and announce that you're his father?"

He sensed the disapproval in her voice but misunderstood the cause. "It was a long time ago, Rachel. Before I met you."

The gentleness in his voice made her gesture impatient. "Leave me out of this. I'm only here to work. Do you intend to be a father to this child?"

"I can't answer that. I suppose it would depend on whether or not he needed a father."

It was the best answer he could give. It didn't fully satisfy Rachel, but she accepted it for now and returned to his earlier statement. "How long is 'a long time'?"

"Twelve years."

"You want me to find someone who left town twelve years ago." She sighed softly. "Where did she go?"

"I don't know."

"Where was she from?"

"I don't know."

"What kind of work does she do?"

He shrugged. "If you'll give me a minute, I'll tell you everything I *do* know about her. Her name is Jenna Elise White. She's thirty-seven, maybe thirty-eight. She was a student at San Diego State at the time. Her major was education. Her birth date is in March. She's five foot five, blond, blue-eyed. Pretty."

"And she was pregnant the last time you saw her."

He nodded once. "With my baby."

Rachel scribbled her last note, then looked up. "That's not much to go on, especially after twelve years."

"If it were easy, Rachel, I'd do it myself."

"Why don't you do it yourself anyway? With your connections in the Department, you could do basically the same things I'll do, and it wouldn't cost you a penny."

"I told you, this is personal. I don't want anything 'official' about this investigation."

She could understand that. If word got out at work that he was looking for the child he'd fathered, it might cramp his style with the female officers who occupied him after hours. "Why did you decide to do this now?"

He could give her several reasons: Shelley's pregnancy. Christopher's impending fatherhood. His desire for a child. The desire to see her. Some she wouldn't understand. The others she wouldn't believe. "I don't know."

Rachel leaned back in the chair. If she was going to handle this search, there were many more questions she needed to ask, but not now. Now she needed to be alone, to deal with the surprises the day had dropped on her: Gabriel, Jenna and his baby. *Their* baby, she corrected. "I'll talk to Mr. Powell and see if he wants to accept this case—"

Gabriel interrupted. "He's already accepted it."

She breathed deeply, seeking a tighter grasp on her control. "What you're asking us to do may very well be impossible. In that event, it would be unfair of us to take the case."

"That really isn't your decision to make, is it? Powell's the boss, and I'm the client. If I want to throw away my money on a hopeless case, that's my business."

She pushed the chair back and stood up. "I'll talk to Mr. Powell," she repeated stubbornly, "and one of us will get in touch with you when a final decision has been made." Picking up the legal pad, she walked to the door and opened it, waiting pointedly for him to leave.

Gabriel stopped in front of her, close enough to smell the faint fragrance of her perfume, to see the rise and fall of her breasts beneath the silk blouse she wore. "I'll look forward to hearing from you, Rachel," he said with a soft smile.

From *her*, not Powell. He was so damned sure of himself, she thought with frustration. It came from a lifetime of always getting what he wanted. Then she thought about Jenna and their baby. Well . . . almost always.

When Russell Powell returned from his appointment, Rachel was waiting. He glanced briefly at her, then turned his attention to the mail Mrs. Shandley had left on his desk. "How did the meeting with Rodriguez go?"

Gone was the hearty, warm friend and back was the man who couldn't be bothered to meet his new employees personally. She wasn't surprised. "I'd like to talk to you about it." It wasn't usual to discuss cases with the boss, but it wasn't usual to receive assignments from him, either.

"What about it?"

"I don't think we should take this case."

She couldn't have said anything that would get his attention more quickly. Laying the mail aside, he raised his narrowed gaze to her. "Why not?"

"The person he's looking for left town twelve years ago, and he has virtually no information about her. Such a search is going to take hundreds of hours and will probably yield nothing."

"You used to be a cop, didn't you?"

She nodded.

"Then you know who Gabriel Rodriguez is. Right now he's a lieutenant in the Homicide Division, but word is that he's being groomed for bigger and better things. Do you understand what I mean?"

"Yes, sir," she answered, her voice subdued. "I understand." She wasn't surprised. No matter what his deficiencies in other areas were—as a man or a human being— Gabriel was the best cop she'd ever known.

"Now, do you really want to tell a man like that that you don't want to handle his case?"

Rachel felt her control slipping again. Gabriel had, in his own arrogant way, warned her what Powell's response would be. She should have accepted his word for it and gone about her business, but she'd had to try. She still had to. "Do you really want to take money from a man like that when the chances of successfully completing his case are infinitesimal?"

Powell's posture was rigid, his expression dark and angry. "Gabriel Rodriguez can throw his money in the San Diego Bay for all I care. He wants a service performed, and, by God, Martinez, you're going to perform it, or I'll fire you so fast that it'll make your head spin. Is that clear?"

She swallowed hard, forcing back the anger, the pure outrage, that was so strong she could taste it. "Yes, Mr. Powell. It's perfectly clear. Excuse me."

By the time she reached her office on the third floor, the anger was boiling. She passed the secretary's desk, ignoring her curious look, went to her tiny private office down the hall and slammed the door behind her. A moment later she emerged, her briefcase in hand.

"Rachel?"

She walked past Elaine to the elevator, punched the button, then returned to the desk. "I'm going home."

Expecting the worst, Elaine asked meekly, "Will you be back?"

Rachel squeezed the bridge of her nose, and her thunderous scowl faded. "First thing Monday morning."

"Thank heavens. I was really starting to worry. Did everything go all right in the meeting with the boss?"

"As all right as could be expected, under the circumstances." The ding of the waiting elevator saved her from making an explanation. "I'll see you Monday, Elaine. Have a good weekend."

Home, for Rachel, was a small stuccoed house outside Lakeside, away from the hustle and the busyness of the city. She unlocked the door, shut off the alarm system, put her briefcase down and headed for the bedroom. Changing clothes was her first priority. It was always a relief to trade the stylishly tailored suits that Powell required in the office for a pair of loose-fitting shorts and a T-shirt, to discard the lingerie and stockings and heels and spend the rest of the evening barefooted and casual.

As soon as she had changed, she settled on the sofa, the television turned on to a low murmur. The house was quiet, with no one else around to disturb the peace. There had been a time when she had needed peace, had craved it, prayed for it, had feared that she would never find it. It had taken months to work through the grief and the guilt of Jack's death, months longer to deal with the heartache and the sorrow, but she had succeeded. She was a whole person again, doing the things a normal person did, feeling the emotions a normal person felt. She was in control of her life again.

But seeing Gabriel today had shaken that control, had threatened that peace. He had breathed new life into the memories that she had struggled for so long to bury. He had made her relive the trauma, had made her feel the pain again, as sharp and deadly as it had been five years ago. She had been wrong to think that she could take his case. If he still had such power over her, how could she possibly consider working for him?

The answer was very simple: she couldn't. She couldn't believe in him, depend on him. She couldn't trust him, and, most of all, she couldn't forgive him. Before he had the chance to destroy her again, she would quit her job, sell her house, move away, start over. It was called survival. She'd done it before. She could do it again.

It was called running away.

Rachel shook her head in protest. There was nothing wrong with wanting to protect herself from the past, from Gabriel. There was nothing wrong with wanting to avoid further pain. She had suffered enough. It was someone else's turn this time.

But there was something very wrong with letting him control her that way. Something very weak.

Did she still care for Gabriel? she asked herself bluntly. After all this time, had anything good and decent survived? She ruthlessly searched inside herself, remembering the love, the happiness, the *joy*.... Remembering, but not feeling, because there was nothing to feel. It had all died so long ago. All the good was gone.

And what was left to feel? Anger. Resentment. Bitterness. Betrayal. They were negative emotions, destructive ones, but they were honest.

So what was she going to do? Quit her job, run away and hide, and hope that he would never come looking for her?

Relinquish her control, lose her self-respect and let him win again?

Or stay. Work with him. Remain in control and take back the power that allowed him to affect her this way. Prove to him that she was an adult, responsible for herself. That she was as capable as any investigator he'd ever worked with. That, in spite of the heartache he'd caused her, she had survived and was strong. That she had learned the lesson he'd taught her. She could protect herself against him, because this time she knew what he was like, knew that he could turn on her, knew that he could take everything and leave her with nothing but pain. She knew not to trust him, not to rely on him, and she knew, as surely as she breathed, that she could never, ever love him.

He would be a client. Just another client. One that she had known a long time ago, in another life. And he would be nothing more.

She picked up a bright yellow pillow and hugged it to her chest. It all sounded so good, except for one minor detail. What if she was wrong? What if she *wasn't* strong? What if, this time, she didn't survive?

Chapter 2

"Phone call, Lieutenant."

Gabriel reached back to rub his neck without raising his eyes from the report he was reading. Murder was a grisly business, but it was *his* business, and he gave it all his attention. "Who is it?" he asked absently.

"Some woman. She didn't give a name," the young detective answered.

"Take a message and tell her that I'll call back later." He turned the page, then suddenly looked up as the man's words registered. A woman without a name. Rachel was supposed to call with the final decision on taking his case, and she had good reason not to give a name to the detective. "No, wait, Johnson. I'll take it," he said, dropping the report on his desk and reaching for the phone. He waited until the other man had left the office before he pushed the flashing button. "This is Lieutenant Rodriguez."

There was near total silence on the line. Gabriel listened for a moment, then said softly, "Rachel?"

A heavy sigh whooshed out. "Yes, Lieutenant."

His chuckle sounded quiet and dark in her ear. "How are you?"

"This isn't a social call, Lieutenant—"

"Can't you be sociable to your business associates?" he interrupted.

He already knew what she was going to say, she thought with a scowl, that she had gone to Powell and he had shot her down. She hated his confidence, his damned self-assurance. "The key word in that line is 'business.' That's all there is between us, Lieutenant."

She sounded prim and snooty and pretty damned assured herself. He couldn't resist a soft retort. "Have I given you any reason to believe that I want anything else, Rachel?"

It was a complete lie. He wasn't sure exactly what he wanted from her—a second chance?—but it was definitely much more than business. Still, the lie had the desired effect.

The silence came again, so loud it echoed. He knew her eyes were wide, her mouth thin and hard. It was an image he knew well, and it made him smile and excuse her from answering. "What do you want, Rachel?"

"I need to ask you some questions. When can you come in?"

He surveyed the paperwork on his desk, mentally reviewing the cases that needed his attention. "Not before six."

"I get off at five."

He knew that was true. He also knew that, according to Powell, she rarely left her office before seven. Working late was a habit with her—to keep her mind occupied? he wondered. To avoid having to go home to an empty house to eat a solitary meal and sleep in a lonely bed? He knew the reasons well, because he had used them himself for a long time.

"What about tomorrow?" she was asking, trying to put off the inevitable. She knew his schedule was rough. Like most other departments, Homicide was overworked and understaffed.

"The same."

She didn't bother asking about the next day. "All right. Six o'clock tonight. I'll be waiting."

"Where is your office?"

"The third floor." Her frown came through in her voice. "It will probably be the only one with a light on."

He laughed again, that soft, shivery chuckle. "Don't worry, Rachel. You'll be well compensated for the inconvenience."

She ignored his amusement and his promise. "I'll see you at six. Goodbye."

At least she hadn't tacked "Lieutenant" onto the end there, he thought with some satisfaction as he hung up. Soon she would stop calling him that at all. Soon she would call him by his name. Soon.

She hadn't exaggerated, Gabriel realized when he stepped off the elevator. The third floor, consisting of two dozen offices and two reception areas, appeared deserted as he walked down the hall. The computers on the secretaries' desks were shut off, the printers covered for the night, and the offices, except one, locked up tight.

He stopped in the open doorway of that office, silent and still as he took in the view before him. She sat behind her desk, looking out the single window. To a casual observer it might look as if she were daydreaming, staring at the city with nothing more important on her mind than the layer of smog and the fluffy clouds above it. But Gabriel wasn't a casual observer. He knew Rachel, and he knew that when she got that distant look on her face, her mind was racing—working, probing, questioning, solving.

He had thought she looked beautiful last Friday, but this evening, in a dove gray suit with a deep rose blouse, with her hair pulled up in a loose knot, she was even lovelier. Softer. More like the woman he had once known. The woman he was going to find once again.

He made no noise, but she became aware of his presence just the same. She turned first her head, then her chair, so that she was facing him. "Hello."

There was another tiny rush of relief that she hadn't used his rank. He was making progress—not much, but some. "Hello, Rachel." He entered the small office, closing the door behind him.

"Sit down, please." There was a faint wariness in her voice that was echoed in her eyes, but she managed to control it. Meeting alone with Gabriel in her tiny office in a deserted building wasn't her idea of a pleasant evening, but it was something that had to be done. As long as she protected herself...

He looked around before finding the only other chair in a corner near the door. Lifting it in one hand, he set it down in front of her desk, then sprawled comfortably on it.

"Do you mind if I use a tape recorder?" She preferred to record her interviews. In addition to giving her an unquestionably accurate record of the conversation for future use, it left her free to watch the other person. Often she learned as much from watching as she did from questioning. Body language, eye movements, nervous habits—all observations were helpful in this business.

Gabriel shook his head. "Not at all."

"How did you meet Jenna White?"

He wanted to delay answering the question, to talk about *her* first, to simply look at her, but her earlier warning echoed in his mind: *The key word... is business. That's all there is between us, Lieutenant.* For now he would have to stick to that. "I was taking a criminal justice class at SDSU. She had a class in the same building."

"Was she a full-time student?"

"Yes."

"In what year?"

"She was a sophomore."

"She was what? Twenty-five? Twenty-six?" She looked at him for confirmation. "That's a little older than your average sophomore. What did she do between high school and college?''

''I don't know.''

Rachel considered it a moment longer, then shrugged and continued her questioning. ''Where did she live?''

He gave her the address of an apartment complex near the university.

The questions went on. How long had they dated? Where did they go on their dates? What did she like to do? What kind of car did she drive? Did she live alone? Who were her friends? What were her plans after college? Did she ever mention parents, brothers or sisters, cousins, aunts and uncles? Did she use any credit cards? Did she take any trips out of town? Did she vote? Go to church? Belong to any clubs on campus? Subscribe to a newspaper or any magazines? Who was her doctor? When did she find out she was pregnant? When was the baby due? Was she happy about it?

As much as he disliked being questioned, as much as he hated being questioned about Jenna, Gabriel was impressed by her thoroughness. She asked all the questions that he would have asked if he'd been in control. It wasn't her fault that too many of his answers were, ''I don't know.'' Except for the last one. He knew the answer to that. He just didn't want to give it.

Rachel waited a moment, then softly asked again. ''Was she happy about having a baby?''

He closed his eyes and recalled the day Jenna had told him she was pregnant. It had been twelve years, but he remembered it clearly. He opened his eyes again and looked at Rachel. ''No.''

It was a flat, blunt, condemning answer, and he felt the need to explain. To justify. ''She was in school, nowhere near earning her degree. Money was tight. She just wasn't ready to have a baby.''

Rachel kept all expression out of her face, her voice, when she asked the next question. ''Do you think she might have had an abortion?''

"She talked about it once." He knew she was watching him, judging his reactions, so he deliberately avoided her gaze. "I don't think she went through with it. I *know* her. I don't think she could have done it."

She leaned back in her chair, listening to it squeak, and folded her hands together. Was that last statement cop's intuition? she wondered. Or the desperate hope of a man who wouldn't accept that his child might have died before it had had a chance to live?

Gabriel seemed to read her mind, because he smiled faintly. "I'm not naive, Rachel. I know women have abortions every day. But not Jenna."

"What if she did?"

He stood up then, shrugged out of his jacket and paced the length of the small office. "She didn't."

"But what if she did?" When he didn't respond, she continued. "I know what a lieutenant makes, and I know the rates Powell charges. Unless you're on the take, this search will probably take every penny you have. What if we never find Jenna? What if we find her, and she admits that she had an abortion?"

"Then I'll deal with it." The money didn't matter. Even if it cost his life's savings—a fair estimate—it would be worth it to know about his child.

He stopped pacing, his back to Rachel, to study the photographs on the wall, and she took advantage of his distraction to study him. Her gaze moved slowly over the white shirt that stretched over his shoulders and down his back before disappearing into black trousers that clung to lean hips and long legs. His revolver rested above his right hip, the compact leather holster threaded onto a black belt. He was a handsome man, she thought dispassionately; then honesty forced her to amend that. More than handsome— he was beautiful. It wasn't a word that she ordinarily applied to men, but it suited him perfectly. He had thick black hair, wicked dark eyes, a brilliant smile, charm, grace and elegance. Because of his name, and because he was dark, most people assumed that he was, like Rachel, of Mexican descent, but she knew that his parents were Indian, and the subtle hints were there, in the flawless bone structure, the slightly exotic eyes. Beautiful.

But that meant nothing to her, did it? His beauty and charm didn't touch her, didn't make her feel anything, and that was good. That showed that she *was* in control, that she *was* strong.

He turned and found her eyes on him again. He tried to read her, but there was no emotion in her expression. Just cool brown eyes in a cool lovely face. "Are you all out of questions?"

She shook her head. "Just one more. Do you have a photograph of Jenna?"

He nodded. "I'll find it and bring it by."

"If you think of anything else that might help..."

His smile was faint, edged with weariness. "I'll let you know." He sat down on the edge of the chair and leaned his arms on the desktop. "That wasn't so bad, was it?"

"It's not *my* past we were discussing."

"I meant talking to me. Being in the same room with me." He saw the muscles in her jaw tense slightly and made a soft, gentle suggestion. "We could talk about your past, Rachel. *Our* past."

She was in control, she reminded herself. She wasn't going to let him take over. "There's nothing to talk about. It happened a long time ago. It doesn't matter anymore."

It matters to *me*. But he kept the words inside him, safe, secret. Rising easily to his feet, he put his coat on again. "Are you going home now?"

The wariness returned. "Soon."

"You shouldn't work here alone at night."

"I carry a gun," she reminded him.

"Guns don't always protect you." Jack Thomas had carried one, too, identical to Gabriel's, but he had died anyway. "Come on. I'll walk you to your car."

"Thanks, but no thanks."

"Don't be stubborn, Rachel. You don't have any work that can't wait until tomorrow."

He was right, as usual, but she still felt the need to refuse. It was silly and irrational—if any other male client had offered to walk her to her car after a late meeting, she would have accepted and been grateful for it. Did her refusal mean that Gabriel wasn't just another client, wasn't just a man?

No. She had spent the entire weekend deciding that he was. He was no one special, no one important to her. Walking to her car with him would mean absolutely nothing.

Reaching across the desk, she shut off the tape recorder and placed it in her briefcase. She locked the desk file drawer, shut off the lamp and moved toward the door. "Are you ready, Lieutenant?" she asked coolly, her hand resting on the light switch.

Gabriel tried not to watch her too closely in the elevator or when they walked into the graveled parking lot. He considered asking her to have dinner with him, but rejected the idea as soon as it formed. Strictly business—that was all she wanted, and, for the time being, that was all he would allow. He wouldn't snoop into her life, wouldn't try to make a place for himself in it...yet. "So...what do we do now?"

Rachel stopped next to her car, a sedate, silver-blue sedan. There was nothing flashy about the car, he thought with a grin, but then, a woman like Rachel didn't need flash. The flash came from inside. "'We' don't do anything, Lieutenant. You do your job, and I'll do mine."

He held out his hand for her briefcase, and she gave it to him while she searched her handbag for her keys. "What will you check first?" he asked.

"DMV, Voter Registration, the university."

"You know the university can't tell you anything—the Privacy Act."

She found the keys and unlocked the door, then glanced up at him. "The university can't tell *you* anything. You use your methods, and I'll use mine."

He suppressed a grin. A private investigator didn't have to work under the same restraints that a cop did, but he knew Rachel too well to believe that she would resort to anything underhanded or illegal to further a case. Maybe borderline, but never illegal. "When will I hear from you?"

Bending, she placed her briefcase and purse in the back seat, then slowly straightened again. "I can handle this case alone. You don't have to check up on me."

"Your boss said you'd give me regular reports. It's called keeping tabs, Rachel. Not checking up."

She sighed and gave in. "A week."

There was a hopeful tone in her voice, a questioning lift of her eyebrows, that he would accept her answer. With a slow, incredibly charming smile, he did. "I'll talk to you then."

He watched her get into the car and drive away without a backward glance. When she had turned the corner, he went to his own car, parked nearby, and started the engine.

She seemed to have accepted the idea of working for him, but he wasn't sure if that was good or bad. He had expected more resistance, more anger. More reason to believe that their past still affected her, because if it did, then she must still care. But, beyond her insistence that their relationship be strictly business and that faint watchfulness that had sometimes slipped into her eyes, she had given him little reason to believe that anything about him mattered to her.

She *had* to still care, at least a little. She felt things deeply, sometimes too deeply for her own good. The anger, the grief, the hurt—those things were still inside her, along with the...

Gabriel eased the car into gear and pulled out of the parking lot. The what? What had Rachel felt for him five years ago? She had never used the word "love." In all the months they'd been together, she had never said, "I love you." But that meant nothing. *He* hadn't said the words, either—his experience with Jenna had taught him caution—but the emotion had been there. He had shown her just what she had shown him: fondness, affection, respect, friendship, desire, lust.

But it didn't matter what label he put on it. The fact was, she had *cared* about him. She had felt something for him that she had never felt for any other man, and, somewhere deep inside her, she had to still feel it. She *had* to. He was betting his future on it.

There was something both frustrating and exhilarating, Rachel decided, about trying to find someone who had disappeared as long ago and as completely as Jenna White had. The frustration lay in checking lead after lead, only to watch each one fizzle into nothing. Voter Registration had never registered a voter by that name in San Diego County. The county tax assessor's office showed no property held in that name. The courthouse records listed no marriages or divorces for Jenna Elise White.

A trip to the state capitol in Sacramento, accompanied by two of Powell's clerks for assistance, had also proved fruitless. There was no birth certificate for a Jenna Elise, under White or any other name, thirty-five to forty years ago. More recently, there was no child born to Jenna White in the state. There was no death certificate—a gruesome possibility that Rachel was glad didn't pan out—and, at the Department of Motor Vehicles, no record of a driver's license or vehicle registration.

The exhilaration came from making progress, in a backward sort of way. The case was like a jigsaw puzzle. She needed all the little pieces of information to create the big picture. She wasn't finding the pieces that fit, but she *was* learning which pieces to discard. Her trip to Sacramento hadn't told her where Jenna had gotten her driver's license or where she had registered her car, or where she'd been born, or where her child had been born, but it *had* told her where those things *hadn't* taken place. It had narrowed the list of states from fifty to forty-nine.

She swiveled her chair around to face the wall map of the United States that she'd just hung. After a visit to the university next week and while she tracked down the former owners of the apartments where Jenna had lived, she would start planning her next trip. San Diego State drew students from all over the country, but the majority were residents of

California and its neighboring states. Her first stops would be Arizona and Nevada, searching for a birth certificate, a driver's license—anything to connect Jenna to a location. Once she found that connection, other information would follow: an address, a place of employment, a relative's name. No matter how outdated the information, it would lead to other information that would eventually lead to the woman herself. And to her child.

Rachel remembered what Gabriel had told her about the child. He only wanted to know if he existed. If he was all right, if he needed anything. When she had asked if he intended to assume the role of father, he had answered honestly. *I suppose it would depend on whether or not he needed a father.*

Still staring at the map, she sighed softly. That answer, honest or not, wasn't good enough. What if Jenna had married? What if another man was playing father to Gabriel's child? How would he deal with that? Would he put the child's interests first and gracefully back off? Or would his ego, the desire that was driving him to find out, demand his rightful place in the child's life?

She could tell him firsthand the problems that could cause. The hurt, the disillusionment, the sorrow, the anger. The betrayal of a man she didn't know claiming to be her father, of the man she had believed was her father but wasn't, and of the mother who had lied about both men all those years. Twenty-one years had dimmed the memories, had dulled the sharp edged emotions, but they were there all the same. Although she resented the lies, she still loved her mother and stepfather. But she hated the man who had devastated her world, who had taken her precious illusion of family from her simply to gratify his own ego.

She could tell Gabriel…but she wouldn't. He had shared in the second traumatic event in her life, but she didn't trust him to know about the first. He was paying her to do a job, and that didn't include giving advice or offering confidences about a shattered little girl who still lived deep inside her.

She sighed again and began clearing her desk. It was long past quitting time, and the peace and solitude of her little house awaited her.

She was almost to her car when she noticed the other car in the lot. She knew it didn't belong to any of her co-workers because she paid attention to that sort of thing. She had seen the car only once before, after Monday evening's meeting with Gabriel. Unlocking her own car door, she laid her briefcase on the floor, then straightened and waited.

A car had never suited its owner as perfectly as the sporty, steel-gray RX-7 suited Gabriel: it was beautiful, sleek and fast, with an aura of recklessness. Carelessness. Danger.

Danger? she questioned silently, then watched as Gabriel climbed out. Yes, she had all the appropriate responses for danger: a tight, panicky feeling in her chest, increased pulse and respiration, clammy hands. He was a dangerous man. But she could protect herself. She was strong.

Sliding her hands into her jacket pockets, she took a few steps toward him. "The week's not up until Monday," she called, pleased that her voice was even and calm.

"I know. I wanted to bring this by." He extended a small manila envelope, releasing it as soon as she touched the other end.

She opened it and saw a photograph inside. After just a glimpse of blond hair and a bright smile, she closed the envelope again. She would look at this woman, Gabriel's lover, the mother of his child, later, when he wasn't standing three feet away and watching her intensely. "You could have mailed it."

He shook his head. "It's the only one I have. I can't afford to lose it." Besides, if he'd done that, he would have had to wait two more days to see her. He had already waited since Monday. "How's it going?"

"That will be in the report next week." She drew the envelope back and forth between two fingers. "Unless you'd rather move the appointment up to this evening?"

"Only if you'd give it to me over dinner."

This time it was Rachel shaking her head. "No thanks. We've both got better things to do on a Friday night than work." She saw the glint of amusement in his eyes and realized that that was exactly the answer he had expected. The invitation to dinner had come easily because he'd known she would refuse. It was tempting to change her mind, to surprise him and make him endure a meal with her. But he would turn the tables on her, and *he* would enjoy, and *she* would be the one to endure—if she was lucky. Briskly, businesslike, she turned back to her car. "Thanks for bringing this over. It should come in handy."

Gabriel took a step closer. He'd offered the dinner invitation halfheartedly, knowing that she would refuse, but he wanted a few more minutes with her. He seized the first topic that came to mind. "You work a lot of late hours."

"No more than you, I imagine."

"Doesn't that bother your boyfriend?"

He was fishing. She had watched him do it too many times on the job to miss it now. "No."

The simple answer both annoyed and amused him—annoyed because he wanted to know if he had any competition other than her memories and her instinct for self-preservation, and amused because she knew the answer would annoy him. "He doesn't mind, huh?" he pressed.

"To be a good interrogator, you have to be able to read the person you're questioning so that you can match your style to his personality," she said in a school-teacher tone. "Some people prefer the straightforward approach. Some like the roundabout way. Others have to be tricked into giving information."

"Which one are you, Rachel?"

She shrugged. "You're the cop. You tell me."

He studied her for a long time. The sun was setting behind her, its rays casting a rosy glow over her creamy white jacket, glinting off the silver combs that held her hair back from her face. She appeared calm, assured, but he saw the nervous tightening of a muscle in her jaw. She didn't like standing still for him, tolerating his long scrutiny, but she did it because it was easier, better, less revealing, than protesting. "I think you'd prefer straightforward questions," he said at last, moving until he could lean against her car. Now little more than a foot separated them. "Honesty."

She nodded once. "I've always preferred honesty...within limits." But he had once overstepped those limits, moving from simple honesty to brutality, and she had paid for it. In some ways she was still paying.

"All right, then, I'll be straightforward. Are you seeing anyone?"

Turning away, Rachel removed her jacket, laid it across the car seat, then rolled up the sleeves of her pale yellow blouse. "I make it a policy not to discuss my personal life with my clients."

"But I'm not just a client," he reminded her in an intimately soft voice. "We were once friends, Rachel." *And a hell of a lot more.*

She was stung by his reference to their affair. It wasn't something she could talk about so easily, so pleasantly. Withdrawing both emotionally and physically, she turned to get into the car. For just an instant, though, she hesitated. "You're still arrogant, Gabriel, and you're still insensitive, and you're *still* the best reason I've found not to get involved with another man." She got in, buckled the seat belt and reached for the door. "Call early Monday morning to arrange an appointment. Ask for Elaine."

Gabriel stepped back and watched her drive away, then shoved his hands into his pockets. Although the conversation hadn't been encouraging, at least she had called him by his name. It didn't offer much hope or consolation, but it was better than nothing, and it was all he had.

He considered going back to his office for a couple of hours—there were always a few unsolved murder cases lying around that he could look at—but he had already worked late every night this week. He could go home to his empty apartment, but there his thoughts had increasingly been turning to Rachel and a time when it wasn't empty, when she had frequently shared the rooms and the space and especially the bed with him. Tonight he needed a few hours of peace, with no gruesome thoughts of murder, no painful remembrances of betrayal.

He just didn't know where to find it.

Rachel sat in the silence of her living room, her bare feet tucked beneath the yellow pillow. Her eyes were closed, her breathing slow and deep. She wasn't looking for peace, like Gabriel, but rather for courage—the courage to open the small yellow envelope he'd given her earlier. Inside was a picture of Jenna White, a woman who had known Gabriel as intimately as Rachel had—maybe even more so. Maybe he had loved Jenna. Maybe that was why he'd never felt anything for Rachel.

She'd been telling herself that she no longer cared for him, but that hadn't stopped the faint twinges of bitterness whenever she thought of him and Jenna as lovers. Was it really bitterness? she wondered. Or jealousy that he had given the other woman what he had refused to give *her*?

If she could take the photograph from its envelope and look at it without feeling anything, then she would know she had been honest with herself. She would know that all her feelings for Gabriel were gone.

And what if she hadn't been honest? What if she had lied to protect herself? What would she do then?

The questions went unanswered as she slid the flat, rectangular photo out of the envelope. For a moment, Gabriel's description echoed in her mind. *She's five foot five, blond and blue-eyed. Pretty.*

As a cop's description, it wasn't bad—sex, height, hair and eye color. As a lover's description, it was woefully inadequate to describe this woman. The photo revealed a slender, delicate-looking woman, with straight, silky blond hair that brushed her shoulders, with clear blue eyes and a sweetly innocent smile. She was the kind of woman people looked twice at, the kind of woman men fantasized about. The kind of woman men loved.

The emptiness inside her was cold, making her shudder uncontrollably. Her hand trembled as she put the picture back in the envelope. She would keep it with her, but she wouldn't look at it again. In those few moments she had memorized the other woman's face. She would never forget it.

Gabriel had claimed that he wanted to find Jenna only to find out about his child. Rachel wondered now if that was true, if he could have had an affair with this woman without falling in love with her, and, if he *had* loved her, if he still did.

It was none of her business. Gabriel was the client, and she was working for him—nothing else. She had no right to question him about anything that didn't directly pertain to the case.

But she needed to know. Lord, she needed to know! An hour ago she had called Gabriel insensitive, but was he insensitive enough, knowing that she had once loved him, to ask her to find the woman *he* loved?

She was terribly, achingly, afraid that the answer was yes.

"Your mind's a million miles away. For all the interest you've shown in this game, we could have left you at home."

Gabriel blinked, then focused on Shelley Morgan, sitting at his side in the crowded stadium. "Did you say something?"

She shook her head and exaggeratedly rolled her eyes. "You haven't even noticed that, for once, the Padres are winning a ball game." She paused for a moment. "Do you need to talk?"

She made the offer easily, comfortably, the same way he had offered countless times to listen to her or Christopher. A refusal was rare, but that was what Gabriel gave. "I don't think talking would help."

Shielding her eyes with her hand, Shelley watched the play on the field below before looking back at Gabriel. "I'm a good listener, and I give great advice."

"I know you do, sweetheart, but not this time." He glanced around, wondering when Christopher would return from the concession stand. He should have offered to go himself and let Christopher stay with his wife, but he'd been lost in thought and had barely noticed when his friend left.

There were literally thousands of people around him, most wearing Padres caps or T-shirts or waving pennants, and one of his best friends was sitting right beside him, but he still felt alone. Loneliness was an emotion he understood and usually dealt with well, but lately it was growing harder to handle. He could put it down to age—at thirty-eight he should have been married, settled down and raising a family—or he could blame it on his job—investigating murders day after day could take its toll.

Or he could be honest and admit that there were only two people who could chase away his loneliness: his child, if he even existed, and Rachel, if she ever forgave him.

Shelley studied his bleak expression, then laid her hand lightly on his arm. "Gabriel, you know I would never pry—"

He laughed a little. "Sweetheart, you're a reporter. You're paid to pry."

She smiled a bit, but it quickly faded. "If I can help..."

He tilted his head, holding her gaze for a long time. "Have you ever done anything in your life that needed forgiveness?" he asked curiously.

"Of—" The rest of her automatic agreement faded unspoken as Gabriel shook his head.

"You've never done anything to hurt anyone. You're a good woman, Shelley. A good person."

She slid her arm around his waist and hugged him tight. "So are you, Gabriel. You and Christopher are the two best men I've ever known."

Her softly given compliment ensured that he couldn't tell her what was on his mind, even if he wanted to. Her reporter's training had taught her not to pass judgment, to find out all the facts, all the extenuating circumstances. But her finding out what he'd done to Rachel might cost him some small measure of Shelley's respect, and he couldn't bear to lose that. There was precious little that he valued, and he wasn't about to give up any of it.

He held her close for a minute. "I love you dearly, Shelley, and I appreciate your concern, but this is something I need to handle on my own," he murmured against her hair. "If I get it worked out, you and Christopher will be the first to know."

Christopher returned a few minutes later carrying a box loaded with soft drinks, a hot dog for Shelley and popcorn for Gabriel and himself. Gabriel relaxed enough to enjoy the last innings of the game, but he didn't join in the wild celebration when the Padres scored the winning run.

"Want to have dinner with us?" Christopher asked, watching his friend stand and stretch.

"Where?" Gabriel replied, only mildly interested.

Christopher put his arms around his wife, resting one hand on her belly. "We're going to La Posta. Shelley's been craving Mexican food every night for the past week."

"Keep that up for the next six and a half months and you'll give that kid a permanent case of heartburn," Gabriel teased her; then he shook his head, turning down his favorite restaurant. "I think I'll head home. Thanks, though."

"Will you be at tomorrow's game?"

"Sure." What else did he have to do with his time?

The Privacy Act had been a bane to law enforcement agencies and private investigators since its enactment, Rachel thought with a scowl. Nobody in the registrar's office at San Diego State was willing to so much as speak to her once they found out what she wanted. She had tried the honest way and failed. That left only the dishonest: bribery or breaking into the computer. Most of her associates at Powell Investigations would try to bribe a lowly clerk into providing them with a copy of Jenna's records; the more innovative ones would find a talented and unscrupulous computer hacker to tap into the university's system. Although she hadn't ruled them out yet, neither idea appealed to her. There was still too much of the cop in her, she guessed.

Her next stop was the university library. A search of the yearbooks for the time Gabriel had said Jenna was attending turned up nothing. She had been one of the many who hadn't bothered with yearbook pictures.

After a hastily eaten lunch, she went downtown again. Tracking down the owners of the apartment complex was going to take some time. She knew it was probably a long shot, but just maybe they'd kept records on their tenants. Wouldn't it be nice if they just happened to have the information that most apartment managers required, listing a home address and next of kin for Jenna? she thought wryly. With that kind of information, she could probably wrap up this case in a matter of days. Instead it looked as if she might still be at it months from now.

Still dealing with Gabriel months from now. She ignored the jerk in her stomach, putting it down to the fast-food lunch instead of the thought of her client. As long as he could afford her services, she would work, whether it was three weeks, three months or three years. She could handle it.

Her appointment with him was at four o'clock. She worked at the courthouse until the last possible minute, then rushed the few blocks to the office. There was no sign of his car in Powell's private parking lot, she thought with satisfaction as she hurried by.

"You barely made it," Elaine said as Rachel stepped off the elevator. "You have a four o'clock appointment."

"I know. He isn't here yet, is he?"

"Not unless I missed him."

Rachel grinned wryly. "Believe me, Elaine, you wouldn't miss him."

"That good-looking, huh?" The secretary twisted her face into a grotesque leer, then gave a sigh. "Is he married?"

"No."

"Nice?"

Gabriel nice? She gave it a moment's thought. Yeah, he could be called nice. He had been special from the first time she'd met him, not like the other cops she'd known—not like the other *people* she'd known. He had been bright, intelligent, a shrewd investigator. He was conceited, but he made the conceit work for him by convincing everyone else that he was as great and wonderful as *he* thought he was.

And yes, he had been nice. He had been aware of the females he worked with as women, but he hadn't let that affect the way he treated them—no special favors or shielding, but no put-downs or come-ons, either. No prejudices. He had demanded that the officers who worked with him be good cops, and it didn't matter whether they were male or female. He had given respect to everyone, had been fair, considerate, willing to work and to help whenever he could.

But he hadn't helped *her*. He hadn't been fair or considerate to *her*. Why? she wondered for the first time in years. Why hadn't he treated her with one half the decency he'd shown everyone else? Why had he been so good to her one night and so brutally cruel the next?

And why was she asking these questions now? They didn't matter. None of it mattered.

"Hey, are you okay?" Elaine touched Rachel's hand and found it cold.

She smiled, but it was cold, too, and sad. "Just thinking. When Lieutenant Rodriguez gets here, will you send him in?"

"I'm already here."

She controlled the impulse to whirl around, but turned slowly instead. "I didn't hear the elevator," she said blandly.

"That's because I took the stairs." He pulled his gaze from her to the secretary, who was watching them both. "I'm Gabriel Rodriguez." He extended his hand, and Elaine was more than willing to take it and complete the introductions.

Rachel stood quietly, glad that he hadn't offered *her* his hand. Since that first meeting in Powell's office, he'd made no effort to touch her, a small thing to be grateful for, but she was, all the same.

When Gabriel and Elaine finished their polite chat, Rachel gestured toward her office, and he followed her inside. The extra chair was where he'd left it after last week's meeting. The setup left the desk between them and kept them apart—much too far apart, in his opinion.

Rachel handed a large envelope to him containing a letter-perfect report, then proceeded in a distinctly professional voice to tell him everything that the report covered. She saw him flinch slightly when she mentioned checking the death records in Sacramento, then avoided looking at him while she finished her spiel.

"Is that it?" he asked quietly.

She shrugged. "I went to the university today but found nothing." She hesitated before asking, "Why don't you go out there, flash your badge and sweet-talk the clerk into giving you what you need?" Being a cop, his chances of learning something were much better than hers had been.

He was shaking his head before she finished talking. "They're not going to hand over the records just because I'm a cop. They'll want to know what my interest in Jenna is, why I need the information. I don't think my answers would particularly impress them. Besides, I told you, I don't want anything official about this. *Nothing.*" He paused briefly. "Anything else?"

"I'm still checking on the owners of the apartments at the time she lived there. Maybe they'll remember her or still have their records or something."

"That's a long shot, isn't it?"

Her words exactly. The fact that, even after all these years, their thoughts ran along parallel paths made her defensive. "You haven't provided a hell of a lot of information. I have to work with what I've got."

He settled back in the chair. "So you'll start looking outside the state now. Arizona first?"

Rachel also settled back, placing the tips of her fingers together to form a steeple. "Why did you come to Powell Investigations?"

She had asked him that question in their first interview, and he had deliberately skirted around it. Now he answered honestly. "Because you work here, and I wanted you to handle this."

"Why?"

Again the answer was painfully honest. "You're good, Rachel. You were a hell of a good cop, and that makes you a hell of a good PI."

Five years ago he had told her that she was responsible for another cop's death. Because of that she shouldn't have felt the rush of pleasure that went through her at his compliment. Because of that she shouldn't give a damn what he thought of her as a private investigator... but she did.

She controlled the pleasure long enough to make her point. "Then why are you trying to second-guess me? I know how to run this investigation. I *know* what I'm doing."

"I'm a supervisor," he said with a charming grin, "so I supervise. It's what I do best. Old habits can be hard to break."

"No," she disagreed softly. "You're an investigator—*that's* what you do best."

The compliment surprised her as much as him. It was the first good thing she'd said to him—probably, Gabriel acknowledged, the first good thing she'd *thought* of him in years. "I still do some of that, too," he said, watching the color flare in her face, then recede. "Would it make you more comfortable if I didn't ask what you're doing?"

"No," she murmured. "You have that right." Taking a deep breath, she looked up at him. "Arizona's first—I'm going this week. After that, Nevada, then New Mexico, Colorado and Utah."

He nodded approvingly. That was the way he'd do it, too, starting with the states that bordered California, then working outward. "When are you leaving?"

"Tomorrow."

"Let me go with you."

The request echoed in the sudden silence of the room. Rachel was staring at him, shaking her head slowly from side to side. She couldn't even find her voice to tell him what an incredibly bad idea that was.

"The work would go a lot quicker with help," he pointed out. "And since I'm paying the bill, and my help is free—"

"No."

"Rachel . . ."

"No," she said firmly. "I prefer to work alone."

He didn't doubt that. She seemed to do everything alone. "Doesn't that get lonely?"

"I like it that way," she insisted.

"All I'd have to do is talk to Powell—"

She interrupted him again. "Don't threaten me, Gabriel. You're paying for my services, not *me*. Don't try to control me."

He raised his hands quickly, palms out. "All right. I'm sorry." He had already forced her into working this case. If he kept pushing, he had no doubt that eventually she would push back—she was too much of a fighter not to. She would quit her job and win, and he would lose a lot. Too much.

"How long do you think you'll be in Arizona?"

"I don't know. It depends largely on how many people were born in the periods I'm checking."

"Do you think you'll be back by Saturday?"

She shrugged, then asked curiously. "Why?"

"I have tickets to the Padres-Dodgers game."

Rachel sat motionless for a long time. Why had he remembered that she was a Dodgers fan? Why had that little tidbit stayed with him all this time? And why in the world was she thinking about how nice it would be to go to the game? "Thanks, but no."

It took an effort to conceal his disappointment, but he succeeded. "One of these days, Rachel, I'll ask you out, and you'll say yes."

She gave a slow but certain shake of her head. "You'll give up asking first. If that's all...?" She stood up and walked around the desk, ready to usher him out the door.

Gabriel rose from the chair and slowly walked toward her. As her hand turned on the doorknob, he laid his own hand, big and warm, over it, stopping the action. She looked up, wariness in her eyes once again, but he ignored it. "I'm a smart man, Rachel. I gave up twice before, and both times it cost me dearly. I've learned my lesson."

She was standing utterly still, afraid to move, because he was so close, touching her, warming her. He raised his other hand to brush over her hair in a curiously gentle way, then lowered his head the few inches necessary to bring his mouth into contact with hers. It was a tiny kiss, a bare whispery touch of lips to lips that lasted only an instant, but it was enough to make her heart pound.

He drew back and looked at her solemnly, his eyes dark and somber. "I never give up, Rachel. Never."

Before she could draw a breath into her aching lungs, he had opened the door and walked through. She was in the same place, motionless, when he returned a moment later.

"I forgot the report," he said in explanation. Picking it up from the desk, he grinned as he walked past. "Spoiled a hell of an exit, didn't I? See you next week, Rach."

Chapter 3

Phoenix was hot, and Rachel didn't like heat. She liked San Diego, with its cool ocean breezes and sandy, crowded beaches, liked working in her own office and sleeping in her own bed. Travel was an unavoidable drawback in this business, one she hadn't grown used to and never would. At least the police department had never sent her out of town, she groused as she unpacked her only suitcase.

Then she smiled faintly. But the Department hadn't paid as well as Powell did. And none of the subjects in her investigations for Powell had ever taken a shot at her. Every situation had its advantages and disadvantages.

The hotel room was small but adequate. A queen-size bed dominated, and along one wall were a desk, a television and a tall armoire. All the comforts of home, she thought cynically, courtesy of Gabriel Rodriguez.

She controlled the tiny shiver that the thought of him sparked. Since he had kissed her yesterday in her office, she'd been having the strangest responses—odd little quivers deep down in her stomach that dangerously resembled desire, faint touches of long-ago memories that she had foolishly believed had been put to rest, twinges of a hunger that no one else could satisfy.

It was all right, she counseled herself—even normal. If he still had the power to cause her pain—and the first time she'd seen him in Powell's office had proved that—then it was only normal that he could make her feel other things. Hell, she'd been alone so long that any kiss from any man would make her feel those same longings. It simply meant that she was alive. It had nothing to do with her love for Gabriel.

Then she thought of the envelope in her briefcase that held the picture of Jenna, of the ugly jealousy that she struggled to contain in the tiny place where it had started. *That* had something to do with her love.

Old love, she argued. Past love. Dead love. Long-gone-and-will-never-come-again love. She was older and much, much wiser. Gabriel would never touch her heart again.

Although she was tired—sleep hadn't come easily to her last night—she picked up her briefcase and left for the state capitol complex. She was here to do a job, and the sooner she got it done, the sooner Gabriel would be, once and for all, out of her life. She would work hard, and she would work fast.

Powell could have saved Rachel the trip by hiring a local PI to conduct the records searches for them. It was common practice, and she had suggested it to him in the report she'd sent up. His veto had been delivered less than an hour later by her supervisor. There would be no significant savings in doing it that way, he had told her, before getting to the real reason Powell was refusing: Rodriguez had been insistent that the case be handled by Rachel and no one else. That didn't mean, Powell had said snidely, letting Rachel hire someone else to do her work for her.

So here she was, in a suit and high heels, in Phoenix, in one-hundred-degree weather. Because Gabriel had been insistent. And if she didn't find anything here, her next step would mean repeating the process in Carson City, Nevada, where the temperature was probably even higher and the search would probably be just as unproductive. At that rate she would be back east by winter, out of the heat and complaining about the cold.

She spent the rest of the day in a room that, while not exactly cool, was at least more comfortable than outside. The records were on microfiche, quicker than files but slower than a computer. By the time the clerk tapped her on the shoulder and told her that they were closing for the night, her neck and shoulders ached, and her eyes were locked in a squint.

"Will you be back tomorrow?" the older woman asked with a friendly smile.

"Yes, I will." And tomorrow and tomorrow, she thought with a weary sigh.

Wednesday was no better. Thursday was outright frustrating. The temptation to forget the search and write Arizona off her list was strong, but she kept looking for a familiar name, for the right date. Friday afternoon she finished without finding a single bit of useful information, scheduled her return flight to San Diego for the next morning, took a long relaxing bath and stretched out in bed to watch television.

The Friday-night cop show was one of her favorites, partly because it had little bearing on reality. The show's Vice cops, in spite of the fact that they weren't assigned to Homicide or Narcotics, routinely worked homicide and narcotics cases. The good guys got shot at on a regular basis, but only the bad guys died. It was unrealistic, often ludicrous, but it was entertaining, and the stars were good-looking. What more could she ask for on a solitary Friday night?

The phone rang halfway through the show, and Rachel absently reached for it. She didn't bother wondering who could be calling when only Elaine and her supervisor knew where she was staying. Answering would tell her exactly who it was.

"Hello, Rachel."

Her first response was a smile, but she quickly turned it into a frown. She wasn't glad to hear from him. She *wasn't*.

Before he could ask how the search was going, she launched into a detailed account of her activities and plans. "I've spent the last four days looking at literally thousands of birth and death certificates, but I haven't found anything. The baby wasn't born here, Jenna wasn't born here, she didn't die here, she's never had a driver's license here, and she's never registered her car here. I'm coming home for a few days, then I'm going to Nevada. If I don't find anything there, I'll go on to New Mexico, then Colorado, then Utah, just like I told you. After that, we'll talk about where to go next, all right?"

He was silent for a long time. "Believe it or not, Rachel, I'm not checking up on you."

She fell silent, too, her eyes locked on the TV screen even though she couldn't follow the action. Her mind was too empty. "Then what did you want?"

"I was calling to check on you."

"But you just said—"

He chuckled at the confusion in her voice. "There's a world of difference in checking on someone and checking *up* on them." The chuckle deepened. "I wanted to hear your voice, okay?"

It wasn't okay, she silently protested. But really it was very much okay. Her voice was soft and hesitant. "You shouldn't say things like that."

"Why not?"

"We're working together—that's all."

"Strictly business," he said. He leaned back on his sofa and propped his bare feet on the coffee table. "You know, Rachel, a lot of people who work together are actually friends. Some are even lovers."

"We tried sleeping together before, remember?" she asked, her voice miserably unsteady. "It didn't work."

Gabriel felt a surge of triumph. She had actually brought their past relationship into the conversation, had brought it into the present for discussion. It was the best sign she'd given him yet. "It *did* work, Rachel," he disagreed. "It would have worked for a long, long time if..." If he hadn't been a cruel, selfish bastard. If he hadn't acted on impulse, saying things that he'd never meant, things that he'd never been able to call back.

"If I hadn't caused Jack's death? That's what you were going to say, isn't it?" she demanded. Tears clogged her eyes, made her voice thick.

"No! Rachel, that isn't what I meant! Rachel?" He sensed that he was losing her, losing this chance. "Rachel, damn it, listen to me! I didn't—"

The quiet click of the phone was all he heard. It took only a minute to redial the number. It rang seven times before it was disconnected. When he dialed a third time, he got a busy signal and knew that she had taken the phone off the hook. He pictured her sitting next to the phone, crying the tears he'd heard over the line, feeling again the grief and the sorrow, and cursed the fact that he was more than three hundred miles away, helpless.

Helplessness was something new to Gabriel, something he didn't like at all. He was used to being the one in control, not the one being controlled. Didn't she understand that he only wanted to apologize, to explain, to ease her pain?

But *he* was the one who had caused the pain. He was the one who had betrayed her, who had turned on her when she had desperately needed his love and support, who had denied her even the smallest comfort. Didn't she have the right to be left alone, to live the rest of her life without the painful reminders that simply seeing him brought?

The question troubled him. If he thought completely disappearing from Rachel's life would magically bring happiness, satisfaction, love and laughter to her, he would do it... wouldn't he? He liked to believe that he could be that strong, that fair, that noble—that he would rather suffer himself than bring her more pain. But he didn't know if it was true. Everyone liked to think well of himself. He liked to think that he was noble, but he would also like to think that he was incapable of inflicting such pain on another person in the first place, even though the past had proven that he was supremely capable of it.

Now, he thought with a weary sigh, he needed to prove— not just to Rachel, but also to himself—that he was capable of healing.

Saturday's flight back to San Diego was brief and uneventful. After taking care of one piece of business, Rachel's plans for the rest of the weekend would also be uneventful: she was going to work in her near-barren yard for a few hours, then spend the rest of the time reading the new thriller she'd picked up in the Phoenix airport. She was going to take it easy and relax. Lord knew, she needed to relax.

The business came first. If she put it off until later, she would lose her nerve, would let it slide until it was too late. Although she hadn't been to Gabriel's Mission Valley apartment in five years, she could find her way there blindfolded. She still remembered his unlisted phone number, too. Some things, she guessed wearily, she would just never forget.

The heavy traffic reminded her that there was a baseball game this afternoon at the stadium a mile away—a game that Gabriel had invited her to. Maybe he would already be gone, and her unpleasant task would have to wait until later.

But he wasn't already gone. He answered the door on her second knock, making no effort to hide his surprise at seeing her there. He stared at her for a long time, and she looked back. He wore white shorts and a gold Padres T-shirt and looked unfairly handsome, she thought, then sternly reminded herself that she wasn't here to look but to talk. Firmly. Determinedly.

His smile, when it came, was hesitant. "When did you get back?"

"A half hour ago."

He looked at the yellow linen skirt and jacket she wore and said with a hint of regret, "I don't suppose you've changed your mind about going to the game with me."

"No. But I would like to talk to you for a few minutes."
She hated sounding so cold and tough, so defensive, but she
had to protect herself. She had forgotten this last week when
he had kissed her, and again last night when he had sounded
so caring, but she wouldn't forget today.

He glanced over his shoulder. "I have company. The only
privacy we'd get is in the bedroom." He saw her flinch, and
his smile grew bittersweet. "No, I didn't think you'd like
that. Well, that leaves the porch, or I could meet you after
the game."

The small square porch where she stood wasn't the ideal
place for what she had to say, but it would do. Gabriel
stepped outside and closed the door behind him, then leaned
against it, his arms folded over his chest.

Now that she had his attention—every bit of it, judging
from the intensity of his gaze—she didn't know where to
start. Finally, moving as far away as she could, she turned
to face him. "I took this case because I felt I didn't have a
choice. I had already quit one job that I liked because of
you, and I didn't want to lose another one. I still don't." She
put her hands in her pockets, where her clenched fists would
go unnoticed.

She hadn't expected it to be this hard. She had thought
about it last night once the tears had finally dried, had considered it all the way from Phoenix to San Diego. She had
known exactly what she would say, the words she would use,
and in her mind they had flowed so smoothly. But in her
mind she hadn't taken into consideration the fact that she
would have to say them to Gabriel face-to-face. Face to in-
credibly-handsome-and-once-very-dear face. She could
hardly think, much less lay out the ultimatum she had
planned so carefully.

He read the discomfort and uneasiness in her features,
noticed the tiny red lines in her eyes from last night's tears
and took pity on her. "You thought you could keep it all on
a business level—forget that we'd ever known each other,
that we'd been lovers, that I had hurt you more than anyone else ever had. You thought you could do a good,

professional job and at the same time show me that you don't give a damn about me, that our past means nothing to you."

She was so surprised that he understood that all she could do was nod.

"But it's not working out, is it Rachel?" he asked quietly. "And it won't. You can't live a lie like that, and neither can I. I won't forget that I knew you before, or that we were lovers, and, God help me, I *can't* forget how I hurt you." Pushing himself away from the door, he took the few steps that brought him close enough to touch her. She tried to shrink away from the gentle fingers on her jaw, but there was no place to go. "I can't forget," he murmured softly, "and you can't forgive. We're a fine pair, aren't we, Rachel?"

Trying to ignore his fingers, warm and hard and comforting, on her skin, she struggled for control. "I don't want to forgive you."

"That's all right." He brought his other hand to her shoulder, simply resting it on the soft fabric of her jacket. "I don't want to forget you."

"It was nothing special."

"It was the best thing that had ever happened to either one of us."

She looked up, her eyes wide with distress, and found his face only inches from hers. "Why are you doing this?" she whispered.

"Because I need to." It was a simplified answer, but it covered all his reasons. He needed forgiveness and peace. He needed to heal and be healed. He needed to love and be loved. He needed *her*.

He let his fingers glide along her jaw, down the slender line of her throat to the pulse that beat rapidly, visibly. "Don't ask me to leave you alone, Rachel. Don't ask me to stay away," he murmured, "because I can't do it. For your sake, I wish I could, but I *can't*." He wasn't strong or fair or noble, after all, he thought with regret. He was just a man. A man who needed *this* woman.

When his lips touched hers, she felt the shock all the way to her toes. She tried to ignore the ripples of pleasure, tried to summon the strength to push him away. She could do it—he wasn't holding her, wasn't forcing her—but her brain refused to issue the command. How could it, when she had wanted this for so long?

Gabriel's hands slid into her hair, loosening the combs that held it back, and he moved even closer. She was so soft, so warm, so perfectly suited to him. He had dreamed for weeks of kissing her this way, of being kissed by her this way, and finally his dream was becoming reality.

His tongue slid between her lips, and she reflexively opened her mouth to it. It had been so long, but it felt so natural, so right. She raised her hands to his shoulders for support, then gave in to the hunger, taking all that he could give, but it wasn't enough. She needed more, needed—

When she made a strangled, helplessly sad sound deep in her throat, Gabriel ended the kiss and took a step back. "I'm sorry." Sorry he had hurt her, sorry she couldn't forgive him, sorry that this was so difficult for her, but not sorry that he'd kissed her. Never sorry for that.

Suddenly she turned her back to him, gripping the rail tightly with both hands, squeezing her eyes shut. She had needed him—his kiss, his closeness, his body, *him*. God, had she lied to herself all this time? Had she deliberately overlooked what she felt for him because it was easier than admitting that she was still weak enough to care about the man who had once destroyed her?

The answers were there, brought close to the surface by his kiss, by his gentle touch and quiet understanding, but she didn't look at them, didn't acknowledge them. She didn't have the courage.

When she was certain that she could speak without her voice breaking, she softly asked, "Do you want someone else to find Jenna for you?"

"No."

"Will you accept that this is—"

"Strictly business?" His smile was wry. "No. I can't pretend, Rachel." He paused a moment, then asked, "Can *you* keep it strictly business?"

How could she, when he wasn't playing by the rules? When maybe *she* wasn't? She ignored the questions, the doubts, her own lies, and stated flatly, "I wasn't trying to be cruel, but I meant what I said. I won't forgive you."

"Even if you did, I don't think I know how to forgive myself."

She turned around then, wanting to see his face. "I can't trust you." She wasn't even sure she could trust herself.

There was no surprise or wounded dismay in his expression. He had expected as much. "Trust can be learned," he said with warm confidence. Reaching up, he gently pulled the two combs he had loosened from her hair and pressed them into her limp hands. The fact that she didn't withdraw from his touch as she would have done a week ago seemed to bear out his statement.

He had an answer for everything, she thought with a touch of frustration, while she had no answers at all. She had been foolish to think that she could come here and settle things to her satisfaction with a simple conversation. Instead, he had twisted and turned everything, and now she was more confused than ever. "Why does it matter, Gabriel?" she asked curiously, dropping the combs into her pocket. "After so many years..."

He dragged his fingers through his hair, tugging at the black strands, then grinned ruefully. "Damned if I know." He restlessly moved away, stopping at the top step. A better answer would have been, damned if he would tell her. She definitely wasn't ready to hear about love, about forever. If those words slipped into the conversation, she would disappear so thoroughly that no one would ever find her again. "Will you change your mind about going to the game?"

She shook her head.

"It's the first in a three-game series. The next one's tomorrow afternoon. I have tickets for it, too."

Again she shook her head. "I really wish you wouldn't ask me to go places with you."

For the first time his grin was cocky and self-assured. "I really wish you'd quit turning me down. It's not helping my ego any."

She didn't smile back, but said solemnly, "I'd better go."

Gabriel hesitated before moving out of her way. "Rachel . . . thanks for coming by."

She gave a shake of her head. "We didn't settle anything." But they had. Now she knew that he wasn't going to leave her alone, and now he suspected that maybe she didn't really want him to.

"Sure we did. We talked." He deliberately refrained from mentioning the kiss that he knew had shaken her even more than him. "Do you know how long it's been since we've really talked?"

She did, right down to the hour, but she didn't answer. "Are you coming in on Monday?"

"We have a four-thirty appointment."

She nodded and walked past him. She was on the third step when he spoke her name softly. She looked up, waiting.

"Be careful."

She paused for a moment, her hand on the rail, then headed for the parking lot and her car. She was going to be *very* careful, and, if she was also very lucky, she just might come out of this in one piece.

Rachel had expected Monday's meeting with Gabriel to be uncomfortable at best, but surprisingly it was almost . . . pleasant. The simple little word made her smile. How Gabriel, with his incredible ego, would hate being described as merely "pleasant." He wouldn't understand that that was the closest thing to a compliment she could manage at the moment. Or, she thought, remembering his insight into everything she was feeling Saturday, maybe he would.

"What?"

She glanced questioningly across the desk at him.

He closed the file she'd given him when he arrived and laid it on the desk. "That's the first time I've seen you smile. What are you thinking about?"

She shook her head, changing the subject instead. "I saw where the Dodgers won yesterday's game."

His grimace was automatic. "Barely."

"Barely?" she scoffed. "The score was twelve to two. They wiped you guys out."

"You could have been there to see it for yourself if you'd accepted my invitation," he reminded her. "If you'd go tonight, I'd tell you all the Dodgers jokes I know."

"I imagine I've heard them all," she said dryly. An L.A. fan living in San Diego was considered fair game by every Padres fan in the city.

This time the subject change came from Gabriel. He didn't want to dwell on yet another refusal. "When are you leaving for Nevada?"

"Sometime this week. Tomorrow I'm going to talk to Mr. Nelson." Bill Nelson had been the owner and manager of the apartments where Jenna had lived twelve years ago. One of the other investigators had tracked him down while Rachel was in Phoenix, and Elaine had arranged an appointment. "He said that he still has some of the records, but not all."

"Where does he live now?"

"Ramona."

"Can I tag along?"

She sighed heavily. "Gabriel—"

"Come on, Rachel, give me a break. Do you think it's easy for me to sit back and let you track all the leads alone? I'm a cop, for God's sake."

"A supervisor," she tartly reminded him. "You sit back and let your detectives track leads on murder cases all the time."

He avoided mentioning the obvious—that she wasn't one of his detectives. She would have made a good one, though. "I'll keep my mouth shut. I won't interfere in any way."

"You can't go."

"Why not?"

"Nelson might not want to cooperate with a cop."

"He won't know that's what I am."

"You *look* like a cop." She paused to study his suit, a tweedy black with a stark white shirt and black tie. It was well cut, the style conservative enough for the Department but flashy enough to suit his personality. "Or maybe a drug dealer," she added thoughtfully.

Slumping down in the chair, he scowled at her. "Rachel—"

"Whichever, you can't go."

"I look like a cop today because that's what I am. Tomorrow I can look like anything I damn well please."

She simply shook her head. She didn't want to admit the real reasons he couldn't go. They were very simple, very silly and very important to her: she didn't want to make the drive to the small mountain town alone with him, and she didn't want to work side by side with him. It would be too painful. Too familiar. Although she'd spent her four years with the Department in Patrol, she had occasionally been involved, on a minor level, in some of his cases. Even when she hadn't been involved, work had been a common topic of conversation between them. Working together again, now... She'd be a fool to agree.

Gabriel's scowl faded. He wasn't really annoyed. He'd known when he suggested it that Rachel would refuse him. He would keep asking, though, because there was always the chance that sometime she would surprise him—and herself—and say yes. That would be worth the repeated refusals and rejections. "Well, if I'm going to get home and changed in time for the game, I'd better go."

Rachel half expected yet another invitation, but it didn't come. When would he tire of asking her, she wondered, and turn to someone else? Someone who didn't have to be coaxed and cajoled? And was that uncomfortable swirling in the pit of her stomach jealousy at the thought of Gabriel with another woman? "I'll see you next week."

He stopped at the door and gave her a charming grin. "You'll see me before then, Rach. I promise."

Her answering smile was both sad and weary. He'd given her promises before: *You can always count on me, Rachel. I'll always be here for you, sweetheart. If you ever need anything, come to me.* They had been pretty words of assurance, but in the end they had meant nothing. When she had needed him, he'd let her down.

When he was gone, she laid her head on the desk and closed her eyes. She was still in that position when the door opened and closed again. Quickly she sat up, relaxing only when she saw that it was Elaine.

"I could have been the boss," the secretary said with a smile, taking the seat that Gabriel had just left.

"With my luck, it wouldn't have surprised me." Rachel removed the pins that held her hair in a tidy bun, shook it out, then fastened it with a silver clasp taken from her drawer.

"How's it going with the hotshot lieutenant?"

"Why do you call him that?" she asked curiously.

"Anyone who has Russell Powell jumping the way Rodriguez does has to be a hotshot. He's awfully good-looking, isn't he?"

"Yes." Awfully.

"Has he made a pass at you yet?"

Rachel felt the warmth that signaled a blush and swore silently. Why couldn't she control her emotions like an adult—reveal what she wanted people to see and hide what she really felt?

Elaine was clearly delighted with the blush. "He *has* made a pass at you, hasn't he? Tell me all the details."

"There's nothing to tell. There was no pass." Her voice quavered only a bit. "You're forgetting, Elaine, that I used to be a cop, too. I've known Lieutenant Rodriguez for nine years. There's nothing between us." Just a lifetime of memories.

The secretary leaned back and crossed her legs. "Strictly business, huh?" she asked, feigning a yawn.

Did she always put such emphasis on business? Rachel wondered. Gabriel often mockingly repeated that phrase, and now Elaine was doing it, too. "That *is* what Powell pays me for."

"Heavens, Rachel, you sound so sanctimonious. You just might be too boring and staid for the gorgeous young lieutenant." When she saw the hurt in the other woman's eyes, Elaine was quick to apologize. "Come on, now, you know I didn't mean that, Rachel. You're gorgeous and young yourself. It's just that you seem absolutely determined to make this job the only important thing in your life. You never even so much as look at men, and heaven forbid that you actually have a life outside this office." She shook her head in exasperation. "You need to have some fun, honey, and Gabriel Rodriguez looks like he could show you a real good time."

Rachel gathered the bobby pins from her desk pad, afraid to look at Elaine for fear she would take it as encouragement to continue.

But the other woman didn't need any encouragement. "He's interested in you."

That, as she had known it would, got Rachel's attention. "Why do you say that?"

"I've seen the way he looks at you. And the way he looks when he's talking about you."

"That doesn't mean anything. I told you, we used to be friends. It doesn't mean a thing." She cringed when she realized that she'd repeated the denial. Who was she trying to convince—Elaine or herself?

"No, you told me that you'd known him for nine years. That's not the same as being friends. Being friends isn't the same as dating, and that's not the same as being lovers." Elaine watched her, her shrewd blue eyes reading all the signs. "Which one was it, hon? Acquaintances, friends or lovers?"

Quickly, clumsily, Rachel began clearing her desk. When her briefcase was loaded and the remaining files were locked in the drawer, she risked looking at her patiently waiting friend. "I can't talk about this, okay?" Her voice sounded young and unsteady. "I *really* can't talk about it."

Elaine reached across the desk and squeezed her hand. "All right, Rachel," she said quietly. "I won't pry anymore. But if you ever need a friendly shoulder..."

"Thanks." It was inadequate, but it was the best she could do. "Thanks a lot."

The drive home took more than an hour in rush-hour traffic. Rachel was relieved to see her small house, to step into its cool, quiet security, where she could relax and let down her defenses.

But tonight the house was too quiet, the security smothering. She sat on the sofa, the stereo tuned to the baseball game, and listened. There was no other noise in the house, not even a dripping faucet. If not for the broadcaster's voice and her own breathing, the place would be absolutely still. Was this what she wanted, night after night, for the rest of her life?

She thought of the house where she'd grown up in east Los Angeles. There had been Rachel, her mother and stepfather, her half sister Estrella and her half brothers Teodoro and Alberto. Never, not even in the middle of the night when the family was asleep, had that house ever been silent. There had been a blaring television, radios tuned to Spanish stations beamed from Tijuana, laughter, discussions, arguments, barking dogs, mewing cats, the creaks and groans of the house itself. It had been a home for a family. This was a house that welcomed no one but Rachel.

She had never imagined, growing up in that crowded, noisy home, that she would end up like this—thirty-three, with a career and nothing else. No one to discuss her work with, no one to share her triumphs or her failures. No one to cheer her when she was down, to encourage her when she was discouraged, to hold her when she was lonely. No one to love.

For a moment she savored the desire to call home, to talk to her mother and absorb over the distance the love and warmth and sounds of a family. But she made no move toward the phone. Rita would be happy to hear from her, but the conversation would revolve around Estrella's pregnancy, or Teodoro's two-year-old or Alberto's new wife. She didn't begrudge her family their happiness, but hearing about it tonight would only increase her sense of loneliness.

This dissatisfaction was Gabriel's fault. She had always been introspective, but not to this degree. Since seeing him in Russell Powell's office, she had spent more time than ever looking inside herself, thinking, remembering, searching for answers, brooding. If only he had stayed out of her life...

Her laugh was harsh. She could have gone on—how had he phrased it? Living a lie. She could have lived the next fifty years believing her carefully constructed lies, patting herself on the back for being so strong, so capable, for healing herself and living a normal life. All lies.

Closing her eyes, she put her mind to work, sorting through years of unwanted, painful memories. She found the darkest, the most painful, and labeled them. The night Jack died. The night innocent-happy-and-in-love Rachel had died, too. The pain was still strong, sharp edged, white hot, but she forced herself to endure, to remember.

Once the shooting team had finished with her, all she'd thought of was getting to Gabriel, drawing on his strength, his warmth, his vitality. He would help her deal with this trauma, would hold her the way he'd held her every night for the past week, would be strong for her until she could be strong for herself.

She had gone to him, the lacerations on her face cleaned and treated, her jacket covered with her blood and Jack's. And he had accused her of letting those men kill Jack. She had looked for excuses to explain his behavior—the grief, the booze. Then he had told her that she should be dead, too, that she didn't deserve to live, and the excuses no longer mattered. Nothing mattered, because *she* hadn't mattered. He had touched her only to hurt her, had spoken only to destroy her, and, in those few minutes, he had succeeded.

She had gone to him, blood on her jacket, looking for comfort, and she had left, blood on her hands, knowing that he was right, that she should be dead, too. She had sure as hell felt dead.

The following month was, thankfully, a blur. There had been visits from friends, mostly cops, who couldn't understand what she was going through, who had been sympathetic but at the same time grateful that it had been her and not them. There had been a note from Jack's widow, kind, compassionate, placing no blame, no guilt. There had been her supervisor's gentle suggestions that she see the Department psychologist, suggestions that had become orders until she had turned in her resignation.

Finally she had returned to Los Angeles, to her home, to her mother and the man who wasn't really her father but loved her like one anyway. There she had followed her sergeant's suggestion and sought out a psychologist. He had helped her cope, had helped her deal with the guilt and the sorrow. But the doctor hadn't been able to help her with Gabriel. He hadn't been able to ease her pain.

God help me, I can't forget how I hurt you.

Slowly Rachel opened her eyes and felt the wetness on her cheeks. He had sounded so sincere... but he'd sounded sincere when he'd blamed her for Jack's death, too. How could she trust him again? How could she even consider trusting him? Maybe her life wasn't perfect—okay, she admitted glumly, not even close—but at least she could wake up every morning without wondering why in God's name she hadn't died, too. It had taken a long time to reach this point, and Gabriel, if she trusted him, could so easily undo all her progress.

But what if he *was* sincere? What if he really *had* cared about her, but had let grief control him that night?

What if she spent the rest of her life alone and lonely because she was afraid to trust the only man she'd ever loved?

She was tired, emotionally and physically. Too tired to face the answers to those questions now. Too tired to face anything more demanding than sleep.

* * *

Wildcat Canyon Road ran only a few hundred yards from Rachel's house. She had liked the house when she'd first seen it a few months ago, and the road's name had appealed to some fanciful part of her nature that rarely surfaced these days, so she had bought the place. After a leisurely breakfast Tuesday morning, she turned onto the road, heading not toward the freeway and San Diego but into the hills. The road, winding through the rugged canyon and the Barona Ranch Indian Reservation, was the back way into Ramona, seldom traveled and never busy.

Bill Nelson's house was easy to find, and the old man was eager to talk. "The wife and I owned those apartments for twenty years," he said, leading her into the living room. "Have a seat there. But when that developer came in and offered all that money for the land, we didn't even hesitate. It was more money than we'd ever hoped to see in our lifetimes, and, to be honest with you, we were getting tired of the work. It was okay when we started, but being around college kids all the time can wear you out. Noisy and inconsiderate, always partying and having a good time. I don't think some of them ever made it to class." He sat down on the sofa that was set at an angle to the easy chair Rachel had chosen. "Now, what was it you wanted to know?"

She opened her briefcase, drew out the picture and handed it to him. "Do you remember this woman? She rented an apartment from you about twelve years ago."

Setting the picture down, Nelson picked up a pair of wire-rimmed glasses from the table and used both hands to fit the curved earpieces into place. Even with the glasses he squinted when he looked at the photograph. After a moment he shook his head. "There were so many.... We had an even hundred units, and they stayed full practically year-round."

"Her name was Jenna White," Rachel said. "She was older than the average student, probably twenty-five or so. She lived there for at least one semester, maybe longer."

Again he shook his head. "I don't remember her. Sorry." He handed the picture to her, and Rachel returned it to her briefcase without even glancing at it. "Why are you looking for her?" he asked curiously as he removed his glasses.

Her smile was faint. "I've been hired by an old friend of hers to find her. Mr. Nelson, you told my secretary that you still have a lot of the records on your tenants."

He nodded slowly. "There's boxes of stuff out in the garage. The wife thought we ought to just toss it in the garbage once we'd sold the place, but..." He grinned sheepishly. "I just don't care to throw things away, you know. Never know when you might need something."

"Did you require new tenants to fill out an information card of some sort?"

"Sure did."

"Could I look through them for Jenna's card?"

He took a long look at her, at her white suit and pale pink blouse, her stockings and white heels, then shook his head. "You go out in that garage and start messing in those boxes, you're gonna look like a coal miner when you finish. That stuff hasn't been touched in...oh, five or six years."

"Could I at least see them?"

Still shaking his head, he led her outside and to the detached garage at the back of the house. There were two stacks of boxes piled six high, the size of the book boxes she had used when she'd moved. "Are they in alphabetical order?" she asked, blowing a layer of dust from the top boxes.

"Nope."

She glanced at him. "By year?"

"Nope. When we cleaned out the offices, the wife just threw everything all together—rent receipts, information cards, maintenance requests, check-in slips. It's all there."

Rachel looked at the boxes again, calculating how many hours it would take to sort through the records. "Mr. Nelson, would you have any objection if I took these boxes to my office to look through? I would give you a receipt for them and bring them back as soon as I finish."

He scratched his head for a moment, considering her request. "Now what exactly is it that you do?"

"I work for Powell Investigations."

"You mean private detectives? Like on TV?"

Smiling, she nodded. "Sort of like on TV."

That idea pleased him. "Well, why not? I'll help you carry them to your car." He picked up a ragged towel from a workbench and began dusting the boxes. "But you're still gonna get that pretty white outfit filthy," he warned.

"I don't think it will be anything that the cleaners can't get out." She would just add it to Gabriel's bill.

It took six trips to load the boxes; then Rachel retrieved her briefcase from the house. She wrote out a receipt on the legal pad, wrapped it around her business card and handed it to the old man, thanking him for his cooperation at the same time.

Since sorting through the contents of the twelve boxes was going to take time, and her suit *was*, in spite of her best efforts, filthy, she decided to take the boxes to her house and work there instead of driving downtown to the office.

By midafternoon she had finished with the first two boxes. Many of the papers were old and yellowed and had to be handled carefully. The cards, fortunately, were of heavier stock, four by six inches, and had survived the years in better condition.

Rachel took a break to stretch and wash the dust from her hands. The house was so quiet. Even the stereo playing softly in the corner couldn't disguise the fact that she was alone. Always alone.

Gabriel could change that.

She tried to ignore the soft, sly whisper in her head, but it was true. He was so dynamic, so vibrantly alive. He could make the tedious task of sorting through the boxes of documents a pleasure. He could bring warmth and light to her empty house. Most of all, he could bring warmth to *her*.

Without considering her actions, without giving herself time to change her mind, she sat down beside the phone and dialed the number.

After a moment's wait there was a distracted voice at the other end. "Rodriguez."

She took a deep breath. "Gabriel, this is Rachel. Is that offer of help still open?"

Chapter 4

Gabriel climbed the three steps that led to Rachel's little tiled porch in one long stride, rang the doorbell, then restlessly shifted back and forth. He had been edgy since her unexpected call two hours ago. Rachel asking for help was enough of a suprise, but was easily surpassed by Rachel inviting him to her home. He was positive that she had never allowed another client even to know where she lived, much less visit. So much for "strictly business," he thought with a wry grin.

When she opened the door, he found another surprise. Gone was the picture-perfect role model for the up-and-coming businesswoman, and in her place was the Rachel he remembered. Instead of a suit, she wore faded jeans and a Dodger-blue T-shirt that stretched tight to follow the lines of her body. Her feet were bare, her hair was pulled into a ponytail, and there was a smudge of dust across her cheek.

Even her greeting was different. The caution was still there, but the professional reserve was gone. "Hi. Do you mind getting some of the boxes out of the car before you come in?'' She extended her keys, and Gabriel took them, catching her hand before she could draw back.

She dropped her gaze to their hands. He was holding hers firmly, but not enough to cause any pain. His fingers were long, slender and could be very gentle. He was a gentle man, yet one who could turn cruel without warning. But wasn't that contradiction part of being human? She was a strong woman, but she could sometimes be very weak. She was weak when it came to Gabriel, too weak to pull her hand away.

''Where are they?''

Her mind was blank for a moment. ''Wh— Oh, the boxes. Some are in the back seat. The rest are in the trunk.''

''Want them all?''

''Please.''

He released her hand slowly, took the keys and moved down the walk to her car. Leaving the door open, Rachel returned to the living room, where the contents of the third box were scattered over the sofa and coffee table. She went back to work, glad that she could sort the papers with only half a mind, because that was all she seemed to be using. The other half was lost in a daze, still feeling the warmth of Gabriel's touch.

He managed the nine boxes in three trips, stacking them neatly at the end of the couch. After returning the keys to her, he pushed his hands into his pockets and looked around the room. ''This will be nice when you get settled.''

From her position on the floor, she had to tilt her head back to see him. Wearing a black-and-white striped T-shirt and snug-fitting white cotton shorts, he was entirely too attractive, she thought ruefully. Her gaze slid on down to his legs, long, hard-muscled, the sexiest legs she'd ever seen on a man. ''I *am* settled,'' she said absently, while the quickening of her heartbeat suggested that she was completely *un*settled.

''There's not much here,'' Gabriel said, looking around again as he sat down on the floor at the end of the table. The furniture was nice, but there wasn't much of it—a sofa, a chair and two tables. A television, VCR and stereo system were stacked on one table, but there were no record albums, no cassette or videotapes. There were no plants, no knickknacks, no books or magazines or newspapers, and the walls were bare. It was nice but impersonal. She didn't live here—it was just a place to sleep.

Without further comment, he leaned across the table to watch her. "What are you doing?"

"All the records for the apartments are here—leases, bills, inspections, everything. I'm sorting the cards that the tenants filled out from everything else." She picked one up from the pile and extended it to him.

"I don't suppose each of these boxes represents one year."

She shook her head.

"And they're not in alphabetical order."

Another shake.

"So we've got to go through every box. And Jenna's card still might not be here."

She nodded this time. "Pick your box and find a place to work."

He obeyed her without further discussion, pulling a box down to the floor in front of him. They worked for several hours, the silence broken only briefly by quiet comments or muttered complaints, until Gabriel leaned back against the chair, stretching his arms over his head. "Is there any rule that says we can't talk while we're doing this?"

Rachel didn't answer immediately but finished flipping through the cards first. When she was done, she looked up. "No, I don't guess so."

"Good. Silence makes me crazy." He dumped all the papers unceremoniously into the box again and shoved it aside with his foot. "Doesn't it bother you to spend all these hours working and finding absolutely nothing to help you?"

She countered with her own question. "Does it bother you when you follow all the leads in a murder investigation and still don't have a suspect or a motive or a weapon?"

He wished, just once, that she would forget everything she knew about being a cop and quit challenging practically everything he said.

"Look, I'm paid to do a job," she explained. "I don't have to enjoy it, and I don't have to be pleased with the outcome. It's a *job*."

"You *do* have to like it," he disagreed. "Maybe not the tedious little jobs like this, but overall you have to like what you're doing."

She neatly repacked her box and carried it to the others against the wall. Bending, she scooped up Gabriel's box and added it to the stack. "Why?"

"Because you couldn't do a good job if you didn't like it."

"People all around the world work hard at jobs that they hate," she reasonably pointed out.

"But not you." He reached for another box, then folded his hands on top of it and looked at her. "You're not the type to stay in a job that you hate, that offers no satisfaction."

Rachel wished that he was right. Technically, she supposed, he was: she *did* like her job, almost as much as she had liked being a cop, and sometimes more.

But in another, more important, way he was wrong. She was living a life that she hated, a life that brought her little or no satisfaction. Her job was the only important thing, as Elaine had said. She had learned the art of self-protection so well that no one could get close enough to hurt her. Her life was as sparsely furnished as Gabriel thought her house was—with no friends, no lovers, no obligations or responsibilities other than her job. There was no personal clutter in her house, and no emotional clutter in her life. She had thought her life was safe, but now she knew that was a lie. It was barren. Empty. In removing all risk of being hurt, she had also removed all chance of being happy.

Realizing that she'd made no response, Gabriel looked at her. She was staring at the tabletop, her eyes glazed with—

Not tears, he thought with a rush of panic. He couldn't

handle tears—not now, not in person. If she cried, he would try to hold her, and she would push him away and would be ashamed of her weakness. He was sure of it. Rachel Martinez didn't cry in front of others—not when Jack had died, not when her own injuries had been treated, not when Gabriel had turned on her. She did her grieving alone, in private, the way a strong person should.

But that sheen in her eyes was definitely the wetness of tears. To ignore it, he seized the first totally unimportant subject that came to mind. "Before we start on these, let's get something to eat."

The sound of his voice pulled her back to the present, back to him. Surreptitiously she wiped a tear from the corner of one eye, grateful that he hadn't noticed it, and agreed to have dinner with him.

Gabriel sat straighter. "Really?"

Her expression was as carefully blank as her eyes when she looked at him. "Really what?"

"You agreed to have dinner with me. See, persistence pays off. I told you that eventually I would ask, and you would say yes, and, as usual, I was right."

He sounded so smugly pleased with himself that she couldn't have changed her acceptance even if she'd wanted to. But the truth was, she *didn't* want to. She was tired of solitary meals. Of solitary life. She wasn't meant to spend so much time alone, and Gabriel was the one she wanted to spend time with. Maybe it wasn't wise—maybe it was weak—but it was what she wanted, and tonight she would take the opportunity.

"I probably have something in the refrigerator that I could fix," she murmured, turning her attention back to the box in front of her.

"Probably? You don't know?"

"I don't cook much." There wasn't any sense in cooking for only one.

"I don't, either, but I can tell you exactly what's in my refrigerator."

"What, beer?" she asked dryly.

He stiffened, then shook his head. "I don't drink anymore."

Her hands trembled slightly, but she didn't dare look at him. She didn't want to ask what had prompted that decision, didn't want to hear his answer. "You never did drink much," she responded in a neutral tone.

That was true, he acknowledged. A shot of whiskey, a few beers a week—that had been his limit. But the night he had decided to surpass his limit, he'd done it with a vengeance. The ache in his head had taken three days to go away. The ache in his soul hadn't stopped yet. His voice was quiet with that remembered pain when he spoke again. "You don't need to cook. Let's go out."

"I'll have to change before we go." Rachel stood up and stepped over the box, then turned back and sat on the sofa. "Would it have made a difference?" she asked quietly.

His eyes asked the question for him.

"If you hadn't been drinking...would you still have said those things?"

He knew what that question had cost her, how painful the memory of that night was for her. Would she take any comfort in knowing that the answer was just as painful for him? He wanted to say no, that if he'd been sober and clearheaded he never would have said them. But the whiskey hadn't been the only thing clouding his mind. There had been grief, sorrow, anger and fear. Fear that someone had killed Jack and had tried to kill Rachel. Fear that the next time she might not be so lucky. Fear of losing her. "I don't know."

She nodded and smiled, a taut, unhappy little gesture, and stood up again. "I'll be ready in a few minutes."

In the bathroom connected to her bedroom, she washed the dust from her arms and hands, then splashed cool water over her face. She changed into a pair of khaki shorts and a loose red top, then replaced the rubber band holding her hair with a red plastic banana clip. It held her hair together vertically, but let it fall in soft, curling waves to the center of her shoulders.

Gabriel was standing near the front door, studying the keypad for the alarm system. "Who installed this?" he asked when he heard her reenter the room.

Rachel gave him the name of one of the best home security consultants in town, a former cop, and he nodded in recognition. "He does good work."

"I was counting on that." She got her purse and joined him at the door, tapping in the sequence of numbers that would turn the alarm on as soon as the door was closed.

"Does it bother you, living alone out here?"

She followed him to his car, waiting while he opened the door for her. "Not really. It's very quiet."

He closed the door behind her and circled around the car. When he'd gotten in and fastened his seat belt, he started the engine, then carefully backed up, avoiding the potholes in the driveway. "And you like quiet."

A few weeks ago she would have quickly and truthfully answered yes. Peace and quiet—that was all she had demanded of her home. But there had been too much peace and quiet, too much time for introspection, for soul-searching, thinking, remembering, feeling. Too much time to regret the past and dread the future, because it didn't hold much promise of being any better than the present. "Sometimes," she said slowly, "you need it."

"And sometimes you need other people."

"Yes," she agreed.

She fell silent then, and Gabriel turned on the tape deck to cover this. Occasionally he glanced at her, wondering what was going on in her mind, whether he was somehow responsible for the pensive look on her face. She stared ahead but didn't see anything, didn't ask where he was taking her, didn't even seem to be aware of him.

"How is your family?"

She blinked rapidly before turning toward him. "What?"

"Your family? Remember—Mom and Dad, your sister and brothers."

"You really meant it when you said silence makes you crazy, didn't you? What interest could you possibly have in my family? You never even met them."

He was interested precisely because they were her family. Because everything about her interested him. "I've talked to your mother before, when we were still together." God, it was hard to say that so casually! "She wanted you to get married. She thought that if you found a nice, dependable man, you would forget about being a cop, settle down and have babies."

That wasn't quite accurate. Rita Martinez had actually said how nice it was that her daughter had found a nice, dependable Hispanic boy; maybe now she would quit the Department, get married and give her mother many grandchildren. And he had politely explained that, in spite of his surname, he wasn't Hispanic, but would a nice, dependable Indian boy do?

Rachel remembered similar conversations with her mother, but, years later, she was embarrassed that her mother had discussed such a personal subject with Gabriel. "Well, I never met any nice, dependable men, and I'm not sure having babies is all it's cracked up to be, but at least she got one of her wishes. I quit being a cop."

His long fingers tightened around the steering wheel. "That's enough. No more tonight, okay?" he demanded, his voice sharp and ragged.

She stared at him, surprised by his outburst. What had she said to provoke him? she wondered, then realized. *I never met any nice, dependable men.* He thought she was getting in another dig, when she had simply spoken without thinking. "I wasn't talking about you," she said softly. "Just men in general."

He left the freeway to cross the bridge that linked San Diego with Coronado, across the bay. "How many men have you known, Rachel?" he asked sarcastically. "In general?"

"Enough." She looked out the window again, allowing him to see only a small portion of her face.

He opened his mouth, then closed it again. He wasn't going to pick a fight with her, not now, when she was finally treating him like a person and not some monster from the nightmare of her past. "Remember the deli on Orange Avenue?"

She heard the forced edge to his voice and recognized the effort he was making to control his temper. If he could try so hard, she decided, so could she. "I haven't been there in years." They had the best avocado and bacon cheeseburgers in the county, and a big-screen TV that was always tuned—*loudly*—to whatever sports event was being broadcast. Conversation was difficult; intimate conversation was impossible.

The deli hadn't changed one bit in five years. They chose a table near the television and talked very little while they ate. Rachel watched the baseball game, and Gabriel watched her.

She was beautiful—really, incredibly beautiful. The lines of her face were delicate, her skin smooth and ageless. Her eyes were soft brown, deep, touched with sorrow and strength and maturity, and her mouth... He remembered the kiss they had shared a few days ago, her passion, his hunger, and his hand clenched into a violent fist. He wanted to kiss her again, to kiss her until she pleaded for him, until she needed him, *wanted* him, as much as he needed and wanted her. *Until she loved him.*

She turned from the game and gestured to his empty plate. "Are you ready?" The noise from the television and the young men gathered around it was making her head hurt, and she was too distracted, too aware of Gabriel, to follow the game.

Nodding, he followed her out of the deli to the car. Instead of turning back toward the bridge, though, he drove along the beach. "Let's take a walk," he suggested suddenly, maneuvering the car into a parking space. "We can watch the sunset."

How long had it been since she'd taken the time to enjoy such a simple pleasure? Too long, she answered wryly, since she couldn't even remember it. They climbed the steps to the top of the seawall, then headed down again, into the soft, warm, shifting sand, before walking toward the water. As the sun began its final descent into the ocean, Rachel stopped beyond the reach of the advancing tide and sat down to watch. Gabriel dropped down beside her.

Vivid hues of rose, pink, purple, blue and gold colored the western sky. Rachel stared at it, fascinated by its beauty, and, once again, Gabriel stared at her, fascinated by *her* beauty. How long would she make him wait before he could touch her, before he could hold her, make love to her, *possess* her? When would she decide that he had paid enough? Or would he ever pay enough to satisfy her?

"Rachel."

The hoarseness of his voice sent shivers down her spine. Slowly her gaze shifted until finally she was looking at him.

"How long are you going to hate me?"

Quickly she turned away and busied herself with removing her sandals and shaking the sand from them. She laid them beside her, carefully arranging them so that they were perfectly straight, side by side. She could have fiddled with them all night if Gabriel hadn't taken her chin gently in his hand and, with great care, forced her to look at him.

"How long, Rachel? Another five years? Ten? The rest of our lives?"

"I don't know," she said quietly. "Maybe."

His chuckle sounded infinitely sad. "Well, that's better than a definite yes." Then he grew solemn again. "I *am* sorry, Rachel—more than you'll ever know."

"I don't want an apology, Gabriel. I've never wanted that."

"What *do* you want? Do you want me to suffer as much as *you* have? Do you want to live your life alone, never touched by anyone or anything?"

"There's nothing wrong with being alone," she bravely lied. "If you don't let anyone get close, then you can't get hurt."

He shook his head slowly back and forth. "That's not true, Rachel. You haven't let anyone get close to you for five years, but you're still hurting. It's in your eyes, your manner. You act like a frightened little rabbit if anyone gets near you."

She scooted back, away from the soft warmth of his hand. "Not just anyone, Gabriel, *you*. And I have reason to be afraid of you."

Groaning, he grasped her hands and held them tight. "No, you don't. I'll never hurt you, honey. I swear to God, I'll never hurt you again."

Her heart was pounding so loudly that it drowned out the waves, and her lungs were too constricted to take in air. "Lies," she whispered. "I can't believe your lies."

"Then believe this." He slid his hands up to her shoulders and pulled her close, claiming her mouth with his. Her small cry of dismay was softened and muted by his kiss. She fought him, but he wrapped his arms around her, pinning her own arms at her sides. She continued the struggle internally, resisting the need to return the kiss, the overwhelming need to give in to him, to give him everything—the anger, the resentment, the passion, the heat—and trust him to handle it all.

He felt the very instant she surrendered. The hands that had been pushing him away were now reaching for him, seeking the warmth of his skin beneath the T-shirt, and the teeth that had been clenched in fury were open, allowing his tongue entry to the dark, moist warmth of her mouth. He gentled his touch, gentled his kiss, as he carefully, awkwardly, lowered her to the sand.

God, he wanted her so badly, he could die! His heart was racing, his body trembling, and he was so hard that he ached with it.

And he was on a nearly deserted but very public beach.

His groan vibrated through her before he forced himself away. "Rachel, honey..."

She stared at him, leaning only inches above her. Her eyes were dazed. She realized that she had given in to need—

heaven help her, had given in to *Gabriel*—and shadows turned her eyes dark. Scooting away, she sat up and began brushing sand from her clothes, began rebuilding the walls around her.

Gabriel stared at her. She was cool and calm, untouchable. He needed her, wanted her, so badly that he was dying with it, but *she* was unaffected. Disappointment turned to anger, irrational, white-hot. He made a brief but futile effort to control his temper; then it exploded.

Rachel was startled when he caught her shoulder and pushed her to the sand again. "What are you—"

He clamped his hand over her mouth. "Don't turn away from me!" he commanded furiously. "Don't you dare kiss me like that, then turn away as if nothing happened!"

She pushed his hand from her mouth, swallowed hard to clear the lump in her throat and took a deep breath to calm her quaking so he couldn't see the hunger inside her. "Nothing *did* happen," she said with feigned calm. "It was just a kiss."

His smile came slowly, and it was ugly. Cold. "Do you just pretend, Rachel?" he asked softly. "Or do you believe your own lies?" Knowing that she wouldn't answer, he didn't wait. "That's a symptom of a serious illness, isn't it? Maybe you should talk to your shrink about it."

His body blocked her right arm, so she raised her left hand and deliberately, powerfully, slapped his face. He flinched, feeling the jarring sensations all the way through his teeth. "You're a bastard, Gabriel," she hissed.

For long moments they stared at each other, the fury that had drained from his eyes now filling hers. Slowly he rolled away from her and sat up, his arms resting on his knees, his hands loosely clasped. "I know." Only moments ago he had promised never to hurt her, and now he had done just that, deliberately, because her rejection had hurt *him*.

Slowly she sat up, too. There was sand in her hair and clothes, but she made no move to brush it away.

"Help me, Rachel."

The plea was soft, tortured, almost lost in the sounds of the ocean. She tried to ignore it, tried not to feel the pain behind it, tried to close herself off again, but none of it worked.

"Help me be the kind of man you want. Show me. Teach me." He turned his head to look at her, letting her see the desperate longing in his eyes. "Please . . . help me."

Frantically she looked away, wishing she were anywhere in the world but here. But she *was* here, and no amount of wishing could change that. "Look, you just feel guilty— that's all it is," she said urgently. "Because of what happened, you feel you owe me something, that you have to make it up to me, but you don't, so you can just forget about it. Forget about *me*. You don't—"

He interrupted her, his voice calm and distant and empty. "Did you know that I was in love with you?"

Rachel's mouth hung open, and, for an instant, the world stopped. So many times she had longed to hear those words from him. One "I love you" would have made everything that followed so much easier, but he had never offered it. Why not? Why had he never said the words when she had wanted them so badly? Why was he telling her now? "No," she whispered. She shook her head so fiercely that the red clip popped open and landed silently in the sand, leaving her hair free. "I don't believe you."

He tilted his head back and stared at the sky for a moment, then sighed heavily. "No," he said, "I didn't think you would." Not when he'd waited so many years to tell her. Not when he'd kept his secret for so long. He had known back then that he should tell her, but he had wanted to wait, had wanted to be sure that her response would be more encouraging than Jenna's. Jenna hadn't wanted his love, had in the end rejected it by leaving. If Rachel's reaction had been the same . . .

But it hadn't been. Because he'd never given her the chance to accept or reject it. To accept or reject *him*.

Giving another deep sigh, he picked up the sandals and extended them to her. While she put them on, he reached for the red plastic clip, handing it to her when she was done.

The walk back to the car was silent. So was the long drive home. When Gabriel brought the car to a halt behind Rachel's own car and reached to shut off the engine, she stopped him. "Don't."

"What about the boxes?"

"I'll take care of them." Opening the car door, she swung her feet to the ground, then twisted to face him. "After all, I'm the one being paid to do it."

He started to reach for her, then curled his fingers into a fist. "I know I really made a mess of things tonight, Rachel," he said in a low, dark voice. "I'm sorry."

She had a ridiculous urge to ease his guilt, to share the blame with him. "I seem to bring out the worst in you," she said with an awkward shrug.

The dim light showed his sad smile. "Not you. You've always been the best thing in my life." Better than Jenna, better even than the child he had fathered. "If you want off this case, I'll talk to Powell. I'll tell him that I've changed my mind. He won't blame you."

He was offering to leave her alone—the very thing she'd been asking for ever since he'd reentered her life. She should be elated, but all she could think of was how lonely and empty she'd been for so long.

She got out of the car and closed the door, then bent to look at him through the open window. "I've never quit a case yet. This isn't going to be the first. Good night, Gabriel."

She worked long into the night, until her eyes refused to stay open and her brain could no longer process the information it was given. Leaving the living room scattered with papers, she trudged down the hall to her bedroom. She undressed in the quiet, dark room, slid between cool, scented sheets and closed her eyes, willing sleep to come.

Did you know that I was in love with you?

She rolled over, fluffing the pillow with a punch that stopped just short of being vicious. It was a lie, a line calculated to get through her defenses. He'd made it clear that he wanted more than a professional relationship with her. This talk of love—this lie—must be his way of getting it.

The house was so quiet that her breathing, rapid and agitated, seemed to echo. She realized that her muscles were rigid, strained to the limit to maintain control. She moved onto her back, took deep breaths, forcing oxygen into her lungs, and practiced the relaxation techniques she'd learned long ago in yoga.

You've always been the best thing in my life.

She made a strangled sound, then unclenched her teeth and concentrated. Start with the toes, the feet, the ankles, she silently instructed. Let them relax, become limp, heavy, sink into the bed.

. . . the best thing in my life.

Next the calves, the thighs, the hips. She allowed a tiny relieved smile when she realized that it was working. She was in control. She was strong.

The heaviness claimed her at last, leaving her still, insensate, on the edge of dark, enveloping sleep. Her mind released its last hold on consciousness, and her breathing slowed into a deep, natural rhythm.

. . . the best thing.

Rachel overslept Wednesday morning. When she awoke, she knew immediately that she had dreamed through the night, but mercifully she remembered only minor details— haziness, blood, fear. She had dreamed a lot in the first months after Jack's death, had considered it great progress when she had learned to sleep through the terrors. Now the dreams came only rarely, and she remembered little and dealt calmly with the aftereffects—the sluggishness, the slow responses, the dull, thudding headache.

After getting dressed, she called Elaine and told her that she would be working at home again today, then returned to the mess in the living room. The last box that she had worked on so meticulously in the weary early-morning hours was a bigger mess than when she'd started. Since she couldn't guarantee to herself, much less Russell Powell and Gabriel, that she'd done a thorough job on it, she went through it again.

Did you know that I was in love with you?

She could hear the question now without the tiny emotional shock waves rocketing through her. It was a lie, of course. She had recognized that immediately, but, oh, how she would have liked to believe it if only for a moment!

He had been good to her. Without the animosity and anger and hurt clouding her perception, she could look back and see that he had treated her well, except for that last night. He had been her friend and confidant. Her lover. He had made her laugh, had held her, had made love to her. He had let her share his life and in exchange, he had made her life better, happier, brighter. And he'd done it all as if he truly cared. As if he truly loved her.

But he hadn't. If he had loved her, he couldn't have said the things he did. If he had loved her, he couldn't have hurt her that way.

So he had lied.

She wasn't disappointed, except maybe in some small secret part of her soul. People did what they had to in order to get by. If Gabriel wanted to lie about his feelings for her, what would it hurt as long as she wasn't foolish enough to believe him? And since she *wasn't* foolish, what would it hurt to spend some time with him the way he wanted—the way *she* wanted? She would keep herself safe, and for a while at least, she wouldn't be alone. What could it hurt?

The apartment records turned up nothing. Mr. Nelson had warned her that they were incomplete, but she had hoped . . .

She closed the last box, interlocking the flaps. Did it bother her, after hours of work, to end up with absolutely nothing? Gabriel had asked her that question yesterday, and she had countered by turning the question back on him, on *his* work. But now she admitted that, on this case at least, the answer was yes. She'd had such hopes that one of those boxes would hold everything she needed to find Jenna White. The hopes had been unrealistic, and now she was paying with her disappointment.

So now she would go to Nevada.

Stretching out on the sofa, she reached for the phone and called the office, asking Elaine to schedule the trip to Nevada for the following Monday. Her next call was to Gabriel. Although it was after five, she decided to try to reach him at the police station. "Is Lieutenant Rodriguez in?" she asked when she'd reached the detective division.

The detective who had answered the phone was the closest to Gabriel's office. Balancing the phone between his shoulder and his ear, he glanced through the open door and saw his boss at the desk. "Yes, he is. Your name?"

She hesitated. So many years later, and she was still uncomfortable talking to police officers, afraid that they might have known Jack, that they might remember her, might blame her, or possibly worse, pity her. After all, she had been through a traumatic experience, one that they risked every day on the job, but she hadn't handled it well. "Rachel . . . Martinez."

There was a brief pause that made her flinch, then, surprisingly, a hearty greeting. "*Rachel?* God, it's been a long time. This is Pat Jones—remember me?"

She did. They had joined the Department at the same time, had gone through the academy together, but she had gone into Patrol, Pat into Traffic. "So you made detective. Congratulations."

"Thanks. The work is harder, but it beats hell out of writing tickets. Are you back in San Diego?"

"Yes, I moved back a few months ago."

In his office Gabriel heard Rachel's name and looked up, his narrowed gaze directed at the younger man. Broodingly he raised his right hand to his face and rubbed the bruises that marked his cheek, four thin lines that formed an incomplete outline of three fingers. No one had recognized the marks for what they were, or if they had, they hadn't had the nerve to comment on it. His mood today could at best be described as dangerous.

"Hang on just a minute." Jones covered the mouthpiece with one hand and called, "Lieutenant, Rachel Martinez calling for you."

His lean finger traced the bruises again; then he said flatly, loud enough for her to hear, "Take a message."

Rachel knew there could be a dozen reasons why he couldn't take her call: he could be wading through the numerous, lengthy reports that each case required; interviewing a suspect or a witness; meeting with other detectives; or handling any of the dozens of other little jobs that came under his responsibility. But none of those had anything to do with it, she was positive. He simply didn't want to talk to her.

Because of last night? she wondered, feeling the tiny ache in her chest. Her dark side was amused. Of course it was because of last night. What man liked being slapped, lied to and then called a liar?

When the detective stumbled over his excuse, she gently interrupted. "I heard, Pat. Tell him—" What message could she leave that wouldn't give her curious old friend too much information? Gabriel didn't want anyone in the Department to know that he had hired her, and he certainly wouldn't want them to think that he had something personal going with her. "Ah, no message, Pat, all right? Listen, it was good talking to you. Take care."

Pat Jones said goodbye, then turned back to the report he was writing. Gabriel left his desk to stand in the doorway. "What did she say?"

"Nothing. No message. How do you spell 'perpetrator'?"

"S-u-s-p-e-c-t." He returned to his desk and leaned back in the chair, folding his hands over his stomach. He should have talked to her, but the last thing he needed now was to hear her voice—soft, dark, velvety warm even when it was totally professional.

When Pat finished the report, he took it to Gabriel, laying it on the desk. "Can you imagine Rachel coming back after so long? Considering what happened, I'd think San Diego would be the last place she'd want to live." He lowered his voice and added in a soft, confiding tone, "I heard that she'd had a breakdown after the shooting."

Gabriel lifted a fiercely cold gaze to the younger man's face. "Don't spread gossip about another officer," he warned in a soft voice. "Do you understand, Detective?"

Belatedly Pat remembered that his boss and Rachel had been much more than just friends, and he flushed uncomfortably. "I'm sorry...I forgot...." The scowl got colder, and Pat squirmed. "Yes, sir, I understand. I'm leaving now, okay?" He rushed the words out, waited an instant for Gabriel to object, then hurriedly walked out.

Breakdown. It was an ugly word, indicative of weakness. Rachel had had problems, Gabriel acknowledged, but she had never been weak. In a matter of hours she had undergone multiple emotionally traumatic events, any one of which would have scarred the strongest man: she had helplessly watched her partner and friend die; she had survived an attempt on her own life; she had killed two men; and she had been rejected and betrayed by her lover. She had survived all four, yet her former co-workers talked with morbid curiosity about a breakdown.

Leaning forward, he fished a file folder from the bottom of the stack that covered his desk. In an edgy, restless mood since last night's fiasco at the beach, he had requested the file from Records first thing this morning, but once it arrived, he hadn't opened it. Now he did.

He had read the preliminary reports as soon as they were completed, had read every supplemental report as it had come in, and everything he'd read had told him what he'd known all along: if anyone carried the blame for Jack's death, it was the man who shot him, and Jack himself. Not Rachel.

Although he would never forget the details, he read the account of the shooting again. It had been a cold February night when Jack and Rachel had stopped their patrol car to question two men parked in the lot of a store that was closed for the night. There had been a rash of late-night robberies in the area, so they weren't taking any chances.

But Jack *had* taken chances. The driver had gotten out of the car to meet him, while Rachel, positioned behind and to the right of the suspect's car, had watched the passenger. When the man had claimed that his license and registration were in the car, Jack had let him return alone to get it—a mistake no rookie should have made. Instead the man had gotten a gun, shot Jack and taken aim at Rachel. Quick reflexes had saved her, although shattering glass from the windshield had lacerated her face. She had returned fire and shot first the driver, then the passenger, who had come out with his own gun. By the time she'd gotten to him, Jack was dead. They were all dead. And Gabriel had left her to deal with it alone.

He could have helped her. He *should* have helped her. But he hadn't, not then, so now he would. She had said last night that she didn't want to quit the case, and he would respect that decision. But she could handle it without him. There was really no reason for her to see him at all—he'd told her everything he knew about Jenna, and the weekly reports could be delivered in the mail as easily as in person.

She had repeatedly asked him to leave her alone, had told him that she couldn't trust him, couldn't forgive him. Now she wouldn't have to. She could forget that he even existed.

But, dear God, how was *he* going to forget *her*?

Chapter 5

It was nearly nine o'clock when Gabriel pulled into his private parking space and shut off the engine. It had been a hell of a long day, and he was tired—maybe, if he was lucky, tired enough to sleep. Tired enough to stop thinking.

The sidewalks that led to each small building were well lit, but the bright lights made the shadows deeper, darker. It was from one of those shadows near the bottom of his stairs that another shadow emerged. His hand flew beneath his coat to his gun, releasing the thumbsnap strap that held it secure and sliding it free of the holster.

Immediately the figure froze, hands in midair, palms out. "It's just me, Gabriel," Rachel said quietly.

He gave an exasperated sigh, wishing he could shake her until her head rattled. Instead he reholstered the gun and fastened the strap.

"Jumping at shadows, are we?" she asked dryly, tucking her hands into her jeans pockets.

"You know better than to sneak up on a cop, Rachel. It's a good way to get your head—" He thought of the report he'd read, complete with pictures of the two men she'd killed, and bit off the rest of the words. "I wasn't expecting you." Not after he'd finally decided to do as she had so often asked and leave her alone. Not when he'd finally discovered that, although it would cost him a great deal, he could be noble, after all, and step out of her life. And here she was, blocking the exit.

"Obviously. I can leave if this is inconvenient."

Still exasperated, he took her arm and pointed her toward the stairs. "Unexpected does not mean the same as inconvenient," he pointed out with exaggerated patience. "I figured you were still working."

At the top of the stairs, he released her and unlocked the door, reaching inside to switch on a light, and Rachel entered the small apartment for the first time in more than five years. It had once been as familiar to her as her own home. She knew the furniture, the prints and photos on the walls, had bought some of the books that lined the shelves.

She waited until he gestured to the sofa before she sat down. "I'm going to Carson City, Nevada, Monday."

"Why not tomorrow?" He had assumed that, after last night, she would want to put as much distance between them as possible.

"If I don't find anything in Nevada, I'm going on to Utah and Colorado without coming back here. If I go tomorrow, I'll only be able to work the afternoon and Friday, then I'll have to wait through the weekend. I don't like wasted time."

"No, I don't suppose you do." He removed his jacket and hung it carelessly over the back of a dining chair. His tie came off next, dangling by its loop from the same chair. Unselfconsciously he unbuckled his belt, slid the holster off and laid it on the table, then discarded the belt, too. Rolling his sleeves up, he sat down at the opposite end of the sofa. He sat sideways so he could watch her, his black eyes shrewdly studying her. Finally, he asked, "Are you here for an apology?"

She nodded.

"All right." Her presumption—that he would even want to see her, much less apologize to her—didn't bother him. When he was wrong, he admitted it willingly. "I'm sorry. I had no right to say—"

"No."

The interruption stopped his words cold.

"I came to apologize to you."

Gabriel smiled slowly until the whitest, most perfect teeth she'd ever seen were showing. "What have you got to apologize for?" he asked lazily.

Rachel couldn't look at him and face the amusement that laced his voice. "Last night."

"I didn't ask when, sweetheart, but what."

Color was climbing steadily up her throat into her face. She had to clear her throat to answer. "I shouldn't have slapped you. Resorting to physical violence is a sign of weakness, and it doesn't accomplish anything."

"I don't know," he disagreed, his eyes sparkling even when he absently touched his fingertips to the marks on his cheeks. "It made me shut up, didn't it? So it *did* accomplish something."

She noticed his movement and leaned closer to get a better look at him. When she saw the bruises, faint, ugly discolorations against his darkly tanned skin, she paled. "Oh, Gabriel..." She raised trembling fingers to touch the narrow lines. "Oh, God, Gabriel..."

He saw the dismay that made her eyes dark shadows in her face and pulled her hand away, clasping it in his. "That sounds good," he teased. "I just wish you were saying it for different reasons."

"I'm so sorry."

He correctly anticipated that she would try to withdraw and held her hand tighter. "I deserved that and more for what I said. Come here, Rachel."

She knew she shouldn't, but when he tugged, she moved closer. He kept her hand and raised his other hand to cup her chin, stopping her from ducking her head. "There's nothing weak about it, Rachel. I provoked you, and you reacted. It's perfectly normal."

She shook her head. "It isn't normal for me to react physically."

"Isn't it?" he countered, his voice low, dark, seductive. "If I kissed you now, would your heart beat faster, like last night? Would your lungs get tight? Would your nipples harden? Would your body get hot and flushed and ready for me?"

She stared at him, her eyes wide, dark and smoky, unable to deny his questions. All those things were happening to her now, with no more stimulus than his voice.

"Those are physical responses, Rachel. I'm provoking you, and you..." He let his hand glide over her throat, feeling her heart beat, then down across the soft cotton of her blouse to her breast, full, aching, hard. "You're reacting. Physically."

And she wasn't the only one, he thought with a grin, finding humor in his own discomfort. He had set out to prove his point by arousing her, but the stronger response was his own. He was growing harder by the minute with a hunger that he knew, as well as he knew this woman, would go unsatisfied tonight.

"I lied to you," she whispered.

Back to confessing her sins, he thought wryly. "About what?"

"I don't hate you," she replied, her face flushing with the admission, "and I'm not afraid of you." Right now the bigger danger seemed to be herself. After all, she hadn't voiced one complaint about him touching her, hadn't pushed his big, gentle hand from her breast where it still rested, sending heated little sparks through her nerves and making her tingle.

"You're entitled to both—the hate and the fear." But he knew she wouldn't claim them, not anymore. She was too gentle to hate him, too strong to fear him.

He moved his hand back and forth, and she stiffened, stunned by sensation. The tiny friction felt so good against her sensitive nipple that it was almost painful. She tried to find the will to push him away, but it had been so long, and it felt so good. "I—I called you a liar." The last word ended on a low moan as his fingers closed over her nipple, protected only by her blouse, and gently squeezed.

"Hey, I'm a big boy now," he reminded her in a husky voice. And if she needed proof of that, he could show her. He could show her so much if she would only let him. "Name calling doesn't hurt me anymore, sweetheart."

He waited to see if she had anything else to confess. When she remained silent, he leaned forward to kiss her. His mouth was sweet, gentle and giving, letting her taste him, letting her control him. She raised her hand, laying her palm against his cheek, and hesitantly stroked his tongue with hers, luring him deeper, making him harder, hungrier.

It would be such a simple matter to slide his hand beneath her blouse to the breast that he knew was bare and needy for his attention; to remove the blouse and sample the hard buds with his lips, teeth and tongue; to guide her hand to the heaviness between his thighs. But such intimacies would frighten her, he was sure. She was ready to relax her vigilance around him, ready even to kiss him, but not ready to make the commitment that making love would require. She wasn't ready to trust him.

Rachel felt him withdrawing and, for a moment, was unable—or unwilling?—to let him go. He released her breast and shifted, preparing to move her away, and she felt his hardness against her hip. The heat penetrated all the way through to her core, shocking, burning, branding her, and her hand fell away from his face.

She blinked at him as if startled awake from a deep sleep; then color flooded her cheeks. Hastily she scrambled to the other end of the sofa, brushing her fingers through her hair to temporarily hide her face.

Gabriel watched her from his end, his eyes solemn, his smile faint. "It's all right, Rachel."

"I—I didn't mean to..." Embarrassed, she looked away.

"Didn't mean to what? Arouse me?" He chuckled softly. "Honey, all I have to do is look at you and I get aroused. You can no more change that than I can change the past." He saw her flinch and open her mouth to change the subject. He interrupted before the first sound was completed. "What bothers you more—talking about the past, or how much I want to make love to you?"

"I—I . . ." She was completely flustered. Her brain was frantically working to find rational arguments to turn him away from both subjects while her body was lamenting the all-too-soon end of the kiss. "This isn't appropriate conversation for business associates," she protested when her voice finally agreed to work again.

"No, it isn't," he pleasantly agreed. "But it's entirely appropriate for two people who used to be lovers and will be again."

"No," she whispered, shaking her head, but she knew even then that it was true. She didn't want to be his lover, didn't want to give him that control, didn't want to be weak, but she needed him. She needed the joy and the light that he could bring her, the laughter and the warmth, the strength and the intimacy and the loving. For just a while she needed to care about someone and believe that he cared about her, too, or the cold, empty loneliness would swallow her up for good.

But becoming Gabriel's lover wasn't the way to keep the loneliness at bay. Her love for him had been so strong, so intense. What if part of it still lived inside her? God help her, what if she fell in love with him all over again? Wouldn't the loneliness be worse than ever once he'd finished with her? She had lost him once and had suffered terribly. Could she survive it a second time?

"Why?" she whispered. "You could have any woman you want."

"Then why is the only woman I want looking at me as if I'm some sort of monster?"

"You don't need me."

His smile was sad with remorse. "Oh, you're wrong there, sweetheart. I do need you." Needed her to mend his heart, to heal his mind and save his soul. But hearing those things would frighten her, so he kept them to himself. "This is all your fault, Rachel. I was prepared to do the *right* thing and leave you alone. I was going to tell you that you didn't have to talk to me or see me or have anything to do with me. But I came home, and you were waiting for me, and..." His gaze dropped to her breasts, her nipples still embarrassingly hard beneath her blouse. "I'm not an honorable man, Rachel. I won't let you go."

She wished she could believe him. She knew he wanted her tonight, but what about tomorrow, next week, next month, next year? When would he get tired and look for someone to replace her? When would he let her down again? "I think I made a mistake in coming here," she said shakily, rising to her feet.

He stood up, too, and blocked her way. "No, the only mistakes have been mine. I was a real bastard to you when Jack died. I let you down when you needed me. I let you go when I should have been on my knees begging you to forgive me. They were mistakes, Rachel, and they were mine. You haven't done anything wrong."

He was touching her with his gentleness, with his sadness—touching her heart and her soul. In defense she struck back, lying. "I didn't need you. You'd done enough to me already."

His smile was faint and sorrowful. "Hating me made you strong, didn't it?"

The idea appalled her, and she opened her mouth to tell him so, but the denial wouldn't come. "Yes," she whispered, stunned by the realization. She turned away from him, walking to the sliding door that led to the balcony, and stared out, seeing nothing. When she spoke again, her voice was so soft that he had to strain to hear it. "I don't think I hated you, exactly, but I wanted you to suffer. There was so much pain and no one to share it with, so I had to find ways to fight it. The only emotions that were strong enough to stand against it were negative—anger, resentment, bitterness. Hatred.''

Gabriel closed the distance between them and laid his hands gently on her shoulders. ''It's all right.''

She didn't seem to hear him. ''I saw a psychologist for a long time.''

''Death is always hard to handle. Violent death is even harder.''

Rachel leaned against him, feeling the warmth of his chest against her back, and he slid his arms around her. He felt strong, she thought. Solid. ''I thought about dying a lot. It would have been easy. There are so many ways to do it— quick or slow, messy or neat. It would have solved all my problems.''

Hugging her tighter, Gabriel hid his face in the sweet softness of her hair and hoped that she didn't feel the shudder that rocked through him.

''But it wouldn't have been fair to my family, or to you.'' She smiled faintly at their reflection in the glass as he looked up. ''I knew you would feel guilty if I did anything stupid. But, more than that, I knew that I really didn't want to die. Life was pretty miserable at the time, but I wasn't ready to give it up yet.''

''Rachel—''

She reached up to clasp his hands. ''Please don't say you're sorry. I told you last night, I don't want an apology. I just want . . .''

''Tell me, Rachel, and, if it's in my power, I'll give it to you.''

Moving swiftly, she released his hands and slipped away from him. ''Friendship,'' she said, looking up at him. ''I'd like to be friends with you.''

She could have asked for his soul, but all she wanted was his friendship. Would she reject it when she realized that it came with strings attached—love, commitment, forever? He grinned, as cocky and arrogant as ever. ''You're hell on my ego, lady. I offer you anything, including my body, but you just want to be friends.''

She smiled a little and waited.

"All right." He extended his hand, and she took it. "I'll be your friend, and you can be mine."

"Thank you," she said solemnly. "I haven't had a friend in a long time."

If you don't let anyone get too close, then you can't get hurt. He pushed last night's words out of his mind. "I'm honored."

He sounded as if he really meant it, and tonight she chose to believe him. "It's late. I'd better be going."

"I'll walk you to the car."

She started to protest, but he laid his fingers over her mouth. "Friends can do that, you know."

A few minutes later, as she started to unlock her car door, he laid his hand on her shoulder and turned her for a kiss. When it ended, Rachel breathlessly asked, "Do friends also kiss each other good-night?"

"That's just for special friends." He traced his fingers along the delicate line of her jaw. "Will you have dinner with me tomorrow night?"

It wouldn't be wise, her protective instincts insisted. Maybe she was strong enough to accept friendship with Gabriel without getting hurt; maybe she wasn't. She should take it slowly, until her strength had been tested and proven capable. "Thank you, but . . . no."

"Friday?"

She shook her head.

"We can't be friends if you refuse to see me."

She hesitated a moment. "I'm going to Ramona Saturday, to return those boxes to Mr. Nelson. Would you like to go with me?"

His grin appeared instantly. A drive to Ramona was even better than dinner. The small town was, after all, only about twenty miles from Christopher and Shelley's house. If he called Shelley tomorrow, he could wangle an invitation that would be the perfect opportunity to introduce his best friends to his newest friend. "All right. Around eleven?"

She nodded, then turned and opened the door. "Good-bye, Ga—"

The rest of his name was swallowed in his kiss. As quickly as it had begun, it ended, and Gabriel was backing away from the car. "Good night, Rachel."

Gabriel called Shelley at the *Chronicle* office the first chance he got Thursday morning. "Are you busy Saturday?" he asked up front, skipping the small talk.

"No. You have something interesting in mind?"

"How would you like to invite me to your house at about twelve-thirty for lunch?"

She laughed softly. "What a wonderful idea. Gabriel, would you like to come for lunch about twelve-thirty Saturday?"

"Yes, I would, thanks. Can I bring someone?"

"Only if she's pretty and single."

"She's beautiful and very single."

Shelley leaned back in her chair, propping her feet on the stool beneath her desk. "You're serious, aren't you? Tell me about her."

"It's Rachel Martinez."

"Oh, that's right—you were asking about her. She *is* pretty. How long has this been going on?"

"A while." He grimaced at the vague answer. If he was going to use Shelley—and, in effect, that was what this request for an invitation was—she had a right to know more than generalities. "I've known Rachel for about nine years—since she joined the Department. We were... involved with each other five years ago, but it ended... badly." Considering the things that she had told him last night, that was a masterful understatement. "I first saw her again a few weeks ago."

Shelley's voice was merry with amusement. "At least that explains why you were so preoccupied at the baseball game. Tell me, Gabriel, are there any women in this city that you *haven't* been involved with?"

"None like this," he replied grimly. "She's still uneasy with me—she doesn't trust me much—so be kind of careful around her, will you?"

"I'll be on my best behavior." Then she spoiled the solemnity of her vow by laughing. "I can't think of anyone who deserves this situation more than you do. If you'll remember, you were none too helpful when I was trying to get Christopher to trust me. You were even more suspicious than he was." After a moment she asked softly, "Is she special, Gabriel?" But it was an unnecessary question. In the nearly two years that she'd known him, he had gone out with many women, but he had never introduced one of them to her and Christopher. Rachel Martinez was very special indeed.

"Yeah," he said bluntly. "She is. I appreciate this, Shelley."

"You can always count on us, Gabriel. You know that."

As he hung up the phone, he wondered, not for the first time, when *Rachel* would learn to count on *him*. Lord, he prayed, please let it be soon. He didn't know how much longer he could wait.

By the time he arrived at Rachel's house Saturday morning, she had all twelve boxes loaded in the car. "I assume we're taking your car," he said, watching as she rearranged the ones in the back seat.

"They certainly won't fit in *yours*. Sometimes I wonder how *you* fit in your car. You're so long and lanky, and it's so...little." She backed out of the car and straightened, wiping her hands on her shorts.

"Don't you know sports cars are supposed to be sexy?" he asked, pretending to take offense.

She tilted her head and looked at him for a long moment, then shook her head. "I don't think you need the car for that."

"Is that a compliment?"

Her blush was her only answer.

"You've given me two compliments in three weeks. I'm impressed."

"I doubt that," she said dryly. She had seen firsthand how women were attracted to him. A few simple, round-about compliments couldn't begin to compare to some of the things they told him.

She started toward the house, but he stopped her with a gentle touch. "I'm very impressed with just about everything that you say and do, Rachel. Don't you know that?"

She knew it. She just didn't trust it. "Let me get my purse and I'll be ready." She went into the house, got her purse, set the alarm and locked the door. "It'll probably be quicker if we go the back way. Do you want to drive?"

He started to refuse but in case she didn't want to have lunch with Christopher and Shelley, it might be better if he was in control when he told her. He accepted the keys.

Rachel said very little until they reached Ramona, then spoke only to give directions to the Nelson home. The old man was sitting on the porch, slowly rocking back and forth. He got to his feet and went to the bottom of the steps to wait for them. "Well, if it isn't the private detective." He gave her a big smile. "Did you find what you was looking for?"

"Hello, Mr. Nelson. No, sir, I didn't. Still, I appreciate you letting me look." She touched Gabriel's arm lightly when he came to stand next to her. "Mr. Nelson, this is a friend of mine, Gabriel Rodriguez."

Gabriel extended his hand, and the old man shook it vigorously. "Pleased to meet you, young man. So you've come to help the girl return all those boxes." He grinned conspiratorially. "Between you and me, she's probably as strong as either one of us."

"Probably," Gabriel said dryly. "Why don't you show me where you want them, and you two can talk while I unload them."

Nelson shook a gnarled finger at him. "I may be old, but I can still carry a few boxes of papers."

Rachel waited on the porch while they moved the boxes from her car to the garage. When they returned, the two men talked for several minutes before saying goodbye.

"Did you ever meet him?" Rachel asked as they drove away.

Gabriel shook his head.

"Why did Jenna leave?"

He stopped at a red light and looked at her until it turned green. "I wondered if you would ever ask that."

"It never seemed very important."

"And now it does?"

She shrugged.

Now would be a good time to tell her the rest of the story about Jenna. That he had wanted to marry her, had gone so far as to buy the engagement ring and set the date. That he had been in love with her. But the words wouldn't come. Did she really need to know that he'd been in love with Jenna? Would it make any difference in her search? Would it make any difference in their newly growing friendship? The answer to the first two questions was definitely no, to the last one . . . He couldn't risk it.

"Why did she leave?"

"I told you before, she wasn't happy about being pregnant. I doubt that she was very happy with me for getting her that way. She didn't want to settle down, to give up school and be a mother."

"Then why do you believe that she didn't have an abortion?"

"Instinct."

"Okay." She accepted that reply with an ease that surprised even Gabriel. Good cops had good instincts, and she had faith in his.

"What would you do, Rachel? If you were in Jenna's place?"

She looked out the window for several long minutes, then exhaled and said, "I wouldn't have an abortion."

He knew that. She would be a wonderful mother, warm and giving and full of love. Once they were married, she would have his children—

His hands tightened on the steering wheel, and he clenched his jaw. He couldn't think about marriage and babies with Rachel now, or he'd never make it through the rest of the day.

Rachel looked around, then frowned. "This isn't the way home."

"You finally noticed that, huh?" Gabriel's chuckle was low. "I'm surprised that anything ever slips past you."

"Where are we going?"

"Do you remember Shelley Morgan?"

The name struck a chord. Rachel searched her memory until she matched it with a face and an occasion. "She's a reporter for the *Chronicle*. She did some articles on private investigators."

"Right. She's also a friend of mine. Her husband and I grew up together in Albuquerque. Then he moved out here a few years after I did. They live a couple of miles north of Santa Ysabel, and they've invited us for lunch."

"What if I don't want to have lunch with your friends?"

"Then smile, be nice, and you can take it out on me when we leave." He glanced somberly at her. "They're good people, Rachel. They're my family."

His words, intended to reassure her, had the opposite effect. She didn't want to meet his family, real or otherwise. It smacked too much of commitment, of an emotional involvement that she wasn't sure she was ready for. Friendship was all she had asked for because friendship was the most she could handle. "I don't think it's a good idea."

"You've already met Shelley, and you'll like Christopher." In a droll voice, he added, "I don't believe I've ever seen a woman who *didn't* like Christopher."

"What's he like?"

"Tall, dark, rich and, according to my female friends who have seen him, 'drop-dead gorgeous.'"

The description, Rachel discovered when they reached the Morgan home a few minutes later, was totally accurate. Christopher was six feet tall, almost as darkly tanned as Gabriel, and incredibly handsome, with thick black hair sprinkled with silver, a hard, muscular body, intensely compelling dark brown eyes and an utterly charming smile. He and Gabriel must have left a string of broken hearts all the way from Albuquerque to the coast.

Now, although he greeted Rachel politely, it was apparent that he had eyes for no woman other than his wife. Auburn-haired, hazel-eyed, freckle-faced Shelley Morgan was about Rachel's age, but a few inches shorter, her pregnancy barely noticeable.

"Since it's so pretty today, we decided to cook out," Shelley said, leading them through the house to one of the multiple decks that surrounded it. "Christopher was about to start the fire. Why don't you go and help him, Gabriel? Rachel, would you like something to drink?"

"Yes, please." She sat down on a chaise and watched the two men move down the steps to the brick-enclosed grill. When Shelley offered her a choice of soda or beer, she chose the icy can of pop, flipping the top carefully with one fingernail. "You have a lovely place."

Shelley glanced around after she'd settled into a padded rocker. "I like it. It's private and quiet. When I first moved to San Diego, I lived in a little apartment, and there were neighbors upstairs and on both sides. It was incredibly noisy. After we got married, Christopher offered to buy another place in town—he used to live in La Jolla—but I love it here."

"It's a long commute to work, though."

"Any place in San Diego is a long commute. I've never seen so much traffic in one place."

"You ought to try L.A." She took a long drink, then stretched her legs out on the chair. "Do you mind if I ask you a personal question?"

"Ask it. If I mind, I won't answer it."

"Is your husband the same Morgan who was involved in busting that spy ring a couple of years ago?" She had followed the story of Morgan's arrest and, later, the investigation that had cleared his name, but with little interest. There had been too much turmoil in her own life for her to care much about the problems in someone else's.

"The same one."

"Then you were the reporter who broke the case."

Shelley nodded.

"Did Gabriel help?"

Again she nodded. "He's very good at what he does."

Rachel couldn't disagree. Even when the mere thought of him had been enough to shatter her fragile mental state, she had always respected him as a cop. Now she was learning to respect him once again as a man, and the lesson wasn't as hard as she'd expected.

"Do you know you're the first woman he's brought to meet us?"

Rachel's smile was rueful. "I didn't need to hear that."

"He can be kind of aggressive, can't he?" Shelley asked with a laugh. "He sort of takes your breath away. But if he pushes too hard, tell him. It probably won't stop him, but he might surprise you and back off a bit." She looked fondly at the two men, lost in their own conversation, then back at Rachel. "I like to tease him, give him a hard time, but there's a lot that I admire about Gabriel. He's a good man, a good friend. He stood by Christopher when everyone else in his life was pretending that they'd never met him. Gabriel's very important to both of us."

Rachel's gaze was long and steady. "Is that a warning?"

"No. It's not my place to warn. Gabriel is my friend, and because you're important to him, I'd like to be your friend."

Rachel smiled slowly. "I could use a friend."

"Good." Shelley's own smile was as bright and warm as the sun above. "Would you mind taking the guys something to drink while I check on dessert? Christopher drinks beer, but Gabriel doesn't."

Rachel got two cans from the nearby cooler and went down the steps and across the uneven yard to the grill. She handed the beer to Christopher and the Coke to Gabriel, who slipped his arm companionably around her waist. "Thanks," he murmured before returning to his conversation. "How much longer will you have to be there?"

"Not a day longer than absolutely necessary. I can't imagine why anyone would want to live in that city."

"Careful. Rachel's from L.A."

Christopher's dark gaze shifted to her. "I hate to speak ill of anyone's hometown, but I hate the place."

"That's all right. I live in Lakeside now." Gently she moved from Gabriel's embrace and took a few steps away.

"So you're a private detective—sorry, investigator." Christopher looked her over, from the top of her braided hair to her sandaled feet. "Somehow you don't fit the image."

"You ought to see her in a suit with a briefcase and a .357 magnum. It'll change your opinion," Gabriel said wryly.

Rachel's smile was unnatural. She didn't belong here. Gabriel was trying to lay some sort of claim to her in front of his friends. Shelley, in spite of her denials, was issuing warnings, and Christopher was looking at her without one degree of warmth in those dark eyes. She raised her head stiffly and said, "I'm used to not fitting preconceived notions. I used to be a cop, now I'm a PI. In between, I was a mental case."

The coldness spread from her to Gabriel, whose eyes were narrowed and hard. Christopher's, conversely, grew warm with a smile. "Yeah, most of us reach that point at some time in our lives."

Rachel spoke to Gabriel without looking away from his friend. "He thinks I'm kidding, doesn't he?"

"Cut it out, Rach—"

Christopher interrupted. "Are you still nuts?"

Slowly she smiled. "Only at times."

"Well, so am I, at times. So we're both normal." He checked the coals, then asked, "How do you like your steak, Rachel?"

"Rare."

"I'll get the meat."

She stared at the glowing coals long after he was gone. When, from the corner of her eye, she saw Gabriel turn to walk away, she suddenly reached out, her fingers grazing the back of his arm. "I'm sorry."

He didn't turn, but he didn't move away, either.

"You shouldn't have brought me here, Gabriel. They think it means something." She sniffed. "Hell, *I'd* think it meant something if I didn't know better."

He turned then, scowling at her. "You don't know anything, Rachel, except what you want to know. Talk about preconceived notions—you have to make everything fit into exactly the spot where you want it, and if it doesn't fit, you don't want anything to do with it!"

She hugged her arms across her chest. "I don't know what you mean."

"I don't want to be your *friend*, Rachel! I want to be able to touch you, to kiss you, to hold you. I want to be your lover. I want to *be* with you."

She shook her head, stunned by the emotion that made his voice heavy. "You don't know what you're saying," she whispered.

"I know exactly what I'm saying. I'm saying that I lo—"

She clamped her hand over his mouth, cutting off the word. "No! Don't say that, Gabriel! Please don't say that!"

Relenting, he raised his hands to her face, gently stroking her skin. "Why does that frighten you?" he asked, then decided that *why* didn't matter. The only important thing was that she *was* frightened, and it was up to him to soothe her fears. "All right, sweetheart." He brushed his lips over hers, then hugged her tight. "Come on, you've got to have a good time today, honey. After all the trouble Shelley went to setting this up for me, she'll have my head if you don't enjoy it."

"You asked her to invite us for lunch?"

He nodded, guilty and not caring.

Rachel raised her hand to his jaw. "She loves you very much."

"I know."

"I don't think Christopher likes me at all."

"Well, as a rule, telling someone that you used to be nuts isn't the best way to make him like you. Fortunately, Christopher is an exception to the rule."

"You're lucky to have such good friends."

"I value all three of you." He heard the click of the door, kissed her forehead, then let her go. "Why don't you find a chair, relax and get some sun while lunch cooks?"

She smiled faintly. "Thanks, but I think I'll see if Shelley needs any help in the kitchen." She passed Christopher on the steps and went inside.

"You *do* have interesting taste in women, Gabriel," Christopher said as he set the platter of meat down.

Gabriel slid his hands into the back pockets of his jeans. "She's nervous," he said in explanation. "She thinks you don't like her."

"Why don't we talk about whether or not *you* like her?" Christopher set two steaks on the grill, then folded his arms over his chest. "I remember a time when I asked you if you had ever been in love, and you said yes, that you might even have a child. You were talking about Jenna."

Gabriel nodded once.

"How did you happen to leave Rachel out of that conversation?"

Gabriel refused to meet his friend's gaze. "I never said that I . . . that I loved . . ." His denial faded away.

"Oh, please." Exasperation rang in Christopher's voice. "You've been my best friend all my life—sometimes my only friend. I know you better than I know myself. I know you wouldn't bring any woman here unless she was damned special to you, and I know you couldn't care that much about any woman without loving her." He picked up the tongs and turned the steaks, then resumed his unyielding stance. "You said that you thought about Jenna every day. Was she more important than Rachel?"

"No." Gabriel tugged his fingers through his hair, leaving it on end, then combed it down again. "A whole lot less."

"So you shut Rachel out and focused on Jenna because it was less painful."

Gabriel's expression was bleak when he looked up. "I used to pretend that she didn't really matter to me. It was the only way I could live with what I'd done to her."

Christopher didn't ask what he was talking about. He knew that Gabriel would tell him when he was ready.

"And now?"

"Now I can live with it. It would just be a hell of a lot easier if I was living with her, too." He watched the meat sizzling on the grill, taking a step to the side when the wind blew smoke in his direction.

"I take it you've hired her to find Jenna."

Gabriel nodded, and Christopher choked back a laugh.

"You went to this woman whom you'd been in love with and asked her to find this other woman whom you'd been in love with who just happened to be the mother of your child? And she agreed?"

This time Gabriel shook his head. "I asked her to find a woman I'd had an affair with a long time ago. I didn't mention that I'd been in love with Jenna, or that we had planned to get married."

"Don't you think those little details might be important to her?"

"Not if she never finds out. Why should she? No one knows but you and Jenna and me. You're not going to tell her, and I'm not, and right now the only thing she knows about Jenna is where she isn't. She may never find her."

Christopher added the two remaining steaks, then finished his beer. "Does that bother you?"

He might never know about the baby, might never know his name or see his face. "Yeah," he answered honestly. But not as much as it would have a couple of weeks ago. Then he'd had nothing. Now he had Rachel.

The sun was setting when they left the Morgan house to return to the city. Rachel settled in her seat, her head tilted back, her eyes closed. "They're nice people."

He made a sound of agreement.

"I'm sorry if I embarrassed you earlier."

He reached for her hand, then pressed a kiss to her palm. "I wasn't embarrassed." When he released her hand, he laid it on his thigh, flat against the worn denim.

"You said they were your family. What about your real family?" All he'd ever told her about his family was that his parents were Indian, both raised in Taos Pueblo, that he'd been born in Albuquerque and had lived there until he'd finished college, and that he rarely saw either parent.

"My mother's in Albuquerque with her third or fourth husband, and only God knows where my dad is," he said with a chuckle. "I guess you'd call him a drifter. He stayed with Mom long enough to marry her and get her pregnant, then moved on. He always came back, though, for a few days here, a couple of weeks there."

She thought of the two men in her own life—the step-father who had always been there, and the father who hadn't even stayed around long enough to marry her mother after getting her pregnant. He had drifted back, too—at frequent enough intervals to damage the relationship she'd built with Ernesto. "How old were you when they divorced?"

"I don't know. Four or five, I guess. But even after Mom remarried, he still visited whenever he was in the area."

"Don't you resent him?"

"Why? Because he didn't measure up to my idea of what a father should be?" He shrugged. "He did the best he could. Settling down wasn't one of the things he could do."

"You're too forgiving," she said flatly. "If the man didn't want to be a father, he shouldn't have had a son."

He slowed to turn off the highway onto the street that would take them to Wildcat Canyon. "Maybe it's better not to judge someone unless you're living his life," he said gently. "Look, he was *my* father, and *I* didn't mind his absences. What difference does it make to you?"

"None," she replied. "None at all." She sounded foolishly stiff and hard. If he didn't care that his father had, for all practical purposes, abandoned him, why should she? "Is that the kind of father you'll be? One who drifts in and out of his kid's life, never there when he's needed and never wanted when he's there?"

"No." He sounded as hard as she had. "I don't resent my dad, but that doesn't mean I didn't learn a few lessons from him. If I ever get to be a father, I'll be the best damn father you ever laid eyes on." Then, suddenly, he grinned at her. "Give me some time and you can see for yourself."

She started to pull her hand back, but he caught it, clasping it tightly in his. "Don't fight me tonight, Rachel. We've had a nice day, and now we'll end it with a nice evening, okay?"

A nice evening doing what? she wondered suspiciously, but didn't ask. "Okay."

Her house was dark and quiet. After shutting off the alarm, she made her way to the lamp on the end table. When she turned the light on, Gabriel closed the door and followed her. "Sit down with me," he requested, catching her arms and pulling her to the couch.

"Why?"

"So I can kiss you." And before she could protest, he did just that, his mouth hard and hungry, taking.

After a moment Rachel raised her hands to his shoulders and forcefully pushed him away.

"Gently," she said in a soft, dark voice. "Like this." She leaned forward, holding him in place, and touched her lips to his while her hands brushed over his skin and into the rich thickness of his hair. She teased him, giving small kisses, tiny samples that ended too soon, avoiding his tongue, nipping at his lip. Then she shifted, gliding her tongue deep into his mouth, exploring, savoring, tasting the heat, the sensuous need.

When she raised her head, he was breathless, his eyes glazed with yearning. "I think I'd like to try that again."

"You think so? What would it take to make you sure?"

He slid his arms around her, twisting at the same time that he lifted her, so that they both lay on the sofa, her slight weight balanced evenly over him. "I'm sure, honey," he replied, deliberately pulling her against his hips and the swelling there. He wanted her to know exactly what he was feeling, how much he wanted her.

He saw her eyes widen, and she became very still. "Maybe we shouldn't do this," she suggested hesitantly.

He pulled the band from her hair and worked his fingers through the braid. "Why? Because you don't want to let me spend the night?"

"How do you know that?"

"Because I know *you*, Rachel." Her hair was soft and smelled sweet. He rubbed the thick, silken strands between his fingers, then used them to pull her head down for a kiss. "Can't I kiss you just for the pleasure of kissing?" he asked, tracing his tongue over her lips. "Do I have to have the ulterior motive of seducing you?"

"But you're..."

"Hard." He claimed her hand from his chest and slid it between their bodies, molding her fingers to cradle him. "I'm hard, and I'm hungry as hell for you, but I can survive a while longer without making love to you. Tonight I want to kiss you, honey, and hold you like this. I just want to be close to you."

She relaxed against him, letting him support her, and brushed her mouth against his. "You're a special man, Gabriel Rodriguez," she whispered. "A very special man."

Chapter 6

Gabriel was on his way out of the courthouse Wednesday afternoon when a familiar voice called his name. He paused at the door until Adam Graves, one of the assistant district attorneys, caught up with him. "What brings you over here?"

"I had to see your boss about the Caldwell case." The murder was one of the few cases he'd been able to solve lately. Either he was getting slower, or crooks were getting smarter. It seemed each case was becoming more difficult to crack.

"Let me buy you some lunch. I'd like to talk to you."

Gabriel hesitated a moment. "As long as you let me choose the place. The last restaurant you took me to served raw fish."

"It's called sushi," the attorney said with a laugh.

"You can call it whatever you want, but it's still raw fish. How about Mexican?"

"Why not? My ulcer's been too quiet lately." Graves looked at the car that Gabriel had stopped beside, then offered, "We can take my car—it's just around the corner."

"What's wrong with my car?"

"No offense, but I don't like driving around in an un-marked police car that everyone can spot as an unmarked police car from a mile away." He led the way to his own car, a silver BMW.

"Nice car," Gabriel said as he slid in. "The D.A.'s office must pay a whole lot better than the Department."

"Are you kidding? I bought this when I was defending the sleaze that you guys arrested."

"Why did you quit? Get tired of setting rapists, muggers and murderers free?"

Adam considered it for a moment, then replied, "Yeah. Maybe I did."

The restaurant was a short drive from downtown. When they were seated at one of the tables, Gabriel asked, "You got anything interesting going on?"

"You cops are the nosiest people in the world, you know that?"

"And you lawyers are right behind us."

Graves leaned back in the chair. "Are you familiar with the Mitchelson investment fraud?"

"No. Should I be?"

The attorney looked pained. The case was one of his biggest, and the name didn't even ring a bell with a cop. "It was in the news every day for a month."

"I have enough crimes of my own to take care of. I don't stick my nose into Fraud's. What about it?"

"It was your typical investment scheme—the guy promised a forty percent return, collected thousands of dollars, but when payoff time came, there was no money, no Mitchelson. Some of the people who got bilked hired a PI firm to locate Mitchelson. They did, and turned him over to us."

"A forty percent return?" Gabriel was skeptical. "I don't know much about investments, but even I know that forty percent is unrealistic."

"So do the victims now. But it cost some of them their life savings to find out." Adam broke off to taste his lunch. "So we arrested Mitchelson, got him on a whole slew of charges, got all of our witnesses set up. There were two PIs who worked the case together—pretended to be husband and wife—but we only needed one, and she wasn't too thrilled with the idea of testifying, so we only subpoenaed him.''

Gabriel wished that Graves would get to the point. In court the man spoke with a directness that Gabriel admired; out of court, he rambled. But years of interviewing nervous witnesses had taught him patience, and he called on it now.

"Now the guy's in the hospital recovering from an emergency appendectomy, so I'm going to have to call the woman. She made it clear in the beginning that she really didn't want to testify, so I'm a little worried about how she'll do.''

"Adam," Gabriel began softly, "is there a reason you're telling me all of this?"

The other man looked surprised. "Of course. There's a reason behind everything I do. I understand that you used to be...ah, friends with her, and I wanted to ask you a couple of questions about her."

For the first time, Gabriel's interest was high. "You're talking about Rachel Martinez, with Powell."

"How did you guess?"

"I'm not 'friends' with too many PIs," he said dryly, giving the word the same questionable inflection that Graves had. "What do you want to know about her?"

"Why was she so set against testifying?"

"I don't know," Gabriel replied, although he could make a pretty good guess. Often, when a police officer went through a traumatic incident such as Rachel had, he disassociated himself from the department—stopped seeing friends who were cops, avoided any contact with the department, closed off the memories. It was a way of dealing with the grief, the sorrow, the guilt. Was it Rachel's way? "Have you asked her?"

"How can I ask her? I've never even laid eyes on her."

Gabriel smiled slowly. "Then you're in for a real treat."

"Is she pretty?"

He nodded.

"Professional?"

"Next to her, you'll look like an amateur."

The younger man wore an injured expression. "Is she intelligent? Impressive?"

Gabriel leaned forward. "Rachel Martinez was a cop for four years, and she's been a PI even longer. She's smarter than you and me put together, and a hell of a lot better looking. Believe me, she'll be impressive."

"I hope so. I was counting on using Wilson, her partner. He *looks* like a private detective."

"And what do private detectives look like?" Gabriel asked with a grin, thinking of Rachel with her long hair, delicate features, sensuous smile and lovely body.

"I don't know—like those TV guys." He sounded morose, then gave a shrug. "Oh well, I'll see for myself tomorrow. She's out of town right now, but her boss promised to get her back in time for me to interview her tomorrow afternoon."

Gabriel smiled slowly. "That ought to be interesting. I wish I could be there." He glanced at his watch. "I've got to get back to work."

"Yeah, me too. Thanks for the information."

As soon as he reached his office, Gabriel called Elaine. "When is Rachel's flight getting in?" he asked after identifying himself.

"About three. How do you know she's coming back early?"

"I had lunch with the assistant D.A. What flight number?"

She checked, then gave him the information.

"I don't suppose you know if she left her car at the airport."

"No, she didn't. Since she didn't have any idea how long she would be gone, she didn't want to leave it at her place— she lives way out in the country, you know—so she left it at my house and took a cab from there. Are you going to pick her up?"

"Sweetheart, I've been trying for a long time."

Elaine laughed softly. "Any success?"

He thought about the last time he'd seen Rachel, all soft and warm and pliant in his arms. "Some. I'm hoping for a lot more. Does she know yet that she's coming back early?"

"No. I left a message at her hotel to call me."

"Don't mention me, okay? She'd come up with a dozen excuses why I shouldn't meet her at the airport."

"Anything you say, Lieutenant." Elaine was all in favor of advancing Rachel's so far nonexistent love life, even if it meant lying a little.

The lies came a few hours later. When Rachel called to check in, Elaine told her about Ray Wilson's appendectomy and gave her the number and time of her flight back to San Diego.

"I don't suppose I have any say in this, do I?"

"Afraid not. You know Powell—he can't resist doing a favor for the D.A. How did it go in Nevada?"

"It didn't," Rachel replied dryly, "or I wouldn't be in Utah." Stretching out on the bed, she returned to the original subject. "The D.A. could have asked for a continuance."

"And waste the taxpayers' money when he can just as easily call you? Rachel, you'll be fine. Don't worry about it."

Why worry over something she couldn't control? Besides, three days of looking at birth and death certificates and motor vehicle records had left her brain numb. This would be a nice little break. A nice chance to see Gabriel. "Any messages, Elaine?"

"A couple." Elaine knew that Rachel wanted to ask but couldn't, so she took pity on her. "Nothing personal."

Rachel held back a sigh. That was the story of her life. *Nothing personal.* "Thanks. When will I be coming back to Salt Lake?"

"Monday morning, provided that the D.A. finishes with you by then. As soon as you get back tomorrow, go straight to his office. It's Adam Graves—have you met him?"

"No." There had been a time when she'd known every lawyer on the district attorney's staff, but now she had no reason to keep track of them.

"I've seen pictures of him. He's nice-looking."

"I'm glad you think so. Why don't you take my notes from the case and pretend to be me?"

"If only I could look like you..." Elaine gave a sigh. "I've got to go, Rachel. Do you need anything else?"

"No thanks. I'll see you tomorrow." She hung up the phone and leaned back against the headboard. She would have liked to call Gabriel and tell him that she would be home for the weekend. Only fear stopped her.

She was on dangerous ground. If she continued to see him, she was definitely at risk of falling in love with him all over again, and if she fell in love with him again... She sighed. The wise thing would be to put an end to the affair before it started, but hadn't she already tried that—and failed? She wasn't strong enough to send him away. That would mean closing the door on light and warmth and happiness, on all the good things in her life. Maybe she was foolish, but she needed those things, even if she had to pay for them later with more heartache.

The flight to San Diego was just the way she liked them— uncrowded and uneventful. She wasn't looking forward to this meeting with Adam Graves, but the sooner she got it over with, the sooner she could go home. The sooner she could call Gabriel.

"Need a ride?"

She looked up, her eyes focusing on Gabriel. For a moment she looked blank, as if she had conjured him up merely by thinking of him, then smiled slowly. "Yes, as a matter of fact, I do."

He took her hand and pulled her to the wall, out of the main traffic in the corridor, then put his arms around her, slowly drawing her to him. "I missed you a lot."

"Did you?"

He shook his head. "Wrong response, Rach. You're supposed to say, 'I missed you, too, Gabriel.'"

"Even if I didn't?"

"You're cutting my heart to shreds with that sharp tongue of yours, lady."

She set her briefcase down, then brought both hands to his face. His skin was soft and warm and smelled faintly woodsy. "Does this feel sharp?" she whispered, touching the tip of her tongue to his lips.

Gabriel didn't wait for further invitation. Wrapping her hair around his hands, he held her head while he hungrily, deeply kissed her, tasting her warmth, feeding it with his own warmth, making her tremble against him. His body responded with its own weakness, with fevered need and heated swelling.

The need was becoming unmanageable. The more he touched her, kissed her, even thought about her, the more he needed to make love with her, to become whole with her, to heal with her.

When he ended the kiss and pushed her back, her breathing was unsteady, her cheeks flushed, her lips bare of artificial color. She rubbed her finger over his bottom lip, wiping away a touch of lipstick. "I did miss you," she admitted.

"I know."

"I have to go—I have an appointment downtown." She touched his lip again, and he wet her fingertip with his tongue. She laughed softly. "Would you like to come over for dinner tonight?"

"Yes. And I'm taking you to see Graves." He released her and bent to retrieve her briefcase.

"How do you know about Adam Graves?" she asked, her voice laced with good-natured suspicion. "And how did you know I was coming back today?"

He held her hand tightly as they moved through the crowd to the baggage area. "Graves is a friend of mine. So is Elaine."

She wasn't surprised. Gabriel had sources—and friends—everywhere. "So Adam Graves knew that you and I had once had a fling, and he told you that I was being called to testify for him and wanted to know..." She tapped her index finger against her lower lip while she thought. "Let's see...he wanted to know if I would make a good witness, if I was reliable, and if I would impress the jury. Am I right?"

He nodded. "He also wanted to know why you weren't eager and willing to testify back in the beginning, when they decided to use your partner."

She watched the luggage on the carousel, unable to look at him. "Did you tell him?"

"Tell him what?"

"That's my suitcase—the tan one."

He easily picked it up, and they started toward the doors.

"Did you tell him about Jack, about the psychologist, about you?" She automatically looked both ways before stepping off the curb, then continued. "Did you tell him that being around cops makes me nervous, that I have this terrible fear of being recognized, of being blamed...or pitied?"

He had been right, Gabriel thought, but he found no satisfaction in it, because her fears were his fault. He'd made her feel guilty for something she'd had no control over. If her lover wouldn't stand by her, without blame, without pity, how could she expect anyone else to?

He stopped at his car and unlocked the door for her, then stowed her suitcase in the back. "And here I thought you were nervous around me because I'm an incredibly attractive man, not because I'm a cop." He slid in and started the engine, then twisted to face her. "I didn't tell him anything, Rachel. I don't know that your reasons are any of his business. I *do* know your aversion to cops is unfounded. Do you think the Fraud guys who are testifying tomorrow are going to point their fingers at you and talk in loud whispers behind your back about what a horrible person you are?''

She smiled reluctantly at the image. "No, I don't guess I do."

"More likely they'll be talking about what a nice back you have…a nice tush…gorgeous legs…and the front's even better." He smiled, but it was more of a grimace. "You told me once that you prefer honesty—remember?"

She nodded.

"Then I'll be honest about what I want, okay?" He paused, cleared his throat and asked solemnly, "What are the chances that you'll let me spend the night with you tonight?"

Once again color flooded her face, and her voice was uneven when she finally made it work. "There's a difference, Gabriel, between being honest and being blunt."

"That was being honest, sweetheart. Being blunt is telling you that I really want to—'' He finished the sentence with a murmured expression that made her burn. He watched her response, saw the heat spread, saw her nipples grow hard beneath her thin blouse, and smiled knowingly. "Hmm. I didn't know you liked that kind of talk."

Rachel turned away from him, sitting straighter in the seat, facing ahead. "We'd better go," she murmured, her voice husky, not quite under control. "I don't want to keep the D.A. waiting."

The meeting with Graves was brief. He asked a few questions about her background—sizing her up, Rachel accurately guessed—then ran down the list of questions he would ask her in court the next day. When he was finished, she found Gabriel in the hallway, passing the time with another cop. He introduced her to the man, a Robbery detective, who studied her carefully before saying goodbye.

"That was curiosity," Gabriel pointed out as they left the building. "Not recognition, not blame and certainly not pity."

She didn't need the explanation. She'd been the recipient of enough interested-male looks to recognize them. "I imagine he looks at all your women that way," she said dryly.

"What women? Don't you know you're the only one in my life?"

She gave him a sidelong look that was filled with good-natured doubt. "Do you know what the first thing I heard about you when I joined the department was?"

"That I was a great cop?" he asked hopefully.

She shook her head. "That Gabriel Rodriguez *loves* women. If a pretty woman came around, the other guys didn't even make a play for her, because they knew that *you* were the one she would choose. You were renowned for having more gorgeous, sexy women than all the other guys in the station combined."

He waited until they were in the car to respond. "It must be true, because you're gorgeous, and you're certainly sexy." *And I love you.*

Rachel fastened her seat belt, then leaned down to remove her shoes. The carpet was thick and soft beneath her aching feet. "You're missing the point. The emphasis was not just on quality, but *quantity*. There were a lot of them."

He couldn't deny it. There had been a time, after Jenna and before Rachel, when he had dated a great number of women, never seeing one long enough to let her think he cared. Rachel had put a temporary and much-welcomed halt to that. She had been the one who made him forget Jenna. She had been the one who had taught him to love again. Now he wanted to teach her the same lesson. "*You're* missing the point. That was in the past, when I was young and foolish. It was before I met you."

"And what are you now—old and wise?" She reached across to squeeze his hand. "I'm teasing you, Gabriel. If you say you aren't seeing any other women, I believe you."

"Why?" When she tried to pull her hand back, he held it. "Why do you believe me? Because you trust me?"

"Because I want to believe you." She tugged her hand free, twined her fingers loosely together in her lap and turned her head away from him.

He tried to hide his triumphant smile from her. If she could believe him simply because she wanted to, then she had to trust him. That was all trust was—believing, having faith. And if she trusted him, then she must have forgiven him without even realizing it, because she couldn't trust without forgiving him. His patience was paying off. Now all he had to win was her love.

"I need to stop at the store." She looked at him out of the corner of her eye. "And I have to pick up my car from Elaine's sometime this evening."

"Why?"

"Because I offered you dinner, and there's no food in my house, and because I have to be at the courthouse by nine o'clock tomorrow morning."

He didn't say a word until he had left the freeway and pulled into a small shopping center. Then he faced her. "I could take you to the courthouse in the morning."

If she let him spend the night. Rachel was flattered by his desire, flustered by his directness, confused by her own feelings. She wanted him—there was no question of that— but could she handle having him? Was she strong enough to survive it?

"I'm kind of tired, and . . . I'm nervous about testifying, and . . ."

Gabriel touched his fingers to her lips, shushing her excuses. "Honesty."

She nodded, and he removed his hand. "I would like to make love with you. . . ."

"But?"

"But I don't think I'm ready. I'm not really sure how I feel about you." She met his gaze, her eyes soft and clouded and filled with pain. "Honestly . . . I'm afraid."

"That I'll hurt you?"

She tried to examine the fear—deep, dark, powerful. Fear that she would love him again. That she was asking for heartache by letting him so near. That she was too weak to say no, for fear of losing him, and too weak to say yes, for fear of losing herself in him. "I'm afraid that I'll get hurt."

She was telling him no, that she didn't want his lovemaking yet, but Gabriel treasured the way she'd done it. A few weeks ago she would have been positive that any pain she suffered in this relationship would unquestionably be his fault. Now she understood that he would never deliberately hurt her. Now she trusted him.

He sighed deeply, a relaxing exhalation. "Okay."

"Are you angry?"

"No. I won't deny that I'm a little disappointed, but...not angry. Honey, no matter how much I want you, you have the right to say no. Now, come on, let's get some food. I'm hungry."

Rachel arrived at the courthouse a few minutes before nine and took her seat in the hallway with the rest of the prosecution's witnesses. Two were detectives from Fraud, men she had known casually for years. They greeted her as they would any old friend, without the slightest hint of blame or pity. Maybe she had been unnecessarily self-conscious all these years, she admitted to herself.

She wasn't called to testify until after lunch. She passed the time reading, working the *Chronicle*'s crossword puzzle and thinking a lot about Gabriel. He had invited her to dinner that night—a real, honest-to-goodness date. She hadn't had one of those in years—not since the *last* time he had asked her out.

And when it was over, he would kiss her and say all those ridiculous things to her about being gorgeous, about how much he wanted to make love to her, and she... Lord, what was she going to do? Could she have an affair with Gabriel without loving him? Could she have an affair with him and pretend that all the good things she felt were purely sexual, that it was her body that wanted him and not her heart?

Because she couldn't love him. Loving him five years ago had almost destroyed her, and she was a different woman now—weaker, needier. She had been broken once before, and like a broken vase that's been glued back together, she would never be quite as strong as she used to be.

Her name was called out by the bailiff, and she went into the courtroom, projecting a calm assurance that she certainly didn't feel. She was sworn in, then took a seat on the witness stand. The questions were simple, her answers straightforward. After Adam Graves finished, Mitchelson's lawyer got his turn. His style was tougher, more aggressive, than Graves's, but Rachel, in her years as a cop, had been questioned by far better attorneys than this man. She remained cool, calm, every bit as professional and impressive as Gabriel had promised Graves she would be.

When she was dismissed, she went straight home. It was the first time she had been in court since leaving the Department, and, she thought, she had handled it rather well—superbly, in fact. She celebrated with a long, relaxing bubble bath, then a brief nap before she began dressing for her date.

"I'll pick you up at seven," Gabriel had promised, and she had never known him to be late, but seven o'clock came and went with no word from him. She waited until eight before trying to call his apartment. There was no answer. When she called the department, she talked to a harried detective who had no idea where the lieutenant was and was too busy to find out. She quietly thanked him and hung up.

Shortly after nine, the phone rang. "Miss Martinez?" an unfamiliar voice asked.

"Yes, this is Rachel Martinez."

"My name is Tony Hatten. Lieutenant Rodriguez asked me to call you. He got tied up on a case, and he said he'll come over as soon as he finishes, if it's not too late."

She was silent for a moment, relieved that nothing had happened to him, disappointed that he hadn't been able to call himself, annoyed because she was disappointed. "Thank you," she said softly. "I appreciate the call."

After hanging up, she went down the hall to her room and removed the burgundy silk dress that she had chosen with such care. She slipped out of the Italian leather heels, the sheer stockings, and pulled a robe over the silver, one-piece teddy that she wore. The dramatic silver hoop earrings went back into the jewelry box, and the silver combs that held her hair on each side came out and landed on the dresser with a soft tinkle.

So much for her real, honest-to-goodness date.

She returned to the living room, turned the television on and curled up on the couch. Even her regular Friday night cop show couldn't hold her attention. She was too busy feeling sorry for herself and even busier castigating herself for that self-pity. It was a fact of life: cops often had to work late. Dinners were missed, dates were broken, and life went on.

When the eleven o'clock news came on, she watched disinterestedly until the screen flashed from a picture-perfect anchorwoman in the studio to the street outside a small, well-kept house. Slowly rotating beacons from police cars and an ambulance cast an alternating red, then blue, glow over the scene, and grim-faced uniformed officers stood in small groups in the background.

Rachel slowly sat up. Someone had died in the little white house—she knew without being told. That explained the stony expressions the cops wore. It explained why Gabriel had missed their dinner and broken their date.

Before the thought was completed, Gabriel, followed by two other detectives, stepped out of the house, into the range of the television cameras. The reporter moved toward him, asking him questions, pushing the microphone in his direction, but he didn't slow his steps, didn't glance at the camera, didn't mutter so much as a single "No comment." The camera followed him and the other two men until the car they'd gotten into drove away, then swung back to the reporter.

The unexpected peal of the doorbell echoed through the room. Rachel moved quietly to the door, peered through the peephole, shut off the alarm and opened the door.

In the news clip a few minutes ago he had looked so stern and forbidding, so hard. Now he looked like a weary man in desperate need of comfort. Hands jammed deep into his pockets, he stared at the floor for a minute, studying her bare feet, before finally raising his gaze to her. "Can I come in?"

"Of course." She closed the door and reset the alarm.

He walked past her, coming to a stop in the center of the living room. When he heard her follow, he gestured to the television. "Film at eleven, huh? Did you get enough gory details? Or is that why you let me come in?"

She ignored his sarcasm and waited, arms folded over her chest.

Gabriel turned to face her in time to see her shiver. He was so damned cold inside that he was giving her chills. Maybe he shouldn't have come here, should have left her out of this nightmare, but he'd had nowhere else to go. There was only Rachel. "Well? Nothing to say?"

"What do you want me to say? Tell me, Gabriel, and I'll say it."

Her voice was too soft, too warm, when he was hard and cold. "What are you willing to offer, Rachel?" he asked derisively. "Condolences? Sympathy? A shoulder to lean on?" His voice grew sharp and ugly. "How about your body? Would you let me find my comfort between your legs, inside you?"

Slowly she walked across the room, stopping directly in front of him. "Do you know what you do when you need someone, Gabriel?"

He answered with a nasty lie. "I don't need you, Rachel. I've never needed you."

She continued as if he hadn't spoken. "You get cold and defensive and abusive. You retreat into your own private little hell to suffer alone, and God help anyone who tries to get close to you. You did this to me the night Jack died. Well, damn you, you're not going to do it tonight."

She was right. He'd done it before, and he had sent her to her own hell, where no one but God *could* help. He stared at her for a long time, then rubbed his eyes with the heels of his hands and muttered a curse. "I shouldn't have come here."

"Yes, you should have." She laid her hands on his arms, afraid he would push her away. When he didn't, she moved closer, sliding her arms around him, holding him in a secure embrace.

"You ought to send me away," he murmured against the silkiness of her hair; then he wrapped his own arms around her, hugging her so fiercely that she could barely breathe.

"How could I do that? This is the first time you've ever truly needed me."

His denial was a soft moan. "I've needed you every day of my life. God, Rachel, living without you is worse than any hell I could imagine. You're the only thing that ever mattered."

She pressed her face against his shirt, hiding the tears that stung her eyes. "Shh, don't talk now. Just let me hold you."

She didn't know how long they stood there in the center of the room before he finally stepped back. "Sit with me," he requested.

She shook her head. "Come to bed."

He almost managed a smile, but it faded away. "Honey, I didn't mean—"

"I do." After all her fear, all her worry, it had been a surprisingly simple decision to make. He needed her, and she needed what he could give. "Come to bed with me, Gabriel, and let me hold you. Let me make you warm."

He let her lead him by the hand to her bedroom at the end of the hallway, not certain exactly what she was offering, and not caring. He stood beside the bed in the dimly lit room and let her slide his coat from his shoulders, then loosen his tie and pull it free. She unfastened his belt, removed the holster and laid it on the nightstand, knowing that he would want the revolver within reach while he slept.

He was tired. Exhausted. Drained. That was the only reason he could think of to explain how he could stand here, with Rachel's thin, delicate fingers undoing buttons, buckles and zippers, undressing him, without feeling the slightest hint of arousal.

She pulled the covers back and gently pushed him onto the bed. His eyes were already closing when he caught her hand. "Stay with me, Rachel. Hold me."

"I will." She turned off the lamp, circled the bed, removed her robe and lay down beside him.

"I'm sorry about our date," he murmured, pulling her snug against his body.

"So am I."

"Sorry I was such a bastard."

"It's all right." She held him, stroked his chest, patted him as if he were a child in need of soothing. But this was no child's body, she admitted reluctantly. The lean chest, hard muscles, flat belly and the slight swelling beneath his navy blue briefs confirmed that. She shifted uncomfortably, the satin sliding roughly over her sensitive nipples. She had offered to make love with him, had admitted finally that she needed him as much as she wanted him, but he had opted instead for sleeping in her arms. For the first time, she was ready, and he wasn't.

She fell asleep slowly, deeply aware of every move he made, every breath he took. And when she slept, conscious thoughts of Gabriel were replaced with intimate dreams, dreams filled with the heat and hunger of loving him, with the pleasure of taking him.

When Gabriel awoke, he lay very still. Although he had never seen this room before tonight, he knew immediately where he was, knew that it was Rachel snuggled beside him, her hair heavy and warm on his arm, her breath moist against his nipple. He moved his hand and discovered that it was her breast he was cupping, heavy and warm beneath smooth satin. Her nipple was hard, and so was he, he realized. Greedily, painfully hard.

What circumstances had brought them together, each partially clothed, in this bed? he wondered; then swiftly, before the memory came, he closed his mind. He didn't want to remember, didn't want to face the ugliness again. All he wanted was this—hunger, arousal, Rachel.

He slid his hand over her breast again, this time capturing her erect nipple between two fingers. Her moan was soft, breathy, and she pushed her breast into his hand, subconsciously longing for more. "Rachel?" he whispered.

No answer came. He tried to remove his hand, but the swelling between his thighs was responding so sweetly to the sensation. He was taking shameful advantage of her. She had offered him comfort, not intimacy, and tomorrow she would hate him for taking both.

At last he released her nipple and started to slide his hand away, but the sound of her voice, husky, heavy with sleep and desire, stopped him. "I was having an erotic dream," she said with a throaty laugh, "but it wasn't a dream at all. It was you.... I want you inside me, Gabriel."

He had to clear his throat before he could answer, before he could respond to her invitation. "Rachel...you're tired...not completely awake.... You don't know..."

She moved her hand over his belly, past the narrow band of his briefs, and found him, heated, straining, too much for her grasp. "If you get any harder, this little scrap won't cover it." She gently eased his length free of the briefs and stroked him. "And if I get any more aroused, I'm going to shatter. Please, Gabriel..."

It was wrong to take her this way, when she was too sleepy, too aroused from her dreams, to realize what she was doing. But how could he turn away from what he'd needed for so long? How could he be noble and leave her alone?

He turned onto his side and pushed her back. In the moon glow that lit the room, he could see her nipples, hard and drawn against the silver satin. He touched his fingertip to one, his tongue to the other, and heard her sharp intake of breath.

"Please..." She struggled to remove the teddy, pushing the straps off her shoulders, baring her breasts to his mouth. He cupped one in his hand, lifting it to his lips, suckling the erect peak until she moaned.

"If we don't slow down, it'll be over so quickly. Too quickly," he warned, drawing the teddy down her body, the satin cool against her hot flesh.

"That's what I want . . . what I need. . . ."

He reached her hips, pushed the satin away and touched her black silk curls. His finger probed beneath them, where she was moist, hot. Ready for him. His fingertip stroked, and she stiffened, tension rippling through the soft lines of her body, a tiny cry escaping her.

He removed his briefs, swept the teddy down her legs and settled between her thighs, poised, waiting, testing. He had no control. Once he was inside her, once he felt her warmth tight and wet around his hardness, he knew he would be lost, for now, forever. "Are you sure, Rachel?"

She felt the blunt tip of him touching her, but barely, and lifted her hips, arching against him, over him, enveloping him. With a low, vicious groan, he completed the movement until he had filled her, and she had taken him completely. She wrapped her legs around his, slid her palms down his back to his buttocks, admiring the feel of the sensual curve, the tightly knotted muscles.

His body, damp with sweat and strained beyond control, covered hers, and he whispered in a tortured voice in her ear, *"Don't move."*

She turned her head only enough to kiss his jaw, then, smiling wickedly, she flexed the muscles deep inside her belly that encircled and cradled his hardness. It wrung a groan from him that tickled her ear, making her shiver.

"I mean it, Rachel, if you aren't completely still..." The muscles flexed again, tautening, easing, tautening, around him. He tried to stand against the shudders, the throbbing, the tightening of his own body, but it was too much. Gathering her close and closing his eyes against the sun-bright explosions, he heard her soft, satisfied laugh and emptied himself, his seed and his soul, into her body.

"Witch."

Rachel heard the low insult, felt it feather against her

throat, recognized the amusement and tenderness behind it, and smiled.

"Now it's your turn."

She tried to look innocent, not easy when her body was flushed, still joined with his, damp with his release. "My turn?"

"You said that if you were any more aroused you would shatter," he reminded her. He paused to glide his tongue over her jaw, then raised both her arms over her head and held them there. "Honey, I'm going to make you shatter."

He left her body and suckled her breast, nibbling, biting, licking, tormenting. She tried frantically to free her arms, intent on pulling him back inside her where she needed him; then he moved his mouth to her other breast, and her arms, her entire body, went limp. He was an expert, teasing, taunting, torturing, making her moan and gasp, offering too much, yet not enough. Not nearly enough.

As he slid down, leaving a trail of wet kisses that burned her flesh, he stayed in contact with her body, letting her feel the growing, taut rigidity of his manhood against her thigh, then her calf. He kissed her hip, then rested his hand lightly over the curls of silk between her thighs. He felt his own wetness against her palm, on his fingers, as he gently delved through the curls to the swollen flesh beneath.

"Gabriel," she whispered, his name an aching plea.

"Does that feel good?"

"Please..."

He stroked her, long, tender touches that started deep inside her and ended on that tiny, hard, heated nub. She tried to protest that she wanted him inside her, but she couldn't wait, couldn't stop the flood of sensations his gentle, talented fingers were releasing.

He watched her, his dark eyes gleaming, his own hunger so great he could hardly stand it. "Come on, Rachel," he murmured in a low, mesmerizing voice. "It's all right. Shatter for me."

Helplessly, she raised her hips, deepening his touch, increasing the torment, until her body contracted, and with a sweet agonizing cry, she splintered into a million, tiny, glistening pieces. Shattered.

"It was an eleven-year-old boy."

Rachel lay on her side, heavy, full, satisfied. It took a few moments for her dazed brain to begin working, to understand what Gabriel was saying. When she understood, she shuddered uncontrollably. The murder victim had been eleven years old. Gabriel's own child would be eleven now, she realized with a sickening rush.

"Almost every bone in his body was broken," he continued in an empty, unfeeling voice. His hands were clasped beneath his head. He didn't want to reach for her while he was remembering the sight that had greeted him when he'd walked into the little white house—the blood, the thin, frail, broken body. He'd felt her shudder, knew she didn't need to hear this, but he needed to tell her. "He was eleven years old, and he was beaten to death by his father. His mother found him." He freed one hand to rub his eyes, then made a harsh sound of protest. "God, isn't it enough that her son had to die, that he had to die like that? Did she have to see it?"

Rachel closed her eyes on his anguish, on her own tears, and hugged him fiercely. If she could give him some of her warmth, some of her strength, if they could share the horror, they would be all right. Sharing made them strong—not handling everything alone, not self-protection. Giving herself to Gabriel made her stronger, because he'd given himself back.

"I'm tired of it, Rachel," he whispered wearily. "I'm tired of seeing the bodies, the evidence of what one human being is capable of doing to another. I'm tired of the murder, the violence, the brutality. Can you imagine the fear, the pain, that little boy suffered?"

She couldn't, and she didn't want to try. "You do the best you can, Gabriel. The only way you can help the victims is by seeing that justice is served."

"Justice isn't going to make that boy live again. It isn't going to help his mother forget what she saw. It isn't going to help his father live with what he's done."

"Did he confess?"

"Yes, to me, the other cops, the coroner's people, the neighbors—to anyone who would listen. The guy is nuts." He rolled onto his side to face her, to get closer to her warmth, and she held him, rubbing his spine, relaxing the muscles in his neck.

"You need some time away," she said softly. "Take a week off. Go to Utah with me."

A week alone with Rachel. God, it would be wonderful—to talk to her, hold her, make love to her. To simply *look* at her. It would be heaven...but, as usual, heaven was out of reach. "I can't. I've got cases."

"Anything that your detectives can't handle?"

"Unfortunately, yes. I'll be in court Tuesday and Wednesday. I'd like to skip it, but I'm afraid the D.A. would frown on that." He separated a strand of her hair and wrapped it around his index finger. "Will you be there next weekend?"

"Either there or Colorado."

"I could probably take Friday off and spend the weekend with you."

"That would be nice," she said with a soft smile. "I don't work on weekends."

She continued rubbing his back. Every long stroke made her breast brush his chest, and every change in position let him feel her heat, smell her scent. "Rachel?" he murmured, reaching up and catching her wrist. "If you want to rub something, why don't you try this?" He guided her hand downward, pressing it snugly against himself.

She smiled with satisfaction. "I was wondering if you would have the energy to make love again," she practically purred as she skillfully caressed him.

"Didn't I satisfy you the last time?" he asked arrogantly. "And the time before that?"

"Every time. All the time." She bathed his nipple with her tongue, then watched it respond, growing harder, much the same way the lower part of his body was responding to her touch.

He returned the favor, teasing her nipples until they were stiff peaks, then moving his caresses lower, stroking, moistening, preparing her with his fingers. She shuddered against him, her limbs heavy, her need great. "Does that feel good?" he whispered, shifting his weight until he was above her, sheltering her.

"Yes."

"Do you want me inside you?"

She arched to meet him, welcoming him, pulling him tightly, deeply, into her, wordlessly answering his question. Kissing him fiercely, she stroked him, her hands spreading fever through his body. She urged him, with her heat, her touch, her soft little cries, to lose control, and he did, forcefully. Her own release came then, leaving them weak, trembling, shuddering in each other's arms.

Rachel was awakened Saturday morning by the soft sound of her name. She moaned, her eyes still closed, and reached for Gabriel, but the bed was empty.

"Rachel?" He was standing next to the bed, wearing only his trousers, his hands clasped loosely behind his back.

"Come back to bed," she mumbled, turning onto her side, her back to him.

He looked at the long expanse of smooth skin that showed where the sheet dipped low and wished longingly that he could obey her sleepy command, but it was out of the question at the moment. "Rachel, would you please wake up, cover up, and tell this man to put his gun away and let me go?"

She stiffened, then whirled around, her hair flying wildly. When she saw the man behind Gabriel, a revolver in hand, she sat up, clutching the sheet tighter. "What— Who— *Webster?*"

The man nodded in greeting. "Do you know this man, Miss Martinez?"

She looked from him to Gabriel, taking in the situation at a glance. He had forgotten about the security alarm—the *silent* security alarm—and had opened the door. She should have warned him about it, and about the fact that one of the security firm's guards lived right down the road.

"Answer the man's question, Rachel," Gabriel said, his voice hard and threatening. He saw the twitch of amusement that crossed her face and swore to make her pay as soon as they were alone.

"Ah, yes, I do know him, Webster." She leaned against the headboard, tucking the sheet firmly beneath her arms.

"I found him coming in the back door after your alarm went off."

She gave a shake of her head. "You should have turned it off, Gabriel."

"How could I turn it off? I forgot it was there." He scowled, thoroughly exasperated with both of them. "I'm glad you both find this so damned amusing. Of course, neither of you is wearing handcuffs." His eyes narrowed on Rachel's face, and he smiled slowly, slyly. "But that's an idea. I just happen to have a pair—"

She turned a shade of deep red and tugged the sheet higher. "Uh, it's okay, Webster. Take the cuffs off. I'm sorry about this."

The man holstered the gun and unlocked the handcuffs. "Any time, Miss Martinez. That's what we're here for. I'll call in and have them cancel the call to the sheriff's department. You'll need to reset your alarm...." He looked from her to Gabriel, who was slowly, methodically, rubbing his wrists and watching Rachel with a devil's gleam in his eyes. "Later. I'll see myself out."

As Gabriel started toward the bed, Rachel started edging toward the other side. "Gee...it's nearly nine o'clock. Time to get up."

He leaned one knee on the mattress, then the other. Just as she swung her feet to the floor, he caught the sheet and tugged. Wrapped around her body as it was, the fabric trapped her, tumbling her back across the bed. Swiftly Gabriel moved over her, straddling her hips, the open stance blatantly revealing his sudden arousal. "You like seeing me in handcuffs, do you?"

"Well..." She let her gaze travel slowly over his face, across his chest, down to his hips. He was lean, strong, virile. Just looking at the masculine perfection of his body made her weak.

"I have a pair of cuffs in my coat pocket," he said, slowly leaning over her. He claimed her right wrist and stretched it high above her head. "I could put this arm here..." He repeated the action with her other arm. "...and this one here, and I could fasten the handcuffs through the bars on the headboard." Bending his head, he brushed his mouth across hers, then pressed her hands together, twining her fingers around one of the brass bars. "Then you would be my prisoner, and I could do whatever I wanted to you. I could kiss you here...." Holding her wrists with only one hand, he brought the other to her face, touching her lips. "And I could kiss you here..." Her nipple grew hard when he gently tapped it with his finger. "And I could kiss you here...." He nudged her legs apart, his hand possessively covering her femininity.

She opened to him, luring him in, and he caressed the dewy softness. "I could make love to you all day," he said hoarsely. "I could make you need me...make you want me...make you love me. I could make you burn to have me inside you. I could make you want it so badly that you'd cry, whimper, plead. I could make you forget that any other man in the world ever touched you here, that any other man ever filled you here. But I don't want to *make* you do anything, give me anything. I want to share with you. Give me what you will, Rachel, and take what you want." He released her hands and rolled onto his back beside her.

Rachel was smiling as she untangled herself from the sheet and rose over him. "Maybe I would like to see you in cuffs," she said. "At my mercy."

He wasn't smiling when he responded. "I'm already at your mercy, honey. I have been all my life."

She licked across his nipple, watched it harden, then repeated it with the other. Then she knelt between his legs, and, with a slowness that made him grit his teeth, unfastened his trousers and discarded them. "I like your underwear," she teased, rubbing her hand over the soft blue cotton.

He swore in a violently low voice, but Rachel just looked at him and smiled. "What do you want?"

"Anything. Everything. You." She could take him any way she wanted, every way she wanted, as long as she did it now.

She moved sinuously, like a sleek, stalking jungle cat, sheathing him in one long, fluid stroke, holding him, teasing him, caressing him, arousing him. Satisfying him.

Chapter 7

Rachel slept again. When she awoke, the room was warm and bright with sunlight, and Gabriel was once again gone. She found her robe on the floor and put it on, belting it loosely, then went down the hall in search of him. "I smell coffee," she murmured, rounding the corner into the kitchen.

"Instant. That's all you have." Gabriel, once again wearing only his trousers, handed her the mug he'd been drinking from, took another from the cabinet, filled it with water and stuck it in the microwave. "How long have you lived here?"

"Since I moved back from Los Angeles. About four months. Why?" The coffee was strong and black, not at all the way she liked it. She added a packet of sweetener and diluted it with tap water before drinking again.

"This kitchen is *empty*. There are no canned foods, no popcorn or rice or spices in the cabinets, no frozen dinners in the freezer, and the refrigerator has a six-pack of Coke, a quart of spoiled milk, a tub of butter, half a head of lettuce from Thursday night's dinner, and one egg that's been in there so long that it's stuck in the egg holder."

"Yeah. I figure it had a little crack in it when I bought it, and the insides leaked out. Egg white makes a good glue—did you know that?"

The oven dinged, and he removed the cup, then stirred a heaping spoonful of coffee granules into the water. "The oven is spotless, the burners don't have even a speck of grease on them, and the dishwasher smells like it's never been used."

"Okay, so I don't cook," she stated calmly, leaning against one of her empty cabinets. "If I don't cook, then I don't have to buy groceries, and I don't have to use the stove or oven, and there aren't any dishes to wash in the dishwasher. So?"

"How can you live like this?" He sounded truly amazed. He'd known the living room was impersonal, and the bedroom wasn't much better, but somehow he had expected the kitchen to look like a kitchen, not like a display model.

She lost interest in the conversation then and turned away. "I live alone, Gabriel," she said, her voice cool and even. "That means *alone*. By myself. Other than the delivery men, the utilities people, the security guys, you're the only person who's ever been here. I have no company, no guests, no friends. If I want to live like this, there's no one to complain. There's no reason to live any differently."

He looked down at the clean-scrubbed tile floor. "I'm sorry."

Her sigh was as soft as his apology. She understood what he was saying. He lived alone, too, in an apartment less than half the size of this house, but with ten times the warmth, the welcome. "At least there aren't things growing in my sink."

He remembered when they were first dating, and she had found, amid the pile of dirty dishes in his kitchen sink, a seed that had sprouted and grown several inches before dying. Slowly he smiled at her. "I have no right to criticize."

She raised her hands in an open shrug. "Criticize my house all you want. Maybe you can even help me get settled in."

He could certainly do that. He could move some of his things over here and have it looking like home in no time.

"Since I obviously have no food here, and it's lunchtime, why don't we get dressed, go by your apartment so you can change, and get some lunch?"

"Huh-uh. The first two, yes, then we're going to the stadium. It's a bright, sunny day, the Giants are in town, and Shelley's bringing the food and meeting us at my place."

Rachel rolled her eyes upward. "A baseball game."

"Unless you want to stay and play here."

Her smile was slow, easy. "Keep it up and I won't be able to get out of bed."

Gabriel took a step toward her, then another, until he was only a breath away. "If I keep it up, honey, you won't *want* to get out of bed."

He didn't touch her, but she could feel him everywhere, imprinted on her body and in her mind. She closed her eyes, but she could hear his uneven breathing, could smell his woodsy fragrance, could feel his heat. Her voice was none too steady when she said, "We'd better go. We don't want to keep the Giants and Shelley waiting."

The instant he stepped away, she knew it. She opened her eyes and saw that he was grinning that cocky, arrogant grin of his that she loved so much. "You get dressed first," he suggested. "Otherwise the Giants and Shelley can wait until hell freezes over."

She returned to her room and changed into a pair of shorts and a faded Padres T-shirt featuring the brown-robed, bat-swinging friar, the logo the team had discarded not long ago in favor of their name in orange and brown. They had no imagination, she thought wryly as she tucked the shirt into her shorts. She carried her shoes into the living room, intending to let Gabriel use the bedroom to finish dressing.

He stared at her, his eyes open wide. "You have a Padres shirt—with the padre, no less. I thought you were a Dodgers fan."

"I am."

"Then why the shirt?"

"I used to date a guy who liked the Padres."

His eyes narrowed suspiciously; then he turned her, checking the size of the shirt. "That's *my* Padres shirt," he accused.

"It certainly is." She'd kept it in the bottom drawer, hoping to forget that she had it, unwilling to throw it away. "Don't you think it looks better on me than you?"

His frown softened into a sweet smile. "Yeah," he agreed. "It certainly does." He drew a deep breath, then backed away from her. "I'll be ready in a couple of minutes."

Barely five minutes had passed before he returned, fully dressed, and they left for his apartment. He drove quickly, confidently, in traffic that grew heavier the closer they got to his exit. At the apartments, he parked next to a red Trans-Am, lifting a hand in greeting to Christopher and Shelley Morgan.

"We were beginning to think you had stood us up," Shelley teased, sliding off the hood of her car as Gabriel and Rachel got out of the Mazda. "Hi, Rachel."

She shyly returned the greeting. Both Shelley and Christopher, she saw, had noticed Gabriel's rumpled suit and reached the same conclusion and were trying valiantly not to let on that they'd noticed, but her face was turning red anyway. Only Gabriel seemed unaware.

"You have the food, Shelley?" Gabriel asked, reaching for Rachel's hand.

"Of course. When have you ever gone hungry around me?" She picked up the cooler and handed it to her husband as they followed the other couple to the apartment. "We're not fond of tailgate parties," she explained to Rachel while they waited for Gabriel to unlock the door, "so I bring the food, and we eat over here."

"We're not fond of parking at the stadium," Christopher corrected.

"Yeah," Shelley agreed, wrinkling her nose. "In the time it takes to get out of the parking lot after a game, we can walk back here and drive all the way home. You don't mind walking, do you? I'm supposed to exercise, and I hate it."

"No," Rachel said. "I don't mind."

Once inside, the two women went into the kitchen to dish up the food. Gabriel changed into running shorts and a T-shirt, then cleared a week's worth of newspapers and mail from the dining table.

"Have a long night at work?" Christopher asked as he glanced through last night's newspaper, which he'd found on the steps.

Gabriel scowled at him. "I can remember a time, right after you met Shelley, when I went to your house early one Saturday morning and found her there, barefoot and obviously not long out of the shower, and I let you both pretend that she hadn't been there all night. So don't say a word."

Christopher was all innocence when he faced his friend. "Me? Say something tacky?" He added the newspaper to the stack that Gabriel was holding. "I saw the news last night. Are you okay?"

He grew somber, remembering what had sent him to Rachel. "Yeah. Thanks."

"How's it going with Jenna? Has Rachel found anything yet?"

Gabriel shook his head. "There's a real good chance that she won't. It's been so long, and I know so little about Jenna." Grimacing, he dumped the papers into a basket and pulled four placemats from beneath them. "I don't know how I got so deeply involved with someone without learning something about her."

"Do you know much about Rachel?"

"I can tell you when and where she was born, where her parents live, what their names and occupations are, her brothers' and sister's names and ages and how many kids they've got, where she went to school, what her favorite food and color and song are, where she's ticklish, how she thinks—"

"Okay, okay, I get the picture. Sort of like Shelley and me, right?"

Sort of like being married. Gabriel liked that idea—liked it a lot.

In the kitchen, Rachel was arranging food on the dishes Shelley had just finished washing. The room, while basically very similar to her own kitchen, was a world apart from it. There were dirty dishes, a few plants, food spilling out of the cabinets and onto the counters, well-used appliances and the smells of cooking—garlic, peppers, spices. A bulletin board hung in the only available wall space, overflowing with notes, business cards, reminders. Above it was a telephone, its extra-long cord a tangle, and, next to that, a calendar, something scribbled into practically every date.

"It's kind of... lived in, isn't it?" Shelley asked, drying her hands on a dish towel.

"I wasn't aware that Gabriel cooked." When they'd been together before, he had often helped in the kitchen but cooking had been her responsibility, one that she had actually enjoyed.

"Not too often, fortunately. He's pretty good—he's fixed dinner for Christopher and me before—but he doesn't just cook," Shelley said, gesturing to the room. "He creates disasters. He can use every single pot, pan and dish in this kitchen to cook a simple meal for three. Let's see... if you'll start taking this stuff out to the table, I'll get the ice."

Over lunch the conversation turned to baseball. Once an avid fan, Rachel had known statistics, rosters and the standings of most of the National League teams. Now the players the other three were discussing were strangers to her. The sport had been one of the many things she'd lost interest in in the past years.

"Are you a baseball fan, Rachel?" Shelley asked.

"I like the Dodgers," she replied.

"Oh, do they play baseball?" Christopher asked, his expression perfectly serious.

"Better than your team does. I hear the Padres are in the cellar again," Rachel said with a smile. "But since they spend so much time there, they must like it."

"I imagine you've heard all the usual L.A. jokes."

She nodded. "I think I have."

Gabriel helped himself to a brownie with rich chocolate frosting. "Did you know that, in L.A., the first time the cops catch you on a routine traffic offense, they give you a ticket to a Dodgers' game?" He paused briefly to take a bite of the chewy cake, then delivered the punch line. "The second time they catch you, they make you go to it."

Rachel rolled her eyes in an exaggerated grimace. "That's *bad*."

"So are the Dodgers," he retorted. He wiped his fingers on a napkin, then began clearing the table. "We need to leave in a couple of minutes."

The stadium was little more than a mile from the apartment, but the streets were clogged with cars. They dodged traffic and other fans, weaving in and out. Once they reached the relative calm of the stadium, Rachel gave a sigh of relief. "I see why you guys don't want to drive in that mess," she remarked, falling in step beside Shelley.

"It's something, isn't it? I guess it's part of the price we pay for living in the big city."

"You're from the South, aren't you?" The accent was faint, fading from exposure to so many other accents, but Rachel could detect it in certain sounds.

"Born and raised in Alabama."

"How did you end up in California?"

"I got a job offer at the right time, when I was ready to make a change."

Rachel considered the change last night had brought in her relationship with Gabriel and wondered if she would be made to pay for it later. "Do you ever regret making that change?"

Shelley answered without hesitation. "No. If I hadn't, I never would have met Christopher." She glanced at her husband, a few feet ahead of them with Gabriel, and smiled gently. "And if I had never met Christopher, I would never have been happy."

Rachel was silent for a long time. Would she ever be as happy as the other woman, with or without Gabriel? She didn't know the answer. She associated him with the happiest time in her life, but she also associated him with the worst time. "It's said that each of us has to be responsible for our own happiness. That if we're not capable of finding happiness alone, then we can't depend on someone else to get it for us."

"Maybe . . . but I don't agree," Shelley said. "We're not meant to be solitary. People by nature need other people, and, for most of us, there's one particular person that we need more than others. If I could be as happy without Christopher as I am with him, then my love for him wouldn't mean a whole lot, would it? Everything in my life is intertwined—my family and friends, Christopher and the baby. How could I be happy with a part of me missing?"

Maybe that was her problem, Rachel thought grimly. When she'd been broken, all the parts hadn't gotten put back together. The part that was Gabriel had been lost, along with the parts made up of trust, faith, hope. Now Gabriel was back, but what did it matter if trust, faith and hope were still missing?

Maybe they weren't. How could she have made love with him last night if she hadn't trusted him to take care with her? How could she have given him the power to destroy her once more if she hadn't had faith that he wouldn't use it? How could she look at him now and think about happiness, about needing and sharing forever, if she didn't have hope?

They reached their seats then, and the chance for private conversation was gone. But Rachel was thoughtful. If she trusted Gabriel, that meant she must also have forgiven him, because she couldn't have one without the other.

For years she had blamed him for turning against her the night Jack had been killed, but had she been fair? She had known from the first time she'd met him that Gabriel was a very emotional man. He reacted first, jumped first, fell first, and considered the consequences later. He loved more intensely, hurt more deeply, was quick to anger and quicker to forgive. His emotionality had been one of the things that had attracted her to him. She was more reflective, cautious and analytical, and she had been drawn to his openness, his intensity, his sheer honesty about his feelings.

His emotions had overwhelmed him last night, as they had the night Jack died, and he had gotten angry, had lashed out at her, offering insults and ugly insinuations. But this time she hadn't let it hurt her, hadn't become defensive and self-protective. This time she had seen his anger as what it was: a defense against grief, against feeling too much.

If she had reacted differently on that long-ago night, if she had looked past her own feelings and needs, she would have known that he didn't mean what he was saying. She would have been able to comfort him, and in giving comfort, she would have been able to take it, too. He hadn't been totally to blame for what had happened that night; she had to accept her share of blame, too.

When the game ended, they walked back to the apartment, where Christopher and Shelley said goodbye, leaving Rachel alone with Gabriel once more. She leaned back on the sofa, a small pillow beneath her head, and sighed. "I had a nice time."

"Really? I thought your mind was someplace else."

Her mind might have wandered, she thought with a grin, but it hadn't gone far—only to the man next to her.

"What do you want to do tonight?" he asked casually. The question made him nervous. If she said she wanted to go home—alone—what would he do?

"I don't know."

"Want to go to a movie? To the beach, to a club, to the mountains, to the desert? For a drive, for a swi—"

She interrupted him. "To bed?"

Gabriel sat still for a long time before questioning her. "Are you asking because it's what you want, or offering because you know it's what I want?"

"Isn't it convenient that we both want the same thing?" She stood up and held her hand out to him, and he took it, letting her pull him to his feet. Then he wound his arms around her and gave her a long, leisurely, arousing kiss.

"It's not a 'thing' I want," he murmured, brushing his lips against her temple. "It's *you*. All my life, Rachel, I've wanted you."

And he could have her, she thought solemnly. For as long as he wanted, for as long as he needed, she was his. And when the need and the want were satisfied... His hands found her breasts beneath the T-shirt, and she shuddered. She wouldn't think about that now. Now she would give, and take, and be happy.

Rachel returned to Salt Lake City Monday morning, welcoming the tedium of the records search that awaited her. The work required little concentration, leaving her mind free to think. All she could think of was Gabriel.

They'd made love more times this past weekend than she could count—making up for five lost years, he had said. She was more comfortable with his casual touch now that she was reacquainted with his intimate caresses. She could talk and smile and laugh with him, could arouse him, be aroused by him, could satisfy him. The only thing she couldn't do was love him.

Except that it was too late for that—had been too late for longer than she cared to admit. She tried to ignore it or call it by other names—lust, desire, friendship, affection—but she was tired of believing her lies, tired of pretending to believe them. She was in love with Gabriel Rodriguez, always had been and always would be, and there wasn't a damn thing in the world she could do about it.

Except keep it her secret. Gabriel wouldn't care. He had never asked for love, had never asked for anything more than the use of her body. Of course, he had used prettier words—had talked about wanting and needing—but an affair was an affair, no matter what words he used. For all she knew, it could end when the case did, when Gabriel had found his child and had no further need, professionally or personally, for Rachel.

But if he ever did fall in love with her, the forever kind of love... She gave a vicious shake of her head. She didn't know what Gabriel wanted in his future, but he'd never given her reason to believe that it was her. He had never offered her anything beyond the present, and she didn't have the courage to ask for more, for fear of losing it all. Because, in spite of her doubts, she was certain of one thing: she might not have much of a future with Gabriel, but there would be no future at all without him.

Jenna Elise Simpson.

Rachel sat motionless for a long time, listening to the thudding of her heart in her ears. The last name didn't match, but the first and middle names and the birth month did. That was too unlikely to be coincidence. She could think of only two reasons for the different surname: Jenna had legally changed it—unlikely—or she had been married. Whatever the explanation, this *had* to be Jenna White.

Blindly she reached into her briefcase, then gave her head a shake to clear it. She didn't need to copy the information; she would simply ask the clerk to give her a copy of the certificate. The woman, used to seeing her every day, would be more than happy to comply.

She realized that her hands were trembling and quickly clasped them in her lap. She wished she could attribute it to her first real progress on the case, but hadn't she decided just this week to quit believing her own lies? Hadn't she also acknowledged just this week that, once she'd found Jenna and her child, Gabriel might no longer need her?

Well, she would soon find out. Finding the birth certificate was a long way from finding the woman, but it would point her in the right direction. If asked to make an educated guess on how much longer the case would take, she would say no more than a month, at the most.

Possibly no more than a month left with Gabriel.

She shut that out of her mind and went to find the clerk. A few minutes later, a copy of the certificate tucked inside her briefcase, she left the office.

It was bright and sunny and hot outside. Rachel glanced at her watch when she reached her rental car. Gabriel's plane was scheduled to arrive at six o'clock. That left her plenty of time to go back to the hotel and change before making the drive to the airport.

Plenty of time to decide what she was going to do about the birth certificate. The next steps in the search were obvious. She would go to Beaumont, Utah, wherever that was, and begin asking questions. She would check the phone book, the city directory if they had one, the high school yearbooks; would talk to neighbors, teachers, the newspaper staff. She would check the marriage records and tax records and show the picture to anyone who would look.

But what was she going to tell Gabriel? He had a right to know that she'd found a solid lead. After all, he was paying for this investigation. But what if it *was* an incredible coincidence and this wasn't the right Jenna Elise? Was it fair to get his hopes up before she had proof? What would it hurt to keep quiet a few days longer, until she'd had a chance to investigate Jenna Simpson?

What would it hurt to have a few more days alone with him, his attention on her and not the beautiful blonde?

She wished she could deny it. She wished she could believe that she wasn't that petty, that selfish, but she was. She wasn't certain that she could compete with the other woman, even her memory, and she was too unsure to try.

She had wondered before if he had loved Jenna, if his desire to find her had as much to do with her as her child. She thought of the questions she had never asked him. *Were you happy that she was pregnant? Did you make the same gesture that thousands of other young men in the same situation have made and offer to marry her? Did you want to*

*marry her? Did you love her? How did you feel when she
left? How do you feel about her now?*

She had never asked him any of those things—because
they had seemed unimportant to the case? Or because she
had feared, even then, the answers he would give?

She let herself into the room, stopping to secure the safety
chain. When she turned and saw the man standing at the
window, she gave a tiny cry before recognizing him.

Gabriel turned around to look at her, rubbing one finger
along the line of his jaw. "It's a good idea to check your
room before you get yourself all locked in," he mildly suggested.

She clenched her fingers around the handle of her briefcase. She wasn't ready for this. She needed time to prepare.
"You caught an earlier flight."

He nodded. "I left a message for you."

She glanced at the phone, where the red message light was
blinking. "You shouldn't have charmed your way in here.
You're lucky I didn't shoot you."

He shook his head. "You don't have your gun with you."

"How do you know?"

"I asked Elaine. She said you don't like the hassle of de-
claring it when you fly. I, on the other hand, take mine
everywhere." He nodded toward the nightstand, where his
revolver lay.

"One of the advantages of being a cop," she said, cross-
ing to the table to lay her briefcase down. Her fingers
cramped when they unbent, and she rubbed them ner-
vously.

"Or disadvantages." He shrugged carelessly. "I never
know when I'll run into someone I sent to prison. Someone
who'd like a little revenge." He slid his hands into his jeans
pockets and rocked back and forth on his heels. "Correct
me if I'm wrong—"

"Of course," she said coolly.

He smiled sardonically. "—but didn't you invite me
here?"

"Yes. Why do you ask?"

"Because I get the distinct feeling that you wish I hadn't come." He was determined not to show it, but her cool displeasure left him feeling hurt and cheated. The last time he had seen her, on Monday morning, he had awakened to her soft hair tickling his belly while, lower, she had intimately kissed him, bringing him such pleasure with her mouth that he'd been left weak and mindless. Now she was acting as if he were a stranger who had wandered into her room by mistake.

She rubbed her hand over the scarred leather of her briefcase. "I'm glad you're here." She took a deep breath, trying to find an expression to match her words. It was just so damn hard with that birth certificate underneath her hand.

"Yeah, I can see that you're just bubbling over with enthusiasm."

She knew he was right, knew he was annoyed, and that his annoyance was justified. She walked across the room to him, laying her hands on his shoulders. "What do you want from me, Gabriel?" she asked softly, concentrating with all her power on him, forgetting the birth certificate, her fears, her doubts. Everything but him.

She had asked the same question over the weekend. He could give the same answer again: *Anything. Everything. You.* Instead he gave her a charmingly wry smile. "How about your gorgeous body?" It was a cheap answer, an easy one that stopped him from mentioning marriage, children, growing old together. There would be a time to discuss those things, but this wasn't it.

"Then why don't you take it?" She rose onto her toes to kiss his mouth, then began undressing. Her jacket slithered to the floor, and, a moment later, her blouse followed. Her bra, sheer and insubstantial, landed on top.

Gabriel dropped his gaze to her breasts, watching her nipples peak without so much as a touch. "Do you know that there's a tall office building across the street?" he asked, his voice soft and husky and aroused.

"So?"

"While I was waiting for you to come back, I was looking out the window. Do you know that some of the guys over there have binoculars on their desks?"

She smiled slowly, moving closer to him. "I'm not surprised. Cops and PIs aren't the only people who like to peep into windows. But as long as you don't move, no one's going to see a thing."

He felt her breasts brush against his chest through the thin cotton of his shirt, and his body responded. "We're going to have a real tough time making love if I don't move," he pointed out.

"Oh." She glanced down at her clothes, too far away to reach. "I don't suppose you'd give me your shirt." She ran her finger along the open throat of the knit shirt.

"I can't get it over my head without moving." Wrapping his arms around her, he pulled her with him while he stretched for the cord that would close the drapes. Darkness fell over the room as the bright afternoon sunlight was shut out. "Can I move now?"

She felt him, hot and heavy, against her belly and gave a soft, longing sigh. "Please..."

"You distracted me."

Rachel rested her head on Gabriel's chest. His skin was damp with sweat that tasted salty on her tongue. "How did I distract you?"

He swept his hand down her body, over her breast and, lower, the soft curls, to rest on her hip. "Did you change your mind about wanting to see me?"

"Of course not."

Raising his free hand, he tilted her head back. "Be honest with me, Rachel. You weren't pleased when you walked in the door and saw me here. Why?"

"It's not you, Gabriel. I really am glad that you're here."

"Talk to me, Rachel, please."

She remained silent.

"Come on. You made love to me hoping I would forget that something's bothering you. Don't use me that way, Rachel. Talk to me."

She stared at his chest, so lean and muscular, then got out of bed and walked naked to the closet. When her robe was belted tightly around her waist, she took the birth certificate from her briefcase, returned to the bed and tapped his chest with one finger. "I made love to you because I wanted to," she said imperiously, then tossed the certificate on his stomach.

He propped both pillows behind his head and held the paper up in one hand. For a long time, he studied it, reading the information several times. "I don't understand," he said at last.

"What's to understand?" It was a struggle to make her voice sound light and normal and unaffected, but she succeeded. "Jenna Elise White used to be Jenna Elise Simpson, and she was born in Beaumont, Utah, thirty-seven years ago. Apparently she got married—and hopefully divorced—some time before she met you."

He laid the paper aside. "What does this have to do with you and me?"

"What does it..." Normalcy fled at his disinterest in the information and was replaced by confusion. "That's Jenna, the mother of your child. It won't be long now until I find her."

He folded his hands over his flat stomach and studied her. "Does the idea of me being a father bother you?"

"Of course not." In fact, she found it rather erotic...if only the children he fathered were hers. Angrily, she brushed that thought away. "Let me ask you some questions, okay?"

"All right."

"When you found out that Jenna was pregnant, did you ask her to marry you?"

The tension that streaked through him was a tangible thing. Rachel could feel it in the air, in the sick feeling low in her belly. He looked at her, raised his hand to touch her cheek and smiled bittersweetly. "You've already guessed the answer to that, haven't you?"

She nodded slowly. She should have realized it before. Gabriel was a man of honor. An offer of marriage would be his natural response to learning that his lover was pregnant. "Did you *want* to marry her?"

"Yes, I did." He knew what her next question would be, knew that it could shatter the fragile relationship between them. He also knew that she had to ask it, and that he had to answer.

Unable to look into his eyes, she stared at the hard line of his jaw. Her hands were clenched into fists, and her voice was strained when she asked the question she dreaded most. "Did you love her?"

Gabriel leaned forward, taking hold of her wrists, and she knew what his answer would be. She tried to pull free, but he held her tight, lifting her across his lap, forcing her to hear his response. "Yes, Rachel, I loved her. I loved her more than I had ever loved anyone in my life."

She sat still, staring at his bare chest. She had heard the worst, and she was still functioning, but barely. So Gabriel had loved Jenna. That meant he probably still did. He cared so deeply, so intensely, with such loyalty. When he loved, he would love forever, and twelve years wouldn't change that.

So, if he loved Jenna, what did that leave for *her*? She squeezed her eyes shut, unwilling to answer that question, unwilling to face the evidence of exactly what he felt for her—the scattered clothes, the rumpled bed, his naked body.

"I have to hand it to you," she said, her eyes open again, her voice low and flat. "Not many men would have the nerve to hire a woman who had once been in love with them to find a woman they had once loved. It worked out well for you, didn't it? For the price of a well-trained investigator, you also got a willing bed partner. Someone to keep you company until you find Jenna."

Gabriel stared at her, his eyes shadowed with pain. When she tugged, he let go of her hands, and they slid easily from his nerveless fingers.

She left the bed and walked to the window, hiding behind the curtains and opening them a crack. "Please leave now."

"Not until you finish your interrogation."

"We're finished." Her questioning, their affair, her hopes. Everything, except the search for Jenna, was over.

"No, we're not. You left out a question. Ask it."

She shook her head. She had found out everything she needed to know.

Gabriel got up and pulled his jeans on, but didn't fasten them. He took a position on the opposite side of the window, one shoulder against the wall, arms folded over his chest, and glared at her. "Ask it."

She shook her head again. "I don't know—" Then she remembered it. The last question on her list of things she didn't want to know about Gabriel. *How do you feel about her now?*

"Ask it, damn it!"

Setting her jaw stubbornly, she turned to stare out the window.

"Do I still love her? Aren't you even the slightest bit interested in that? Because if you're not, maybe you're right about yourself. Maybe all you're capable of being is a willing bed partner. Maybe you've got nothing else but your body to give." He saw her flinch and felt her pain, mixed deep inside with his own. "Ask me, Rachel."

She was staring straight ahead, her features hard and unyielding. Gabriel reached across, touching his fingers lightly to her jaw, and felt the nerves tighten, felt her tremble. "If you give a damn about me, Rachel, ask the question."

His touch was so gentle, his voice a soft plea. Slowly she turned her head to look at him, forced her muscles to relax and asked quietly, accusingly, "Do you still love her?"

He closed his eyes, feeling the relief move through him. If she hadn't cared enough to ask that most important question, he would have been devastated. He let his fingers slide down her throat until his hand rested on her shoulder. "No, I don't love her. I stopped loving her a long time ago."

She wanted to believe him, wanted it so badly that she ached with it, but she was afraid. Maybe he really didn't still love Jenna. Or maybe it was just easier for him to believe that—the way Rachel had believed for years that she didn't still love him. The hurt and loss had been so great that the only way she had been able to survive was by denying the love. Maybe he had survived losing Jenna the same way.

Finally she risked looking at him and murmured, "It's none of my business."

"You can't hide behind business anymore, Rachel. It's personal now. It's so damn personal that it hurts." He was quiet for a few minutes, then asked, "Were you really in love with me?"

Quickly she turned her face away from him. She couldn't talk about her love for him in the past tense without him knowing that it existed in the present, too. Yes, she had been in love with him, and it had never ended, had never died. But she hadn't told him then—she had been waiting, she supposed, for some sign that *he* cared about *her*, that the playboy of the department might actually love *her*—and she wouldn't tell him now. It had to be her secret.

"You said that not many men would have the nerve to hire a woman who had once been in love with them. Were you in love with me?" He heard the hopefulness, the outright plea, in his voice and winced. In a matter of minutes, he'd gone from demanding to pleading. At this rate, he would be reduced in no time to begging for something, anything to let him believe she cared.

"What was between us ended a long time ago," she hedged.

He glanced at the bed, then back at her. "It hasn't ended yet."

"It doesn't matter anymore."

"It matters to me."

She was starting to get edgy. If she refused to answer, he would know that she had something to hide and would guess what it was. If she lied, he would know that, too, and would guess the truth. "Practically every woman who knows you is half in love with you."

"I'm not interested in other women. Only you."

"Why?" she challenged. "What makes me different?"

He smiled slowly, wryly. This wasn't the way he'd hoped to say it—not the time or the place or the mood—but he couldn't keep it in any longer. "Because *you're* the only one *I'm* in love with."

Chapter 8

She stared at him for a long time, then moved away. Her arms were folded across her chest, her hands clenched into tight fists. "Please don't say that again," she said quickly.

Gabriel shifted to watch her walk across the room. She reached the mirrored closet door and stood there, staring at his reflection. "Is it such a terrible thing to hear?" he asked.

She made no response.

"Or are you afraid that if you hear it very often, you'll begin to believe it? That would be a disaster, wouldn't it, Rachel—to trust me enough to believe that I love you?"

"You don't know what you're saying."

"I don't?" Slowly he started toward her. "I may not be the most intelligent man in the world, but they're pretty simple words. I think I can understand every one of them."

"What about Jenna?" she asked when he was only a few feet behind her.

"I told you, I don't still love her. I love *you*."

She shook her head impatiently. She knew, and he didn't. She knew what it was like to love someone, to lose him and, in defense, deny the love. If she had never seen Gabriel again, she could have lived the rest of her life believing that she no longer cared for him. She might even have been able to convince herself that she loved someone else, but it would have been a lie. She would have been settling for less than the real thing. Gabriel had lost Jenna, and he had convinced himself that his love was gone, too, that he loved Rachel instead. But what would happen when she found the other woman? What would happen when he saw Jenna again?

The same thing that had happened to Rachel when she'd seen him again. The memories would overwhelm him—the love, the happiness, the joy. Jenna could give him all those things, and his child, too, and he would realize that his "love" for Rachel was nothing but a poor imitation.

He was behind her now, his breath warm on her neck. "Don't you think you deserve to be loved?"

"Yes," she replied, still holding his gaze in the mirror. "And someday I'll fall in love with someone, and he'll love me, too. But it won't be you, Gabriel."

"What makes you think I'll ever let you go long enough to fall in love with someone else?" He reached around her, taking hold of her clenched fists and gently forcing her arms to her sides. "You're mine, Rachel. You may not stay with me willingly, but you *will* stay with me."

She watched him untie the belt of her robe and push the soft fabric to one side. She knew she should push his hands away, shouldn't let him touch her like this, make her feel like this, but she was too weak. She couldn't believe in his love, but she could believe in this. She needed this. "Don't you think that Jenna might object to that?" she asked in a breathy, trembling voice. "Two is company, three—"

"Is kinky." He bent his head to trace her ear with his tongue, making her shiver. "Jenna can't object to anything that she's not going to be a part of, and she's not going to be a part of my life. This is between you and me, honey."

His hands touched her breasts, rubbing gently over them, avoiding the straining peaks until she moaned, low and pleading. Then he took her nipples between his thumbs and forefingers, twisting, teasing, making them harden even more, while his mouth played a different tormenting game with her ear.

Rachel twisted her head to claim his mouth with her own, but he denied her the victory. Instead he kissed the long line of her throat, down to the shadowed hollow of her collarbone and up again. He touched his lips to her cheeks, her closed eyes, briefly to her mouth, then raised his head. "Look at us, Rachel."

Her head was resting on his shoulder, too heavy to hold erect, but she lifted it and opened her eyes. His left hand still caressed her breast, but the other was moving downward over her belly with a touch so light that she barely felt it. When he reached the juncture of her thighs and continued probing, her muscles contracted involuntarily, sending ripples across her satiny skin.

He had told her last weekend that he could make her burn, and now he was proving it. "No," she protested helplessly, but she made no effort to stop him. How could she stop him when she wanted him this way more than anything in the world?

"That feels good, doesn't it?" he murmured in her ear. He felt her body weaken, felt her lean against him for support. His own legs were none too steady, but he couldn't move away. Being able to see what he was doing to her was too tantalizing to give up yet. "Have you ever had sex with a man, Rachel?"

She couldn't answer. The knot of need in her belly was expanding, filling her, threatening to consume her.

"It's not the same as making love," he continued in a softly erotic voice. "Having sex is physical, meaningless, empty. But you're not empty, Rachel. I'm going to fill you—your body, your life, your heart, your soul. I'm going to love you, honey, right now... forever... always...."

He slid the robe from her shoulders, letting it fall to the floor, and carried her, limp and weak, to the bed. His jeans came off easily, and he joined her on the bed, joined her intimately, greedily, lovingly.

* * *

Rachel lay on her back, her head tilted to one side, supported by one fist. Her eyes were closed, her breathing slow, even shallow. Gabriel pulled the sheet over them, then settled on his side and watched her sleep.

He was in a hell of a position—in love with a woman whose response to his declaration of love had been a quick "Please don't say that again." He had always thought such a disclosure was supposed to bring happiness, not wariness. He hadn't expected her own vow of love, but he had wanted more than this.

Maybe she would feel better if he told her that Jenna hadn't seemed much more pleased with his love. Maybe he was doing something wrong—saying it wrong, or showing it in the wrong way. Hell, he hadn't had much experience at it. Jenna had been the first, and Rachel would be the last, because if he lost her, there wouldn't be anything left to give anyone else.

Someday I'll fall in love with someone, and he'll love me, too. But it won't be you, Gabriel. He closed his eyes against the pain. She couldn't love someone else. God help him, she *couldn't.* He wouldn't allow it. He would keep her so busy, so tired, so satisfied, that she would never look at another man. Someday she would have to believe him. Someday she would have to love him.

She shifted, bringing his attention back to her. Behind closed lids, her eyes moved rapidly, side to side. She was dreaming, he realized, wondering what kind of dreams disturbed her tonight. Once she had dreamed about making love with him. She had awakened, aroused and needy, and had seduced him. But now, he suspected, her dreams were unpleasant—a replay of this afternoon's revelations?

Her movements became agitated, her breathing increasing, and soft, frightened cries escaped her. Gabriel laid his arm over her, hugging her close to his warmth, and she grew calm, peaceful. Then suddenly she cried out, and her eyes opened wide, glazed with fear. She stared at him for a moment, then flung her arms around him and hid her face against his chest.

He held her close and unquestioningly stroked her, comforted her. "It's all right, honey," he whispered. "It's all right."

He held her until the shudders had stopped, until the fear was gone from her face. He wanted to ask about the nightmare that had disturbed her, but it was clear that she didn't want to discuss it, that she was still edgy, so instead he asked about dinner.

They settled on a restaurant near the hotel and got dressed. Their conversation as they walked to the restaurant was brief, uninteresting, unimportant. But once they were seated in a private corner of the dining room, Gabriel asked the question that he couldn't keep inside any longer. "How often do you dream?"

Rachel pretended great interest in the menu she was looking at. She couldn't look at *him*. "I suppose every night. Don't most people?"

Under the table his hand formed a fist. Why was she always pretending? Why wouldn't she let him help her? he wondered angrily; then the answer came, draining the anger and leaving him empty. Because she had gone to him for help once before, and he had turned his back on her. She was afraid to count on him again. "You were whimpering," he said quietly. "When you woke up, you looked at me as if you were seeing a ghost. Jack's ghost?"

The waiter's appearance saved her from answering for a few minutes, gave her time to come up with a suitable lie. But when they were alone again and she started to tell it, the words came out all wrong: she told him the truth. "I don't know. I usually don't remember much when I wake up. There's fear, blood . . . death." She shrugged in mock indifference.

"The dreams started after Jack died."

She nodded. "I prefer to call them nightmares. Dreams are pleasant, soothing. These aren't."

"Are you afraid of them?"

"The first few months, I'd wake up every night screaming. It was kind of tough on my parents and my sister." She smiled, but there was no humor in it. "I thought for a while that maybe I really was going crazy. But gradually they came less often, were less graphic. Most of the time now I can't remember any details when I wake up." The smile was more convincing this time. "What do you dream about?"

You. But he didn't say it, didn't want to see the disapproval in her eyes again. "I don't have nightmares."

Reaching beneath the table, she found his clenched hand and laid it on her leg, flattening and relaxing the fingers. "No," she said softly. "You get your nightmares when you're awake. Like that little boy, and all the other cases you've worked."

"I usually handle them better."

"You do okay." She glanced around the restaurant, her gaze skimming over the other diners. She knew Gabriel was watching her—knew that he watched her most of the time—but she didn't object. "Tell me about her."

"Who?" he asked absently. He couldn't be blamed for not realizing that she meant Jenna, not when all his senses were filled with *her*.

"Jenna White."

He sighed softly. He wished she would let it rest. If he knew that she had been in love with another man, he wouldn't be asking for information about him . . . or would he? He had to admit that he would be so consumed with jealousy he would want to know everything. Maybe *she* was jealous. But how could she be jealous if she didn't care about him? he wondered, and immediately countered that with another question: if she didn't care, why did knowing that he'd once loved Jenna upset her so much? "What do you want to know?" he asked with a slight smile.

This time it was Rachel who sighed. Emotionally, she didn't want to know anything, didn't want to hear a single word about Gabriel and another woman and love. Intellectually, though, she wanted to know it all. "You said you were both in school when you met."

He gave a shake of his head. "I was taking an evening class. I was in the Navy then, and I'd been thinking about joining the Department when I got out, so I signed up for a criminal justice class at SDSU. She had a class in the same building, and one night I offered her a ride home."

She could imagine it well—the gorgeous young blonde and the handsome Navy officer. "Love at first sight," she said, unable to keep the mockery out of her voice.

"Not hardly. I thought she was pretty, and she thought riding with me beat the hell out of walking home alone at night."

"And?"

He shrugged. "I asked her out, and we began dating."

"Was she deliberately evasive, or did you just never get around to asking her about her background?"

"I never gave it much thought at the time, but . . . yeah, she was evasive. I should have realized that she was hiding something, but . . ." He finished with a shrug. Rachel had a vivid imagination; she could fill in the blanks.

She smiled absentmindedly at the waiter when he served them and just as absentmindedly tasted her dinner. "You must have been hurt when she left."

"Yeah," he agreed with a wry look. "I must have." The pain had been bad at the time, a deep, relentless hurting that he'd thought would never go away. For a long, long time it had been a constant companion, always there, hovering in the shadows, waiting to catch him at a weak moment. But now there was only a curious emptiness. Time was a healer, as the old saying went. So was Rachel.

"How did you find out that she was gone?"

"She had told me that she was pregnant and had rather reluctantly agreed to marry me. We set the date, started making plans. I was supposed to meet her at her apartment one Saturday afternoon to iron out the final details, but when I got there, the apartment was empty. Her neighbor told me that she had moved out a couple of days earlier. He didn't know where she had gone, just that she wasn't coming back."

"Were you surprised?"

He picked up his water, took a drink, then rolled the glass back and forth between his palms. "Yeah, in a way I was, but in another way, maybe I sort of expected it. You see, Rachel, Jenna didn't love me, and she really didn't want to marry me. She had agreed because I bullied her into it, and because she felt it was her only choice. Marriage to me was better than coping with the baby alone." He was silent for a moment before finishing. "But, apparently, she changed her mind. She found a better alternative and took it, and left me to deal with it."

Rachel didn't doubt that he was being totally honest this time, but she couldn't understand it. The idea of knowing Gabriel and not loving him was beyond her comprehension. What was in Jenna's past that had prevented her from returning his love, that had prompted her to run away, taking herself and his child from him?

"Maybe she wasn't alone," she suggested quietly. "Maybe she was still married at the time you knew her." That would explain why Jenna had disappeared after Gabriel's marriage proposal. Marrying him would have been difficult if she was still married to another man.

Gabriel didn't like the idea, didn't like thinking that he could have fallen in love with a woman who would betray both him and her husband. "A lot of people get married and divorced."

"And a lot of married people separate, go their own ways, then get back together again. Jenna could be one of them."

"You think she left her husband, moved to San Diego, went to school, had an affair with me, then went back to her husband?" He shook his head skeptically.

"If she married young, it would explain why she started college so late." Rachel reached out to lay her hand over his. "I'm just guessing, Gabriel. I'm probably wrong."

He rolled his head back to ease the tension in his neck. "I don't know. I'm tired of answering questions, Rachel. I came here to relax and spend some time with you, not undergo another cross-examination. It seems most of my life involves questions. Either I'm questioning suspects, witnesses and cops, or being questioned by D.A.s and defense attorneys and you. Can't we just talk?''

She responded with an amused smile. "It's hard to carry on a conversation without asking and answering questions.''

"We can try.''

They were both silent for several minutes, then Gabriel chuckled. "You're right—it is hard. Everything that I want to say to you comes in question form. You know what I would really like to do?''

She shook her head.

"Just look at you…hold you…touch you…'' *Love you.* "Can we go now?''

This time she nodded, laying her napkin on the table as she gracefully stood up.

The hotel was across the street, but they turned away from it, walking in the opposite direction instead. Rachel's hand was clasped securely in his bigger one. It made her feel warm, safe.

They were standing at an intersection, waiting to cross the street, when a police car pulled in behind a parked car and a female officer got out to talk to the driver. "Why don't you come back to the Department?'' Gabriel asked suddenly as he pulled her across the street. "They would rehire you in a flash.''

"And give up these lovely business suits for a khaki uniform?'' She laughed softly. "No thanks.''

"You were a good cop, Rachel. If you hadn't quit, you would have made detective a long time ago.'' He stiffened then, troubled by his own words. If she hadn't quit… If *he* hadn't failed her.

She knew the reason behind his sudden tension as surely as if he'd said it aloud: guilt. His guilt was probably the largest part of his so-called "love'' for her. He had hurt her and needed, for his own peace, to make it up to her. "You are so incredibly arrogant and egotistical that you think everything that happens, happens because of you. Well, it just isn't true, Gabriel. I quit the Department because I was afraid. That was the first time anyone had ever pointed a gun at me. It was the first time I had ever fired my gun except in practice, the first time I had ever seen anyone die. I'll admit that you didn't help any, but even if you'd been there for me, even if you had supported me fully, I don't think I could have remained a cop. I was so shaken up that I would have been a liability to anyone foolish enough to work with me, and I didn't want to be responsible for anyone else's death."

Gabriel shook his head in denial. "You weren't responsible."

"*I* pulled the trigger."

"If Jack hadn't let the guy go back to the car alone, if he had been wearing his vest..." If *he* had been patient and caring, if he had controlled his temper, things would have turned out differently. He was sure of it.

"There are a million different *ifs*," Rachel said. "You'll drive yourself nuts if you dwell on all of them. *I* did."

He released her hand and hugged her close to his side. "You were never nuts, Rachel," he disagreed, his dark eyes mirroring his impatience with her statement. "You're probably the strongest person I know."

Although she laughed it off, she treasured the compliment. "Maybe I'm just resilient. Or maybe I don't know when I've had enough." After a moment, she returned to the original subject. "I liked being a cop, but I like what I'm doing now better. It's interesting, challenging, always different, and safer. I know most cops work their entire lives without ever drawing their guns, much less shooting someone or getting shot at, but it *does* happen. But when is the last time you heard of someone taking a shot at a private detective?"

"Yet you carry a gun."

"I carry a gun in San Diego for the same reason that you're carrying one now." She could feel it, secure in its holster, between them. "I *was* a cop, and I never know when

I might run into someone who remembers that. You don't need to feel badly, Gabriel. Even if Jack hadn't died, I probably would have quit sooner or later. I could have stayed, gotten promoted—I probably could have made lieutenant by now," she added with a teasing smile. "But that wasn't the life I wanted for me."

If that wasn't the life she wanted to live, could she accept that kind of life for her husband? he wondered. For the first time, it was something he had to think about. Before, there had been no one else to consider, no one else who was affected by his long hours and heavy caseload and often difficult moods. Now there was. "I don't think I could quit being a cop," he said cautiously.

"Of course you couldn't," she agreed. "Being a cop was my job—I got up every morning, put on the uniform and the gun belt, went to work and collected a paycheck. But it's different for you. It's what you *are*. You're good at it, and it makes you happy." She just hoped that, when they found her, Jenna understood that. If she hadn't wanted to marry Gabriel the Navy officer, she might not be any more willing to marry Gabriel the Homicide detective.

She wanted him to be happy—she truly did—but deep down inside, a part of her hoped that was the case. If Jenna didn't care about Gabriel, if she didn't welcome him into her life and that of their child, then maybe he would settle for Rachel. Maybe he could pretend forever that he loved her, or maybe it would last only until his lust was satisfied and his guilt was resolved. Either way, she would accept it. As long as *she* didn't pretend, too, as long as she didn't believe in his love, she could deal with it. She would survive.

"I'm tired, Gabriel," she said softly as they approached the hotel. "I'd like to go back now." She would like to do as he had suggested earlier: look at him...hold him...touch him. Lord, she wanted to love him.

The rest of the weekend was relaxed, enjoyable. Gabriel made no demands other than physical ones, ones that Rachel could fulfill without hesitation. But when she took him to the airport Sunday evening and it came time to say goodbye, he made it blatantly emotional. He held her tight, her body wedged between his and the wall, and gave her a long, leisurely kiss. "I love you, Rachel," he murmured, then kissed her again when she opened her mouth to protest.

"Gabriel, please..." She was breathless, dismayed by the impact of the simple words.

"I'm not asking you to say that you love me. I'm not asking for anything, Rachel. I'm just telling you that I love you."

"'But you don't,'' she whispered. "You can't."

"Why not?"

"You feel badly about the way our affair ended," she tried to explain, "and you think you owe me something because of it. But—"

He laid his fingers over her mouth. "And so I'm telling you that I love you out of guilt, and I'm willing to sacrifice the rest of my life to make it up to you—is that it?" He shook his head slowly. "And *you* call *me* arrogant. At least I don't try to tell you what you're feeling and why—although I think I could do it with a great deal more accuracy than you can. I think you're damn close to falling in love with me, and I think it scares the hell out of you. You're afraid that you can't count on me, that I'll hurt you again. You're afraid that, if you get hurt again, it will be more than you can handle."

He released her and pushed his hands into his pockets, walked a few steps away, then returned. "Let me tell you something, Rachel. I'm sorry about what I did to you, but I'm not going to let it rule everything that I do now. I'm not going to *pretend* to care about you, and I'm not going to beg you to believe me. The only thing I'm going to do is try. I'm going to try to love you the best way I know how. I'm going to try my damnedest not to hurt you. I'm going to try to make it work for us this time. But if you don't care enough to try, too . . . well, we both lose, don't we?"

He scowled as the final boarding call for his flight was announced over the loudspeaker. Frustration lacing his actions, he pulled her to him and kissed her quickly. "Be careful," he commanded.

She nodded mutely.

"I love you."

This time she almost managed a smile, but not quite.

He kissed her one last time and started to walk away, but her voice stopped him.

"Gabriel? Call me."

His smile was worth the twisted knot of nerves in her stomach. "I will," he promised.

Monday morning she returned to the capitol, this time checking for death certificates for Henry and Maggie Simpson, Jenna's parents. Henry had died ten years ago and was buried in Beaumont. There was nothing, there or in the motor vehicle records, on Maggie. Maybe the woman had moved following Henry's death from Utah to wherever Jenna was living. It wasn't unusual for a widow to want to live near her only child and grandchild. Now there were two names to check, two sets of information to work with.

She checked out of the hotel, got directions for Beaumont, a hundred miles almost due east of Salt Lake City, and set off. It was a lovely drive through mountains and the Ouray-Uinta Indian Reservation and ending in the desert. The arid surroundings contrasted vividly with the thousands of brilliant flowers that lined every corner and every storefront and filled the park in the center of town.

She hoped the myth about small towns—that everyone knew everyone else's business—held true in Beaumont. It would certainly make her job easier if she could find a few gossipy old men who could tell her everything about the Simpsons.

But she wasn't certain that she wanted her job to be easier. In fact, she wasn't certain that she wanted to find Jenna White at all. As long as the woman remained lost, Rachel's chances of holding on to Gabriel were much higher.

But did she want him that way? Did she want him to stay with her only because Jenna wasn't available?

Of course not. She didn't want to be second best, didn't want to win by default. He had to have another chance with Jenna before Rachel could take a chance with him.

She parked her car in front of a café that advertised home cooking and crossed the street to the library. The woman behind the desk directed her to the reference section, where yearbooks from Beaumont High for the last forty years filled the shelves. She found the three books for Jenna's high school years and carried them to a nearby table.

Jenna Simpson was pretty, petite and blond. At the moment that Rachel recognized her picture, she realized how nervous she had been that it wouldn't be the same woman. The relief she felt was almost tangible.

The yearbooks listed activities for each of the graduating seniors, and Rachel listed Jenna's in a notebook: cheerleader, drama club, homecoming queen, honor society, debate team, even a club for future teachers. Next she paged through the book, looking for other cheerleaders, the queen's court, other club members and their faculty advisers, adding their names to her lists. She also added the names of two young men, one in Jenna's class, one a year ahead: Charles and Mike White. One of them was very likely her husband.

Then she turned to the phone books. The library had Beaumont's slim directories for the last five years stacked next to each other. She started with the most recent and worked her way back, finding addresses and numbers for several of the people on her list. She also checked the listings for Simpson and White, copying several names under each. Even though Jenna and her mother had moved away, it was possible that at least one relative remained. She would start making phone calls when she checked into a motel later.

It was after one o'clock when she finished. After eating lunch at the restaurant across the street, she headed for the county courthouse three blocks away.

The marriage license was easy to find. She started with the year Jenna had graduated and found it there, with four other June weddings. Jenna Simpson had married Chuck White on the seventeenth of June. According to the records, if she had divorced him later, it hadn't been in Beaumont.

As long as she was there, she ran down the list of students whose names she'd copied from the yearbooks. A half dozen had married within a few years of Jenna; with their husbands' names, she should be able to find them more easily.

At last she left the courthouse and checked into a motel. There were only two in town, the court clerk had told her, both shabby, both overpriced and only the one with phones in the rooms. She had chosen that one and found that it lived up to the clerk's description. The room smelled musty, and the carpet was dirty. There were holes burned into the bedspread, a hideous yellow and purple floral thing, the bathtub was stained a permanent rust color and the only way to lock the door was to secure a chair beneath the knob, but the sheets were clean, and the phone worked.

She worked her way down the list of Simpsons and Whites in the area, repeating the same spiel to each one who answered. "My name is Rachel Martinez, and I'm trying to locate Jenna Simpson White, who used to live here in Beaumont. Do you know Mrs. White? Is she a relative?"

She got one definite no, three children whose parents weren't home from work yet, and two young women who both thought the name sounded familiar, but if she was a relative, she was their husbands' relative, and they weren't home yet. Rachel thanked them and said that she would call again later.

She got lucky on her last call of the evening. She remembered Karen Dalton Thompson from the yearbook—another pretty, blue-eyed blonde who had also been a cheerleader and honor student and had served as princess in Jenna's court.

"Sure, I knew Jenna," the woman said, her voice echoing through the phone over the sound of a television and arguing children. "What did you want to know about her?"

"I have quite a few questions, Mrs. Thompson. Maybe it would be more convenient if we met tomorrow to talk."

"No problem. Did you see the little park near the center of town?"

Rachel hadn't noticed it, but she could find it.

"I always take the kids there about eleven o'clock. It makes them tired so they'll take a nap after lunch. Why don't you meet me then?"

She agreed, hung up and began making notes. Gabriel hadn't mentioned a report, but Powell would want one, and she couldn't afford to leave anything out. She was on the second page when the phone next to her rung shrilly.

It was Gabriel. "How did you know where I am?" she asked curiously, putting the pen down and rubbing her neck.

"Give me a break, Rachel. I'm a cop, remember?" There was amusement, soft and warm, in his voice. "I knew you were going to Beaumont, and there are only two motels there. It was pretty simple."

"Oh. How was your day?"

"The same as usual. Long and busy and lonely. How was yours?"

"Productive. I'm meeting a friend of Jenna's tomorrow."

He was silent for several long minutes. "Have you learned anything?"

"Not much. I just got into town around noon. I did find her marriage license." She waited for some signal that he wanted to hear more—or didn't. When he said nothing, she continued. "She got married the summer after she graduated from high school to Charles White, same age, a local boy."

"Anything in the divorce records?"

She searched his voice for a sign of hopefulness, but found none. "No, but that doesn't mean anything. These records cover only this county. They could have gotten the divorce anywhere in the United States.''

''Or maybe they didn't.'' His chuckle was low and laced with bitterness. ''I never would have believed that I would have an affair with a married woman. I thought I had higher principles or something.''

''*If* she was still married. You don't know, Gabriel. Even if she was, you can't blame yourself. You couldn't expect yourself to know what she didn't tell you,'' she said gently. She wondered how it had felt to find out that the woman he'd been in love with might have been married to another man at the time. Probably a lot like finding out the man you loved was very likely in love with another woman, she concluded philosophically.

''So what now?''

She detailed everything she'd done so far, ending with her scheduled meeting with Karen Thompson. ''We know that Jenna still had ties with Beaumont as recently as ten years ago—that's when her father died, and he was living here at the time of his death. There's a very good chance that I'll find someone who knows about the baby.''

It made sense, he acknowledged. Jenna had probably returned to Beaumont for her father's funeral and would certainly have taken her baby with her. Surely someone would remember. ''I wish I was there,'' he said with a hint of longing.

Rachel tried to ignore her own longing. ''I can handle this myself,'' she said softly. ''I'm not going to make any mistakes, Gabriel, or miss any leads.''

''I was referring to being with you, sweetheart, not watching over you. I don't care about your work. I know you're doing a good job.'' He knew her too well. She thought he loved Jenna, so, by God, she was going to find Jenna for him. She wouldn't be happy until she'd succeeded, and neither would he. *Then* she would see that Jenna meant nothing to him. *Then* she would have to believe that it was her he loved, and only her. Then they could be happy. ''I miss you.''

She let the warmth of his low words wash over her, and for just a moment, she let herself believe. Then common sense returned, bringing with it cool reason. "You just saw me yesterday."

"But not today." He rubbed wearily at his eyes. "Come on, Rachel, be honest. Don't you miss me at all? My wit? My charm? My handsome face?"

"Your gorgeous body?" she asked dryly. Then she gave him a serious, honest answer. "Yes, I miss you. Very much." As she'd known it would, her honesty stunned him into silence. She took advantage of it to say a hasty goodbye. "I'll call you tomorrow evening, all right? Take care of yourself."

Before he could recover enough to say anything, she had hung up, and there was only a soft buzz in his ear. With a grim shake of his head, he hung up, too. She'd done that deliberately, so she could get off the phone before he had a chance to tell her that he loved her.

"Run while you can," he murmured, stretching out on the sofa, a pillow tucked beneath his head. Soon this case would be over, and she would know how he felt about Jenna. More importantly, she would know how he felt about *her*. He just hoped he could wait that long.

In spite of the heat, the park two blocks off Main Street was a hive of activity when Rachel arrived the next morning. She recognized Karen Thompson from the twenty-year-old photos she'd seen in the yearbooks and approached her, extending her hand to the older woman. "Mrs. Thompson, I'm Rachel Martinez."

Karen shook her hand, then looked her over slowly. "So you're a private detective."

She knew she didn't look the part, as Christopher Morgan and a host of others had pointed out, but today she was even farther from the image than usual. She had broken Powell's strict rule about presenting a professional appearance at all times by dressing in khaki shorts and a tailored red shirt. Her hair was pulled up in a ponytail, she wore no makeup, and instead of heels her shoes were flat-soled sandals. But, damn the rules, Powell had never conducted an interview on a hot summer day in a park in the Utah desert wearing a suit, panty hose and heels.

"Have a seat," Karen invited, gesturing to the quilt she'd spread beneath a tree. "This is Casey and Kristin, and that's Max."

Rachel sat down cross-legged, saying hello to the two older children and smiling at the fat-faced baby. The children seemed awfully young, she noticed. Karen Thompson hadn't started her family until rather late in life. Casey appeared to be about five years old, which meant his mother must have been . . . thirty-three, Rachel's age, when he was born.

Was that what people would say about *her* when she got pregnant? *Aren't you a little old to be having a baby?* She hadn't given it much thought—when there was no man in your life for so long, what was the use in thinking about starting a family? But even after Gabriel had come back, she hadn't really thought about it, either. That was why they'd made love so many times without the slightest bit of protection. He probably assumed that she, an intelligent, mature woman, was taking care of it herself. After all, it was her body, her life that would be forever changed by pregnancy—but she had never given it a moment's concern. Maybe subconsciously she *wanted* to get pregnant. Maybe her subconscious mind figured that was the only way she would have some part of Gabriel to keep forever.

She slowly became aware of three pairs of curious eyes on her. Apparently Karen had spoken to her. . .repeatedly. She felt her face color and smiled uneasily. "I'm sorry. I was just thinking. You have a beautiful family, Mrs. Thompson."

"Thanks. And please, call me Karen. What was it that you wanted to talk to me about?"

"Jenna White. My firm has been hired by an old friend of hers. I was hoping you could give me some information that will help us locate her."

"Whatever I know. Casey, take your sister over to the playground. And mind that you stay inside the fence, understand?"

The boy nodded solemnly, reached for Kristin's hand and led her across to the playground. Rachel watched until they were lost among the other children, then looked back at their mother. "Did you know her well?"

"We were best friends in high school."

"Do you know where she's living now?"

Karen shook her head. "About a year after she and Chuck got married, they moved to New Mexico—he was going to school there for a while. We used to write, call, exchange birthday and Christmas cards, but that gradually stopped. You know how it is when you're living different lives."

"Is she still married to Chuck?"

"I don't know."

"When was the last time you saw her?"

"Um...about a year after her dad died. That would have been...nine or ten years ago."

Nine, Rachel thought. When the baby was about two. Cautiously she asked, "Did she and Chuck ever have any children?"

Karen's expression grew secretive. "Kids?"

"Yes." Rachel gestured to Max, chewing his fist. "Kids."

"She had one."

She had one, she'd said. Not "they." Did Karen know about Jenna's affair with Gabriel, that Jenna's child wasn't her husband's? "Was it a boy or a girl?"

"A boy."

So Gabriel had a son. Did he look like his father? Had he inherited any of the characteristics that Rachel loved so much in his father? She wanted to see him, to find out. How much more would Gabriel want that? She reached out to cup Max's bare foot in her palm. Laughing, he pulled it free, then waited for her to take it again. "He's awfully cute. How old is he?"

"Nine months."

"How old would Jenna's son be now?"

"I'm not sure. I guess . . . about eleven or twelve."

"Her husband must have been pretty happy. Most men really like having sons."

Karen was silent for a long time, staring across the grass toward the other two kids. Finally she glanced at Rachel. "Why are you looking for her—really?"

"I told you. An old friend of hers hired us."

"Do you have a business card?"

She found one in her purse and handed it over.

Karen studied it, then tucked it into the diaper bag. "You're from San Diego," she said flatly.

"Yes." Rachel was holding her breath. The city seemed to mean something to the other woman—because she knew that Jenna had met her son's father there? A moment later, Karen confirmed it.

"Is it him?"

"Who?"

"The guy who hired you. Is it Todd's father?"

This time it was Rachel who fell silent. As a general rule, they promised confidentiality to their clients, but she knew Gabriel would trust her judgment. If telling Karen Thompson everything would help her get more information, he wouldn't object. But she wasn't prepared to be completely candid, not yet. "What makes you think that Chuck isn't Todd's father?"

"The first couple of years that they were married, everything was fine, but after that . . . well, they fought a lot. And they split up a lot. Jenna would come back here and spend weeks at a time with her parents before going back to him. Finally she left him for real—just packed up and disappeared. No one knew where she was, not even her parents."

The baby's sudden wail interrupted her, and she paused to search through the diaper bag for a box of animal cookies. When he was quiet again, she continued, never looking at Rachel. "Then one day she called me—out of the blue. She wanted to know how her mom and dad were, but she couldn't call them herself, because they would ask so many questions. She told me that she was in San Diego, that she'd met this man, and that she wanted to divorce Chuck. Well, the divorce talk was nothing new—I heard that every time she left him. But the man...that *was* new. As far as I know, she had never been unfaithful to Chuck. Then, the next thing I heard, she was back in New Mexico with him, and pregnant. She pretended that the boy was his, but I've seen him. Chuck is as fair as Jenna is, and that boy is dark—dark hair and dark eyes. He looks like he's part Mexican or..."

Or Indian, Rachel finished silently. She folded her hands together and stared down at them. "Did you get the impression that she cared for this man?" she asked, her voice the slightest bit unsteady.

"She talked like she was in love with him. Frankly, I didn't ask her anything because I didn't want to know. I'm no saint, but...she was a married woman, and that didn't seem to matter to her *or* him." She shook her head in dismay. "It just seemed cheap."

"Maybe he didn't know that she was married." Rachel smiled sadly. "So, as far as you know, Jenna is still married to Chuck. Is there anyone in town who might know where they're living now?"

Karen gave a shrug. "You might talk to some of the older ladies—Sophy Morris, Thelma Adamson, Liz Wilkes. They were Maggie's friends for years and years. They might know where she moved when she left Beaumont, and I'd guess that you would find Jenna and Todd nearby." She wiped Max's chin before handing him another cookie. "This man—he's not going to start any trouble, is he?"

Rachel shook her head with more confidence than she felt. "He just wants to know." At least, that was what he'd wanted in the beginning, but then he'd been talking about some sexless, nameless, faceless being who might or might not exist. When he knew that the child was a boy, that the boy had a name and resembled his father, would he be able to stay away? Would he let Jenna and Chuck continue their pretense, or would he force his way into his son's life, the way her own father had done? She hoped Gabriel was a wiser man, a better father than hers had been, but she couldn't swear to it.

"So Jenna ran out on him without saying goodbye, too," Karen remarked with a sigh. "She seemed to make a habit of that."

Rachel shook hands with the woman. "Thanks for everything, Karen. I appreciate it."

"Good luck in finding her. And if you do find her, tell her to give me a call sometime. I'd like to hear from her."

"I will. Thanks again."

She got to her feet and crossed the lawn to her car. She would have liked to sit in the park a while longer, playing with Max and watching the children and chatting with Karen, but she had work to do. She might be leaving for New Mexico soon, but first she would talk to everyone in town who had been friends with Jenna or Maggie Simpson, starting with the three ladies that Karen had mentioned.

Then tonight she would call Gabriel and tell him the good news: that he had a son, a dark-haired, dark-eyed son named Todd, and that Jenna had loved him, after all. She was sure that he would consider it very good news, indeed—so good that maybe he wouldn't notice that her heart was slowly but surely breaking.

Chapter 9

I have a son."

Christopher stiffened, grew still, then slowly swiveled his desk chair to face his friend. He studied him for a long time, searching for some hint of how he felt, but Gabriel's expression was blank. "A son?"

"Named Todd." Gabriel stared out the window, seeing the bay some distance off, blue and hazy. That was how he felt—hazy. His mind hadn't been functioning quite properly since Rachel's phone call Tuesday night, which had left him suffering from a mixture of elation, disappointment and annoyance. All along he had hoped that the child was alive, that Jenna hadn't had an abortion, but he had been afraid to believe. Now he could. And all along he had hoped that Rachel would begin to trust him, begin to believe in his love, but now he was starting to doubt that it would ever happen.

Considering the importance of her news, Rachel had kept the call short, hadn't given him a chance to touch on anything the slightest bit personal, until the very end. "By the way," she had said, her voice every bit the professional, "her friend thought that Jenna was in love with you. I thought you'd like to know." Then she had told him that she would probably be going to New Mexico soon, that she would call him again, and had hung up.

He had started to call her back, but he hadn't. He had been too stunned by the news of his son to deal capably with Rachel's fears about Jenna. He had decided to wait until the next evening to confront her. Tonight. He wasn't looking forward to it.

"Has Rachel found him?" Christopher asked, bringing Gabriel's attention back to him.

He shook his head. "She found a friend of Jenna's. Later this week she's probably going to New Mexico. That's where Jenna was living when Todd was born."

"What are you going to do when she does find him?"

Gabriel turned his head to look at Christopher. "You sound like you might regret starting this."

"Not regret. I'm concerned. Come over here and sit down and look at me while we talk."

Christopher could read him like an open book, Gabriel thought with a humorless smile. Christopher wanted to judge his expressions as well as hear his words. That way he could reach a more accurate conclusion about how Gabriel felt. Since he felt the same way—it was easier to talk to Rachel's face than to the back of her head or over a long-distance telephone connection—he willingly obliged Christopher, taking a seat in front of his desk.

"So what are you going to do?"

"I don't know."

"Have you talked it over with Rachel?"

"Should I have?"

Christopher looked exasperated. "Are you going to deny that you're in love with her?"

"I never said that."

"No, and I don't remember ever having to tell you that I was in love with Shelley, either, but you knew it—practically before I did," he said with a scowl. "You sure as hell act like a man in love."

"But what difference does that make when not only does she not love me, she doesn't even want to hear that I love her?" he asked with a cynical shrug.

Leaning back in his chair, Christopher shook his head. "I don't believe that."

Gabriel's grin was only halfhearted. "Neither do I." He believed what he had told Rachel at the Salt Lake airport—that she was scared as hell because she was falling in love with him. It was a hollow victory, though, when she refused to acknowledge what he was certain she was feeling. "But *she* believes it. It's kind of complicated."

"Relationships usually are." Christopher toyed with his wedding ring, twisting it around his finger. "Have you given any thought to what you want, as far as the boy is concerned?"

"I don't know. I thought at first that it would be enough to know that he was alive, that he was all right. But I can't deny that I'd like to see him. According to Jenna's friend, he has dark hair and dark eyes." Like his father. In what other ways was Todd like him? he wondered wistfully.

"Have you talked to Rachel about it? If you're planning to take an active part in this kid's life, and if you're planning to marry her, she deserves to help make the decisions."

Gabriel shook his head, remembering their first meeting in Powell's office. Her behavior had been hostile, but particularly so when she'd asked the same question Christopher had. *Do you intend to be a part of his life? To come in, at this late date, and announce that you're his father?* Her disapproval and antagonism had been so strong that he had, consciously or subconsciously, avoided the subject again. "I can't discuss it with her."

"Does she dislike the idea of you being a father so much?"

"No, I don't think that's it at all. In fact, she didn't seem too surprised by it. As if she didn't expect any better from me." He tilted his head back and rubbed his jaw. "Why isn't it ever easy?"

Christopher smiled gently. "If it were easy, it wouldn't be worth anything. There's a lot involved in relationships—friendship, trust, faith, support, acceptance, love."

And the first time around, Gabriel had failed Rachel on all of those. He had broken their friendship, destroyed her trust and faith, denied her support and acceptance, and had refused to even acknowledge his love. Was it any wonder that she was having trouble believing in him now? "She knows about Jenna—that I asked her to marry me."

"How did she find out?"

"I told her." He scowled at Christopher's reproving glance. "She *asked* me. What was I supposed to do—lie to her? She'll never learn to trust me if I'm not honest."

"So now she knows everything."

Gabriel nodded.

"Well, at least there won't be any more unpleasant surprises. Was she upset?"

"Yeah, a little," he replied sardonically. "She tried to throw me out."

"Tried?"

"I'm bigger than she is." He looked down at his hand for a minute, stretching his fingers wide, then clenched them into a fist. "She has this crazy idea that I might still love Jenna, that I'm hanging around *her* only because I feel guilty for what happened before and want to make it up to her."

"And what happened before to make you feel guilty?"

Gabriel was silent for a long time. There had been a time—most of his life—when absolutely nothing had happened that Christopher hadn't immediately known about. That had changed with Jenna, and again with Rachel. "You were still traveling a lot, I guess."

Christopher nodded. The company he'd started right out of college had grown rapidly, with offices in his hometown, Phoenix and San Diego, and he had divided his time among the three cities before finally settling in San Diego.

Even though he knew his friend would never judge him, Gabriel didn't want to talk about this. He had been over it a hundred times in his mind, and nothing changed. It was still an ugly story. But quietly, unemotionally, he related it to Christopher—every detail, every mistake, every failing—and when he finished, he swore he would never go over it again.

Guilt could be a powerful motivator, Christopher acknowledged, especially to a man with a strong sense of honor, like Gabriel. But he didn't for one moment believe that his friend was mistaking guilt for love. Still, he could sympathize with Rachel, too. Once your trust has been betrayed, it's not easy to give it again. He had learned that through personal experience.

"So give me the benefit of your wisdom," Gabriel said with a crooked smile. "I don't want Jenna, I don't still care about her, and I've lived with both guilt and love long enough to know the difference between them. But how can I convince Rachel of that?"

Christopher raised his shoulders in a helpless shrug. "Damned if I know."

Gabriel couldn't help laughing. "Thanks a lot, buddy. You've been a great help." Glancing at his watch, he got to his feet. "You should be getting home to your wife." And *he* should be getting home to wait for a phone call.

"Shelley's meeting me here when she finishes at the paper." Christopher walked to the door with him, his hand resting lightly on the other man's shoulder. "If you need anything..."

"Thanks."

The call came at precisely eight o'clock, San Diego time. Gabriel thought he was prepared for the cool, unemotional tone that she'd been using with him lately, but when he heard it again, it stabbed through him like a knife. This was the woman who had shared his bed, the woman who had laughed and cried with him, had moaned and pleaded, the woman he loved, and she sounded as if he were just another client.

He let her finish the rundown of her day, the information she'd given him fading away forgotten. When she was done, he said softly, "I've missed you, Rachel."

She was silent for a long time. Did he know how badly she needed to see him, to feel his arms around her? Needing anything that badly couldn't be good, especially when it was likely that she would lose him soon. The next time she saw him, she would have found Jenna, and he might easily forget that Rachel even existed. He would remember his love for Jenna and recognize his guilt and be grateful that Rachel had let him go so easily. "Gabriel—"

She was going to say something he didn't want to hear—he could sense it, could feel it in the sudden, empty chill across the distance. He interrupted her, saying the one thing that she was dreading, the one thing he couldn't stop himself from saying. "I love you, Rachel."

She closed her eyes, feeling the hot tears on her cheeks. Why had he said that? And why couldn't she believe him? Just once, why couldn't she be foolish and take what she so desperately wanted, even if it was only for a few days?

"Are you leaving for New Mexico?"

She wiped her cheeks with one hand, took a deep breath and tried to sound totally normal. "Yes. Tomorrow afternoon, I imagine. So far, no one knows exactly where they moved to. There are only a few more people I need to see here, and I can probably take care of them in the morning. I'll drive to Salt Lake City and catch an evening flight from there."

"Where are you going?"

"Santa Fe. I want to get a copy of Todd's birth certificate, and I'll check the motor vehicle records for driver's licenses for Chuck and Jenna. Where I'll go next depends on what I find out there."

"Spend the weekend in Albuquerque." The idea had come swiftly, rationally, completely formed. He had plenty of vacation time, no court dates for the next few weeks, and he needed to see her.

"Why there?"

"Because that's where I'll be."

"Gabriel..." A fresh tear slid down her cheek.

"Please, Rachel."

"You're not being fair."

"I've got too much at stake here to bother with fairness." If he didn't see her, he was going to lose her. The closer she got to finding Jenna, the farther she withdrew from him, trying to protect herself, to prepare herself for the pain and loss that she was certain would come. He might not be able to convince her that she was wrong, but he could try. He could stop her from slipping even farther away, and maybe he could find a way to bring her back to him.

"Wait until I find Jenna, until you see her.…." Then he would know, and so would she. If he came to her after he'd seen Jenna again, she would know that he really did love her.

"No."

"Then you'll be able to make a rational choice—"

"Rachel, I've made my choice. You just can't accept it." There was sharp tension in his voice, and he made an effort to ease it. "Will you call me tomorrow before you leave Utah?"

"I don't know," she whispered sorrowfully.

"Please?"

She sat silent for a long time, then murmured, "All right, Gabriel." Before he could respond, she had hung up.

By the time she left Beaumont Thursday afternoon, Rachel was exhausted, physically and emotionally. She hadn't slept well the night before—hadn't slept well since Gabriel had left her alone in Salt Lake City.

She had talked to practically every person in Beaumont, and half the people in the county, too, and the myth about small towns had held true. Everyone she'd talked to had known Jenna or her parents, and everyone had had some little bit of information to add to her report.

She had heard more about Jenna and Chuck's rocky marriage and frequent separations, had gotten the name of

the university where Chuck had gone to school and learned
that he had attended on a scholarship. She'd heard an ear-
ful about the scandal when Jenna had come home for her
father's funeral with her dark-haired, dark-eyed baby, and
how no one had been fooled into believing that he was
Chuck's son, but everyone had pretended, just as Jenna and
Maggie had pretended. *She* had been luckier, Rachel
thought, sympathetic to Gabriel's son. All three of her parents were Hispanic, so no one had looked closely at her. No
one had guessed that Ernesto was not her father.

The three older women that Karen Thompson had directed Rachel to had all lost touch with Maggie after Henry's death, but they had all been certain she had moved to
New Mexico, to be close to Jenna and her grandbaby.
Chuck's parents had moved away, too, but it had been so
long ago that no one remembered where they'd gone, and
his friends had long since moved or lost track of him.

But she had plenty of solid leads. Once she got a copy of
Todd's birth certificate, it would be only a matter of days
before she found him and his mother.

She arrived at the airport with plenty of time before her
flight was scheduled to leave. She tried sitting quietly, but it
was impossible. She paced back and forth in front of the
plate glass window, watching planes taxi back and forth.
Finally, unable to resist any longer, she walked to the nearby
pay phones, dropped some coins in one and dialed a number.

Gabriel practically pounced on the phone when one of the
men called his name. "This is Rodriguez."

Leaning against the wall for support, Rachel tried to
mimic his greeting, but it sounded flat. "This is Martinez."

He was unashamedly relieved to hear her voice. "I didn't
think you would call."

"I said I would."

"I'll be at the . . ." He searched his desk for the note pad
he had scribbled the information on and gave her the name
of a small hotel not far from his mother's house. "Will you
meet me?"

"I don't think it's a good idea."

"You don't have to stay with me, Rachel. Just meet with me. Talk to me for a while. Let me see that you're all right."

She wanted to cry that she wasn't all right, that she was falling to pieces and it was all his fault. She had known from the beginning that she couldn't get involved with him and come out of it whole, but she had wanted... "I don't know, Gabriel. I'm sorry." She hung up and walked away quickly, not knowing or caring where she was going. When she reached the end of the concourse, she turned and more slowly returned to the gate assigned to her flight.

If she spent this weekend with him, she would fall even more in love, knowing that it was hopeless, that it would soon end. It could take her forever to recover.

Or she could have one last time with him, two days and two nights to remember, to treasure, to last the rest of her life. She could pretend that her heart wasn't breaking, could have a good time and make sure that Gabriel did, too. It was one last gift she could give, to both him and herself.

What was she going to do?

When Gabriel left the plane in Albuquerque and found that Rachel wasn't waiting, he wasn't surprised, just disappointed. He claimed his luggage and took a cab to the hotel, checked in and went to his room to wait.

Sometimes he felt as if he'd waited most of his life for Rachel. All those years of seeing one woman after another—he hadn't been simply trying to forget Jenna. He had been looking for the *right* woman, the one who could fill the emptiness in his life, and he had found her in Rachel. When he had first asked her out, he had never imagined that she would be any different from the countless others. He had known her for years, since her first week in the department, and had never had the slightest hint that he would love her.

But he *had* loved her and, through those long years without her, had never stopped loving her. How long would it take to convince her of that? How long would he have to wait?

He watched the sunset from his window and continued to look out. The lights came on slowly, twinkling and shimmering in the desert heat. Darkness settled completely over the valley, and still he waited.

The knock came shortly after ten o'clock. Gabriel crossed the room with impatiently long strides and jerked the door open. When he saw Rachel standing there, he closed his eyes and said a brief prayer of thanks, then stepped back so she could enter.

"I—I'm sorry," she began in a shaky, husky voice, but he ended her apology with a kiss. He held her face in his palms, and his mouth gently covered hers, taking her voice, giving her his warmth, his hunger and love. When he released her, he closed the door, then led her further into the room.

"I'm glad you came."

Slowly she shook her head. "I tried not to." Lord, she had tried—for her own protection, her own security—but she'd had no choice. She loved Gabriel, wanted him, needed him. If it meant hurting more later, all right. But for now she would take what she needed.

"I know." He could see it in her face. There were lines bracketing her mouth, shadows beneath her eyes, and her eyes themselves were bleak, reddened, heavy. She was hurting, and there was nothing he could do to help her except love her . . . and speed up the search for Jenna, so he could prove to her, once and for all, that he didn't love the other woman. Those were the reasons why he was here. "You look tired."

Somewhere inside she found the strength to smile. "You're supposed to tell me that I look beautiful."

He smiled, too, brushing a strand of hair from her cheek. "You do look beautiful, but you look tired, too. Have you been having the dreams again?"

"You can't have nightmares if you don't sleep." She looked around the room, noticed his two suitcases, removed her jacket, then sat down in the single chair. "Do you want to hear what I found today?"

He knew that she had found his son's birth certificate, knew, too, that seeing it could wait a while longer. He took a seat at the foot of the bed, leaning his arms on his thighs, his hands clasped loosely. "I'd rather hear why you're not sleeping."

She gave him a slight smile that was achingly sad. "I guess I've been missing you."

"I'm here now."

"But not for long."

He wondered if she was talking about reality—that the weekend would soon be over—or her fears—that he would leave her for Jenna. He had deliberately let her believe that this visit was just for the weekend, aware that she would accept two days with him far easier than she would accept two weeks. He shook his head. "I don't know what to do with you," he murmured.

This time her smile was real, bright and amused, and it warmed his soul. "You knew exactly what to do with me last weekend," she reminded him. "Have you forgotten so soon?"

"We always seem to make love first and talk later," he said wryly.

"There are some things you just can't say with words."

Again he shook his head. "Oh, I know the words to say everything I want to say. I just don't know the ones to make you believe me."

She reached out to clasp her hands around his. "Is it so important that I believe?"

"Is the rest of my life important?" he countered.

"Don't think about the rest of your life this weekend." She wasn't going to. She was going to concentrate on these two days and nights, and this man. "Just think about me."

"They're one and the same thing. You *are* the rest of my life."

"You want me now, but in a couple of weeks..." She shook her head. Not after they found Jenna.

Gabriel pulled his hands free and leaned back on the bed. "You think that I would tell you I love you, and in a couple of weeks leave you for another woman?" He didn't even have the energy to be angry with her. He had expended it all in fear and worry. "You really don't think much of me, do you?"

She recognized the insult too late to call it back, and she couldn't find the words to make him understand that she knew, better than he did, what he was feeling. "Gabriel—"

He raised one hand to stop her. "No. We'll do it your way. No more declarations of love, no more talk about the future. Just sex, and friendship."

"Gabriel—"

Again he interrupted. "That's what you want, isn't it? You don't want to give me anything—not your trust, your love, your forgiveness, your respect. Nothing but your body. All right. I'll agree to that." He reached for her, pulling her onto the bed beside him.

Angrily she pushed his hands away from the buttons on her blouse. "I respect you more than any other man I've ever known!"

"No you don't." He tugged her blouse free, located the side zipper on her skirt and pulled it down. "You don't respect what I say—hell, you don't even listen to it! It doesn't fit into your neat little slots, so you tell yourself that I don't know what I'm talking about, that I don't mean it, that I'm pretending, that *you* know how I really feel." He succeeded in maneuvering around her hands and undoing the buttons on her blouse. "If you don't want me to love you, Rachel, okay, but have the guts to say so. Don't hide behind Jenna, or the past, or the future. Tell me, right now, that you don't want my love."

She stared into his dark eyes for a long moment, then shook her head. She couldn't tell him something that was so obviously a lie. More than anything in life, she wanted him to love her the way she loved him. "I do want it," she whispered, touching her fingers to his jaw. "Show me, Gabriel. Love me . . ."

He kissed her briefly, hungrily, then drew back to look at her again. "Believe me," he demanded hoarsely.

"I'm scared."

He raised his hand, and she saw that it was trembling. "So am I. I'm afraid of losing you, Rachel. I'm afraid that even if you stay with me, you'll never trust me, never believe me. You'll never really be mine. I'll spend the rest of my life trying to convince you, and I'll fail."

"I don't want to get hurt again." Her whisper was half plea, half heartache.

Gabriel touched her gently, carefully. "You're already hurting, honey. You're dreading the end, and it hasn't come yet. You're dreading being alone again, yet you're pushing me away with both hands. Please..."

Why shouldn't she believe him? part of her silently pleaded. She was so arrogantly certain that she knew his heart better than he did, that his love for her was just a poor substitute to fill the emptiness losing Jenna had created, but what right did she have to make that judgment? If Gabriel or anyone else presumed to judge *her*, to tell her that she couldn't possibly know how she really felt, she would be incredibly angry. Yet that was exactly what she'd done to him. Did she have so little faith in him? In herself?

She loved him, didn't she? What kind of love could she offer without faith, without trust, without believing?

She caught his hand and pressed a kiss into his palm. "I'm sorry I've hurt you," she murmured.

Was she giving in, or backing away? He studied her face, looking for clues. The bleakness was fading from her eyes, but she still looked as if she would cry at any moment. "Is that 'I'm sorry I've hurt you, but I believe you,' or 'I'm sorry I've hurt you, but you're not worth my time'?"

She sighed softly. "When you first came to the agency to hire me, I decided that the only way I could possibly work with you was to keep it strictly—"

"Business," he finished with a wry smile.

She nodded. "There had been so much pain. Simply seeing you in Powell's office brought it all back so clearly, and every time I thought of you, I remembered all the bad times. You don't know how many times I was tempted to pack it in and run away, but I was strong. I thought I could handle a business relationship with you. But you wanted more." She was silent for a few moments, not certain why she was telling him these things, just aware that they had to be said. "And the frightening thing was that *I* did, too. I convinced myself that I could have an affair with you, one that would end when the case ended, or when you got bored, or when you found someone else. I didn't dare hope for anything more."

When she stopped, he quietly asked, "You still don't, do you? You're afraid to hope for love, for permanence, for a family, a future."

"I thought I was so damn strong, but I'm not, Gabriel," she whispered, turning her face against his chest. "I'm weak and cowardly."

"No, you're not," he disagreed, stroking her hair. "There's nothing strong about living alone, needing no one, counting on no one, and there's nothing weak about needing someone. If there is, then I'm incredibly weak, Rachel, because I need you—tonight, tomorrow and every day after. Forever."

Forever. That sounded like heaven. She'd had a taste of heaven before. It had kept her going through her time in hell. "Gabriel?" She tilted her head back, meeting his eyes. "Make love with me . . . please?"

He hesitated a moment, then shook his head. "You're tired, honey. You've had a long, hard week." Then he clenched his teeth as she slid her hand intimately between his thighs.

"Speaking of long and hard . . ." Her smile was anything but tired. "It's been five days since we made love. And five nights. I thought I would have to face the rest of my life without that."

Closing his eyes, he let his body go limp while he savored her gentle caresses. "Be honest," he commanded in a rough, husky voice. "It's just my gorgeous body you want, isn't it?"

With a slight nudge, she pushed him onto his back, then rolled onto her side, leaning over him. "All of you," she whispered, her breath warm against his jaw. "I want all of you."

She tugged his T-shirt up, getting it as far as his shoulders, then abandoned it for him to dispose of while she explored his chest with her hands and mouth. Her tongue flicked across his flat, brown nipple, making it rise in eager anticipation. "You *are* gorgeous," she murmured. "It's not right, you know—that a man should be so beautiful."

He slid his hands into her hair, dislodging the pins that held it in a chignon at her nape. Fanning his fingers wide, he combed through her hair, at the same time pulling her head closer to his chest. Laughing softly, she took the hint and kissed his nipple again while her hands continued to stroke him.

Freeing herself from his loose hold, she knelt beside him, unfastening his jeans. Each button slid free with a tug, exposing a pair of low-riding briefs of deep burgundy. She slid her hand inside the waistband of his jeans, fingering the soft cotton, then moved away from him.

Gabriel started to pull her back, but she shook her head. Standing next to the bed, she removed her clothes, neatly folding each piece and laying it on the chair. When she was naked, she came back to the bed, unlaced the heavy leather running shoes he wore, dropped each shoe to the floor, peeled off his thick white socks and dropped them on the floor, too, then, with his help, tugged his jeans off. Surveying what she had accomplished, she smiled. "Umm, nice."

He reached for her, but she playfully slapped his hand back. "Don't be in such a rush," she admonished. "We have all night."

"Al*ways*," he corrected. That was what forever meant, wasn't it?

She stroked and kissed him, taunted and teased him, until his need was as great as her own. When his muscles quivered, when his flesh ached in response to the slightest touch, she slid the briefs over his long, lean legs and moved over him, taking him deep into herself.

He felt her heat enclose him, and a shudder rippled through him. "You are beautiful," he whispered, raising his hand to touch one fingertip to her breast.

She moved against him cautiously, feeling the curling sensations building in her belly. "I bet you say that to all your women," she teased in a breathlessly needy voice.

"To my *only* woman." He arched into her, making her gasp. "See how well we fit together? How perfectly I fill you? There couldn't be anyone else, Rachel. Not for me, not for you. You're mine, and I'm yours, and nothing—" He groaned as she moved again, taking him deeper. "—nothing will change that."

She leaned down to kiss him, her breasts brushing sensuously over his chest. "Nothing," she agreed. Whether they were together always or not, nothing could change the fact that she would always be his.

He moved into her again, then stiffened and, with a low groan, filled her. A moment later her own release, sharp, vital, draining, followed. "I love you, Rachel," he murmured, pulling her down beside him. "I'll always love you."

Gabriel roused himself to turn out the lights, and the darkness in the room was almost complete. Not a hint of light could penetrate the heavy drapes at the window. Rachel had once feared the darkness, because that was when the nightmares had come, but tonight it was a safe, secure cocoon of warmth. She lay on her back, her eyes open, while Gabriel drew random patterns over her bare skin. When he reached her belly, he laid his hand flat, his fingers spread wide. "If we keep this up, one of these days I'm going to get pregnant," she remarked with forced nonchalance.

Gabriel was still for a long time. Although they had never discussed it, he had assumed that she was using some sort of contraceptive. That was one of the reasons he had never made any effort to protect her himself. The other, he admitted with a slow grin, was simple: if she *wasn't* using birth control, he wanted to see her grow big with his baby. "I'd like that. Would you?"

"I'm thirty-three years old. It would be nice to have a few babies before I'm too old."

"It would be nicer if we were married first." He was very still, gauging her breathing, the level of tension in her muscles, trying to judge whether the idea caused an unfavorable reaction.

But there was no increased tension, no change in her steady breathing. "Yes," she agreed softly, unable to stop her smile. "It would be."

The breath he'd been holding escaped in a whoosh of relief, and he returned to moving his fingers lightly over her stomach and breasts, around but not touching her nipples. He was grateful for the darkness, because it hid the idiotic grin of elation that he wore. "I'm glad you came here tonight, Rachel." He bent to kiss her forehead. "I love you."

I love you, too. But her whisper was soundless, just a breath against his skin. She was ready to believe him, ready to trust him, but some small part of her held back from that final step. Just in case she was wrong, just in case *he* was wrong...

It was for his protection as well as her own, she rationalized. What if he realized, once he saw Jenna, that he *did* still love her? He was an honorable man—after going to such lengths to win Rachel's trust, if he knew that she loved him, he would feel obligated to stay with her.

Soon, she promised herself. She would find Jenna so Gabriel could see her. Soon she would know how he felt. And soon she would tell him how *she* felt.

Rachel awakened the next morning to the delightful feel of Gabriel's hands touching her gently—her breasts, her belly, her hips, between her thighs. She stretched, eyes still closed, then snuggled back against him, spoon-fashion, to let him continue. "Now," she commanded sleepily, trying to turn to face him, but his arms held her tight.

"Now," he agreed in her ear. "Like this." He shifted her position to make his entry easier, gliding deep into her, then began stroking her again. Turning her face toward him, he kissed her and murmured to her in a soft, erotic, arousing voice that made her shiver.

It was different—slow, gentle, with no wild passion, no frantic need, no uncontrollable rush to completion. There was an easy, lazy pleasure that started deep inside and spread gradually outward until its warmth touched every part of her. Instead of sharp cries, there were soft moans; instead of a shattering explosion, there was a gentle peak, a tiny rush of sensation that rippled through her, then faded.

Gabriel nipped her shoulder, then kissed the slight redness left by his teeth. "Are you awake now?" When she didn't answer, he touched her sensitive flesh beneath the damp curls, and she stiffened. His chuckle tickled in her ear. "Yes, you're awake. We've got to get up, honey. We've got places to go."

She shifted and felt the satisfying fullness as his manhood responded. "Go where?"

"I want to show you Albuquerque."

"I saw Albuquerque yesterday. I drove around for four hours trying to decide whether or not to meet you. Show me something else. Something that doesn't require getting out of bed."

"And I want you to meet my mother."

As he'd known it would, that statement brought a prompt reaction. She carefully moved away from him, rolled over and looked blankly at him. "Your mother?"

"Yes. She lives here, remember? I have to go see her, and I want you to go with me. She'll be hurt if she doesn't get to meet you."

She combed her fingers through her hair. "That's not fair. I've never asked *you* to meet *my* mother," she said reproachfully.

"I'd like to meet your mother, and your father and your brothers and your sister." He rolled onto his back and propped his arms beneath his head. "It might be nice if I meet them before the wedding, don't you think?"

Scowling at him, Rachel responded darkly, "I never agreed to marry you."

"That's all right, honey," he said with a grin. "I never asked you. Mere technicalities. We'll take care of them when the time is right."

She stared at him for a moment, then laughed. "I would like to meet your mother, Gabriel. I'd like to meet the woman who could produce a child like you."

Eyes narrowed, he studied her. "When I figure out if that's an insult, I'll let you know. Do you want the bathroom first?"

Gabriel's mother was working in the yard, cutting dead buds from the flowers that lined the sidewalk, when they arrived. She was a lovely woman, Rachel thought. Her short black hair was streaked with iron gray, her dark eyes bright and lively. Nearing sixty, she was tall and slim, like her son, and radiated the same joy that Rachel admired so much in Gabriel.

She greeted Gabriel with a hug and kisses, scolding him at the same time that she welcomed him. "Why didn't you let me know that you were coming? It's been so long. Where are you staying? How long will you be here? Why didn't you call me?"

Ignoring her questions, Gabriel kept one arm around her shoulders and extended his other hand to Rachel. His mother hadn't noticed her before, but now she gave her a quick, intense study as she took Gabriel's hand and joined them.

"Mom, this is Rachel Martinez. This is my mother, Louise . . . what is it now?" he teased.

"It's still Warren," she replied with a haughty air. "It has been for fourteen years and will be for many more," she added for Rachel's benefit. "Just because I married recklessly a few times in my youth . . ."

"A few times?" Gabriel interrupted. "Christopher and I used to speculate that you were trying to outdo Liz Taylor."

After jabbing her elbow in his ribs, Louise left his embrace to get a better look at Rachel. "She's a pretty one."

Gabriel agreed. Rachel blushed.

"Rachel Martinez." Louise nodded approvingly. "Do you know that you're the first girl my son has brought home to meet me since he was in the eighth grade?"

"You can remember that long ago?" Rachel asked, feigning awe.

Louise burst into laughter, causing Gabriel to give both of them a wounded look. "I'm not that old," he protested.

"Old enough to have an eighth-grader of your own," his mother retorted. She ushered them into the small house, not noticing the faint tension that passed through Gabriel's eyes. Rachel saw it, though, and hugged him tighter.

David Warren was the opposite of his wife—quieter, shorter, heavier, with blond hair and blue eyes. He said hello to Gabriel, greeted Rachel politely, then returned to the ball game on television when Louise led them into the kitchen.

"Of course you'll stay for lunch," she said, washing her hands in the sink. "Gabriel, I'll need you to run to the store and pick up a few things for me."

"Why don't you let us take you out?" he suggested.

"Nonsense. It won't take any time at all." She dried her hands, wrote out a quick list, then went to get her purse.

"Mom, I don't need any money," he protested, but she left the room anyway. Shaking his head, he turned back to Rachel. "Be prepared."

"For what?"

"The reason she doesn't want to go out to lunch is because that wouldn't give her any time alone with you. That's also why she's sending me to the store. She wants to talk to you."

Rachel looked faintly alarmed. "About what?"

He gave her a teasing leer. "She probably wants to know if your intentions toward me are honorable. I *am* her only son, and her only chance for grandchildren."

She put her arms around his neck and rose onto her toes to brush her lips over his. "I intend to honor every dishonorable intention I have toward you," she murmured before kissing him seriously.

Louise politely coughed before she reentered the room, giving Rachel time to step away. She pressed some money into her son's hand, along with the list, and shooed him out of the house. "Have a seat, Rachel. Would you like something to drink?"

"No thanks. Can I help you?"

"No, you sit down and relax."

Rachel went to the table pushed against the far wall, took a seat and waited for the questioning to begin.

Louise brought a cutting board, a knife and a bowl of vegetables to the table and sat across from Rachel. "So... how long have you known my son?"

"Nine years."

"That long? And it's taken him until now to bring you home to meet his mother?"

Rachel smiled at her surprise. "We *met* nine years ago. We hadn't seen each other for the last five years until just recently."

"Oh, well... Are you serious about him?"

She could trust this woman, Rachel thought. She reminded her a great deal of her own mother—warm, friendly and maybe a little bit nosy at times, but she had her son's best interests at heart. "Yes," she said softly. "I am."

Louise beamed with pleasure. "That's wonderful. Has he asked you to marry him?"

"Aren't you forgetting something?" At the older woman's frown, Rachel prompted her. "Is he serious about me?"

"Well, of course he is. He wouldn't have brought you here if he wasn't. So... has he?"

Rachel remembered this morning's conversation. *Mere technicalities. We'll take care of them when the time is right.* "No, he hasn't."

"Well, he will. Don't worry about it." She finished slicing the onions, set them aside and reached for the green peppers. "Tell me about yourself. Where are your people from? Where do you live? Do you like children? What do you do?"

By the time Gabriel returned forty-five minutes later, Rachel knew exactly how the people she interviewed in her cases felt. "Your mother would make a good PI," she murmured when he sat down beside her. "She can come up with more questions off the top of her head than most people can when they sit and think about it for a few hours."

"She's had a long time to prepare," he replied with a grin. "I bet your mother asked at least as many questions of the girls your brothers married."

"I'm fixing *fajitas*," Louise said, preparing a marinade of fresh-squeezed lime juice and spices. "How do you fix them, Rachel?"

Her expression was blank. "I buy them at a little Mexican place in town," she replied.

"Rachel doesn't cook," Gabriel added.

Louise turned to stare at her, her hands stilled in midair. "You can't cook?" The idea obviously shocked her. That a woman could reach adulthood without learning to cook was beyond her comprehension.

"I didn't say 'can't,' Mom. I said she *doesn't*," Gabriel explained.

"I know how. I just don't like to bother with it, since I live alone."

The woman turned back to her work while she thought that over. She had learned to cook as a child, Rachel guessed, and had done it practically every day since then.

Gabriel stood up and tugged at Rachel's hand. "Come in here with me. We'll be right back, Mom." He led her down the hallway to the room at the end. "This was my room."

Leaving him in the doorway, she walked to the shelves that lined the wall. There were books, pictures of friends and athletic teams, trophies for football and track, mementos of a long-ago life. She picked up a framed photo of him in a UNM track uniform. He was younger, and his hair was longer, but he was still lean, still brash and confident. "You were handsome."

"I still am."

With a smile she returned the picture to the shelf. "Did you go to college on a track scholarship?"

"Yeah. I was fast."

She glanced at him over her shoulder. He was leaning against the doorjamb, wearing a striped T-shirt, white shorts that left his long, powerful legs bare, and running shoes, and again she smiled. "You still are." In the next picture she reached for, he was a few years older, and his hair was much shorter. He wore a Navy uniform with shiny gold buttons, a high, tight collar and white shoulder boards with two wide gold stripes. "Why did you join the Navy when we were still in Vietnam?"

He came to stand behind her, laying his hands on her shoulders. "'I joined the Navy to see the world,'" he recited.

"'And what did I see? I saw the sea.'" She leaned back against him. "Why did you join, really?"

"I look good in white." He tapped his finger on the dusty frame. "*This* is the best-looking uniform in all four branches of the military combined. It's called full-dress whites, although those of us who wore it preferred to call it by a more appropriate name: choker whites. That collar was a killer." He grew serious then, resting his chin lightly on the top of her head. "I joined the Navy because it was what I wanted to do. It seemed...right. I didn't want to go to Vietnam, but I had a..."

Duty. He had been prompted by old-fashioned and, at that time, out-of-style patriotism. Smiling, Rachel returned the frame to the shelf, then turned in his arms. "You're an honorable man."

"No, I'm not," he denied, his eyes dark and grim. The things he had done to her couldn't be mentioned in the same sentence with honor. "I just do the best I can."

Pushing the memories back where they belonged, he pulled her to the window, into the wedge of space between the bed and the wall. "See that light blue house across the street? That's where Christopher grew up. We've been best friends since we started school. He's a year younger than me, so we were in different grades, but it never mattered much."

"Do his parents still live there?"

"No, they're dead. He's alone except for Shelley."

"And the baby."

Gabriel pulled her more snugly against him. "And the baby," he agreed softly.

Louise called them to lunch then. David left the television long enough to eat, chatting casually with Gabriel. David treated him as if he were an acquaintance rather than a stepson, Rachel thought curiously, then realized that that was exactly what they were—acquaintances. Gabriel had been twenty-four and living in San Diego when Louise and David got married. He had never lived with them, and had never even seen them often.

There was a big difference from the way Ernesto treated *her*. No one would guess that she wasn't his daughter. He gave her the same love and affection that the younger kids received. If she had felt that she didn't belong, that she wasn't a part of the family, it was her own fault, and her natural father's, rather than Ernesto's.

And she *had* felt that way. She had looked at her brothers and sister and known that they were the real children, the real family. She was Rita's daughter, but Teodoro, Alberto and Estrella belonged to both Rita and Ernesto. Once she had learned about her father, she had lost that sense of family and had never completely belonged again.

Was that how Todd White would feel?

Chapter 10

When they left Gabriel's parents, he offered Rachel a tram ride to the top of Sandia Peak, a tour of Old Town or a visit to the Indian Pueblo Cultural Center. She chose to return to the hotel, to discuss business. She saw the tensing of the muscles in his jaw and laid her hand on his bare thigh. "It won't take long, I promise."

He knew that. He was just afraid it would ruin the rest of the day. Either Rachel would get scared by talk of Jenna, or he would get depressed, because he knew what she had to show him: a birth certificate for *his* son with another man's name on it. But he made the short drive back to the hotel and grudgingly followed her to their room.

Rachel took the copy of the birth certificate from her briefcase while he opened the drapes. He sat down at the table in the only chair and she laid the piece of paper in front of him, then moved to stand behind him. She rubbed his shoulders, kneading the taut muscles there, muscles that tightened even more when he reached the block of information designated for the father.

How it must hurt to see another man listed as his son's father. She ached inside for him, but didn't say a word, just continued rubbing away the stiffness.

After several long moments he pushed the paper away. "Rachel."

"What?"

He reached for her hands, lifting them from his shoulders, and pulled her around so he could see her. "What do you think are the chances that he's not my son?"

She shook her head slowly. "She left her husband, had an affair with you, went back to him pregnant, and gave birth to a son who, by all accounts, looks nothing like either of them but just like you. I think the chances are so slim as to be nonexistent."

That was what he thought, too. "What else did you find?"

"Driver's licenses for both Jenna and Chuck, but they expired about four years ago, so they've apparently moved again."

He glanced again at the birth certificate, at the Albuquerque address listed as their then-current residence. "That's on the northeast side of town. Is that the same address as on the licenses?"

She nodded.

"So Monday we'll talk to the neighbors...." His voice trailed off when she began shaking her head. "What?"

"Sunday you go back to San Diego. Monday *I* talk to the neighbors."

His smile was halfhearted. "Uh, Rachel, there's something I've been meaning to tell you. About this weekend..."

Her gaze was steady, waiting.

"I'm staying for two weeks," he said in a rush.

She continued to look at him for a long time, then slowly went to the bed and sat down, facing him. Her only response was to shake her head again.

"See, I had a lot of vacation time saved up, and I really needed a break, and you're the only person I wanted to spend the time with, so...I thought I would come here...and stay with you...." He gave up.

"No, Gabriel."

Leaving the chair, he sat on the bed in front of her. "Why not? We need some time together—you can't deny that."

"No."

"I can help you."

"I don't need help."

"You know how you hate traveling. The sooner you find Jenna, the sooner you can go home. Back to your own house and your own bed and your own routine."

She didn't ask how he'd found out that she disliked traveling—probably Elaine, she thought with a scowl. "You can't stay, Gabriel."

"Why not?"

"Because I'm working this case, not you."

He noticed the stubborn set of her jaw, the obstinate gleam in her eyes. She wasn't going to give in easily on this. If she didn't come around by Monday morning, he might have to take drastic measures—like calling Russell Powell. No matter what it took, he wasn't leaving her. "We'll discuss it later."

She folded her arms over her chest. "There's nothing to discuss."

"Come on, Rachel, don't be mean." He leaned forward to kiss her, brushing his mouth across her unresponsive lips. "Let's go sight-seeing."

"No."

"You're in a beautiful city in a beautiful state. Surely you're not going to sit here in the room and sulk for the rest of the weekend." He grinned charmingly. "What would you like to see? Old Town? Mountains? Petroglyphs? Dinosaurs?"

She relented slowly. "Dinosaurs?"

"Sure—at the museum."

"Oh." She sniffed. "Bones."

He gave her a wry look. "Yes, bones, and models. They had to get rid of the real ones. They scared away the visitors."

"What's Old Town?" She raised her hand when he started to answer. "I know, it's a section of town that's old. What's there?"

"Restaurants, gift shops, galleries. You could find something to hang on those depressingly bare walls at home."

"Okay, let's go there." She let him pull her off the bed, then held up a warning finger. "Just because I've decided to enjoy the rest of the weekend, don't think that means I'm going to let you stay."

He smiled as he escorted her out the door. "We'll see," he murmured softly. When she looked sharply at him, he was as innocent as an angel. "I didn't say a thing."

Sunday afternoon they visited the Indian Pueblo Cultural Center, eating in the restaurant, touring the museum, browsing in the gift shop and watching the ceremonial dances. "You have a wonderful heritage," Rachel murmured as they left.

Gabriel shrugged. "I suppose so. I don't really know."

"What do you mean, you don't know? The history, the dances—"

"Are as different to me as they are to you. Rachel, my father moved to the city when he was seventeen. My mother came when she was eighteen, and as far as I know, she's never been back. I have relatives in Taos Pueblo, but I've never been there. I've never seen the dances, I don't know the history or the culture or the traditions, I've never heard the language. I was raised in a predominantly white city, in a white neighborhood, with white friends and white stepfathers. By birth I'm Indian, but my background is no different from the white kids I grew up with."

He unlocked the car door and opened it for her, then walked around to the driver's side. "It was different for you, I bet. You grew up in East L.A. You learned to speak

Spanish when you were a baby, and you were surrounded by other Hispanic families who had strong ties to Mexico. You visited relatives there when you were younger, and you celebrated all the Mexican holidays, didn't you?"

"Yes," she acknowledged.

"Well, I didn't do any of those things. The extent of what I know about the Pueblo people is what we just learned in that museum."

After a few minutes Rachel broke the silence that had fallen. "You need to make your reservations to go home."

Gabriel didn't look at her. "I'm not going home."

"You're not staying with me."

"I am."

"I won't let you."

He gave her a sidelong glance. "How are you going to stop me, sweetheart? I'm seven inches taller than you, and a good deal heavier. Besides that, I'm on a first-name basis with your boss."

"Are you threatening me?" Disbelief echoed in her voice, and she turned as far as the seat belt would allow so she could see him.

He grinned boyishly. "Well . . . I guess I am."

"You would really call Russell Powell."

"Yeah."

"And tell him what?"

Pulling into the hotel parking lot, he shut off the engine, then turned, as she had done, to face her. "That I'm madly in love with you and need to spend every possible minute with you."

She resisted the urge to laugh. "You wouldn't tell him that. He would think you were nuts."

"You're right. He doesn't strike me as the sort of person who believes in love. I could tell him that I'm consumed with lust for you. He would damn sure believe that."

She touched his hand, and he wrapped his fingers tightly around hers. "Tell me one thing, Gabriel. Do you trust me?"

His good humor faded, and he became totally serious. "With my life."

"You don't think that I might help Jenna and Todd stay hidden from you?" It was an ugly thought, one that had occurred to her earlier, one she hadn't been able to get out of her mind. It also held a certain temptation. If she never "found" Jenna, even though she knew where the other woman was living, Gabriel would never have to choose between them.

He raised her hand to his lips, kissing the palm, then the back. "I honestly believe," he said slowly, "that, at this point, finding Jenna is more important to you than it is to me. No, I don't think you'd help them hide."

"I would still be in charge."

"Absolutely."

"You would do whatever I told you."

He raised his hand in a mock salute. "Anything you say."

She was studying him skeptically, not quite certain whether to trust him. She didn't expect him to interfere with her investigation, but there was no denying that he could create problems. After all, she found it difficult to concentrate on business when he was around. Sight-seeing, talking, making love with him, were all more interesting than work. It was especially difficult to concentrate on Jenna when Gabriel was with her—difficult and still somewhat painful. She would probably get the job done faster without his dubious "help."

"Well?"

She nodded grudgingly. "You can stay." She just hoped that she wasn't making a mistake.

There *was* one advantage to having Gabriel's help, Rachel discovered Monday. Although he hadn't lived in Albuquerque for many years and it had grown a great deal in that time, he was able to find his way around the city with little trouble. She had no need for the map she'd bought Friday afternoon.

On Monday morning they drove to the most recent address they had for the Whites, in a neat, middle-class neighborhood in northeast Albuquerque. After knocking on a half-dozen doors and getting no answers, Gabriel gave an impatient curse. "Have you ever noticed that you and I work days, when most of the people we need to talk to are also at work?"

Rachel smiled calmly. "That's why you and I also work a lot of evenings. There's a car in the driveway over there. Let's try it. If there's no one home, we'll leave and come back this evening."

There was no answer to their knock. "Now what?" Gabriel asked as they walked back to the rental car.

"Let's check the county records."

"For what?"

"We can check the property tax and divorce records. We also need to see if they were registered to vote, or if either of them was licensed to do business of some sort in the county, and go by the library to see if they were listed in the city directory. And, as long as you're here, it would help if you'd take your badge and your charm to the local P.D. and see if either of them was ever arrested."

He nodded agreeably.

"You might also see if you can get a little assistance in getting their credit history." That information, giving employment background as well as debts, would be helpful, but Rachel would have trouble getting it on her own. She could do it, just not as quickly or as easily—or as legally—as a local cop could.

"Everything we need is downtown. Why don't I show you where to go, then I'll go to the Department and get started there?"

On the drive downtown, Rachel pulled a small notebook from her purse and began making a list of everything she wanted to check. Just as she finished, Gabriel was pulling into a parking garage. A few minutes later he slipped his arm easily around her shoulders as they stepped into the sunlight.

"Okay, that's City Hall there," he said, gesturing to a building across the street. "And across from it are the police station and Municipal Court Building. The county offices are down there—" he pointed to the left "—nd the library is a couple of blocks beyond, on Copper between 5th and 6th."

"I'll start with the county records," she decided, "then go to the library and finish up at City Hall. When and where do you want to meet?"

"Give me . . . two hours. I can't walk in, flash the badge and ask for information without talking a while first," he said with a grin. "Why don't you meet me in front of the county building at twelve-thirty, and I'll help with whatever you've got left."

"Okay." Rachel started to walk away, but he caught her hand and pulled her back for a kiss.

"I'll see you soon."

"All right," she murmured. She was smiling idiotically as she headed toward the Bernalillo County Office Building. Her first stop in the Court Clerk's office was Divorce Records. Since she knew that Jenna and Chuck had still been married when Henry had died ten years ago, she started with the nine-year-old records and worked her way forward. When she reached the current year without finding anything, she breathed a sigh of relief. It would please her immensely to discover that Jenna was still happily-ever-after married to Chuck White.

The tax assessor's office was her next stop. She dutifully copied the tax information on the property they had visited that morning. She got a lot of information on the house, but none that would help her learn where the Whites were living now.

She glanced at her watch and decided she had just enough time to check the voter registration records before meeting Gabriel. Half an hour later she went outside, found a shady place to lean against the building and waited.

"Sorry I'm late," he said when he joined her.

"You're not as late as I expected," she said dryly. "I know how you cops talk. How about lunch?"

They stopped at the first restaurant they came to and went inside. As soon as they had placed their orders, Gabriel asked, "What did you find out?"

"There's no record of a divorce. I got the tax information on the house, and I have Jenna's former employer and—" she pulled a slip of paper from her purse and handed it to him "—her social security number. Chuck didn't seem to be a responsible citizen. He wasn't registered. You can run that and see what turns up."

"If we're lucky and she's worked since they left New Mexico, we can get an address and her employer's name," he said, glancing at the nine-digit number, then sliding it into his pocket.

"How did you do?"

"No arrests, no field interview cards. But I did get the credit history. I didn't want to carry it around, so I left it in the car. They never borrowed much, but they did have one outstanding loan when they moved away—a car loan financed through a local bank. The forwarding address that the credit bureau got from the bank is in Colorado."

Rachel sat back to allow the waiter to serve their lunch. In Utah, she had estimated another month at the most before the case was finished. Now she revised that guess. She would be very surprised if they hadn't located Jenna and Todd within the next few days. "Why don't you have your buddy at the Department run a DMV check in Colorado? There's no sense in following up the leads here if we can get a current address on them that easily."

He was silent for a long time, then nodded. He'd heard the somber tone in her voice and understood its cause. She was ambivalent about finishing this case. As much as she wanted to get back home, to resume her routine, she was also dreading the end. She didn't want to see Jenna, didn't want to be there when *he* saw her. In spite of her best efforts, she was still insecure, still in fear of losing him, of being hurt.

Rachel reached for his hand, clasping it firmly in her own. "Thanks. You've been a lot of help."

He shook his head. "I didn't do anything that you couldn't have done yourself. There isn't a cop in that Department who wouldn't have done the same things for you. All you would have had to do was introduce yourself as a former officer, chat a bit while they checked you out, then ask for the moon, and they'd have given it to you."

She smiled ruefully. She wasn't comfortable with the idea of taking advantage of the unique camaraderie shared by current and former officers alike. "I couldn't have asked. I would have ended up bribing a clerk at the credit bureau, and that would have cost you a pretty penny."

"Fifteen or twenty thousand of them, more likely."

They finished their meal and walked the few blocks back to the police station. This time Rachel went inside with Gabriel, following him to the offices that housed the Homicide Division. It was the first time she'd been in a police station since the day she had resigned from the Department. She was surprised to find a comfortable, familiar feel to the surroundings.

Gabriel found the detective who had gotten the other information for him.

"Need something else?" the man asked after his greeting.

"Can you run a DMV check for driver's licenses in Colorado for me?"

"Same names as before?"

Gabriel nodded; then Rachel spoke. "Could you also check Maggie Simpson?"

The detective looked at her with interest. "Another San Diego cop?"

"Used to be," Gabriel replied. "Rachel Martinez, this is Pete Myers."

She nodded politely.

It was only a matter of minutes before the computer printed out three responses. Rachel glanced at Gabriel, then looked away. She had seen the city listed on each of the three—Denver. Tonight or tomorrow they would go there, and they would see Jenna no later than Wednesday. Two more days.

Gabriel thanked the detective and steered Rachel outside once more. "Do you want to fly or drive?"

"How far is it?"

"About eight hours."

"Let's drive." It would delay their arrival, delay their meeting with Jenna. "We should see your mother before we go."

He slipped his arm around her shoulders. "See how naturally that came out? It's not so hard thinking in terms of you and me, is it?"

"No, Gabriel," she said with a soft sigh. "Not hard at all."

They took Louise and David Warren out to dinner that evening, then returned to their small hotel. Rachel spent the night in Gabriel's arms, too despondent to make love but needing his closeness, drawing from his strength. She was going to need it to get through the next few days.

Tuesday morning they left for Denver. It was a long drive through beautiful country. It left them plenty of time to talk.

"We should be back in San Diego this weekend," Gabriel remarked, glancing at Rachel, who was quiet and still beside him.

She gave a soft sigh. "Technically, I should go back as soon as I'm sure it's the right Jenna White. My job was to find her, not stay while you meet with her."

"I want you to stay. This isn't a job anymore, Rachel. Forget that I'm your client and think of me as the man you love, who needs you at his side." He spoke in a playful voice to disguise the knotted nerves in his stomach. Her response could tell him everything he needed to know . . . or nothing at all.

"I never said that I loved you," she said in a flat voice.

Relief seeped through him. She *did* love him. Even though she hadn't admitted it, he'd been right. "Another technicality. You'll remedy that when the time is right."

"You are such an arrogant, conceited man, Gabriel. Sometimes I wonder how people stand your ego," she said with a scowl. She wasn't angry with him, but she was in a somber mood and didn't want to be teased out of it.

He grinned. "At least you didn't deny that you love me."

No, she hadn't. She couldn't lie to him like that.

"I'll have a week of vacation left. Can you take some time off and spend it with me?"

Her refusal was automatic. "I've been on the road for weeks now. I just want to go home."

"I wasn't thinking about going anywhere, except maybe to Los Angeles, so I could meet your family. We could spend the rest of the time at home, just the two of us."

She felt the tension that had turned the muscles in her neck into granite relax slightly. He was so certain that seeing Jenna again would mean nothing to him that he was willing to continue planning a future with *her*. She wished she shared his faith. "We'll see," she said, then changed the subject to the one she hated most of all. "The first time I see Jenna, I want to go alone. If you showed up out of thin air, it would probably shock the hell out of her."

He sighed deeply. "You can see her alone the first time and every time after. All I want to know about is Todd."

After a moment, she nodded. They needed to talk about Todd, to discuss Gabriel's plans for the boy, but now wasn't the right time. Then she frowned fiercely. In all the time that they'd been together, she had never found the "right" time. She dreaded hearing that Gabriel had decided to be a part of his son's life, dreaded finding out that he could be selfish enough to shatter Todd's world to satisfy his own need to be a father.

Soon, she promised herself. They would talk about it soon.

* * *

Leaving Gabriel at the hotel Wednesday morning, Rachel drove to the address listed on Jenna's driver's license. All the way over she rehearsed what she would say to the woman, but the words disappeared the instant the front door opened.

Todd White was tall for his age, handsome, slender, darkly tanned, with black hair and smiling dark eyes. There was a strong resemblance to the high school pictures Rachel had seen of Gabriel. Yes, she thought, somewhat dazed, he was definitely his father's son.

He waited impatiently for Rachel to speak, then said, "You want to see my mom?" Turning his head, he hollered, "Mom, you got company! I'm going over to Zeke's house, okay?" He stepped out, then gestured for Rachel to enter. "Go on in and close the door, or she'll yell about letting the cold air out."

"I don't yell, young man," a feminine voice scolded, then its owner appeared. Although she was twelve years older and twenty pounds heavier than in the photograph in Rachel's briefcase, Rachel would have recognized Jenna White anywhere.

"Well, you sure fuss a lot. What time do you want me back?"

"How about next month?" she responded with an affectionate grin. "Check in about four." She watched him leave, then turned to Rachel. "Can I help you?"

Rachel glanced at the diamond and gold wedding ring on the woman's left hand. She really should have checked the divorce records first, but she had been too anxious to get over here. "You're Jenna White?"

"Yes, I am."

Rachel moistened her lips with her tongue. "My name is Rachel Martinez. I'm a private investigator. Can I talk to you?"

Jenna's sharp blue eyes took in the expensive suit, the briefcase, the all-business expression Rachel had finally managed. She stepped back and let her enter, directing her to the family room at the back of the house, where she offered iced tea or lemonade. Rachel refused both.

"What is it you want to talk to me about?" she asked, settling into a comfortable chair.

Rachel chose the sofa, laying her briefcase beside her. She took a moment to look around the room, gathering the thoughts that seeing Todd had scattered. It was a big room, homey, comfortable, divided from the kitchen by a wide tiled counter. Pictures of Todd were everywhere, including a recent family portrait on the wall. "Mrs. White—"

"Please, call me Jenna."

She smiled faintly. "It's about your son, Todd."

The brief moment of friendliness disappeared behind a mother's protective shield. "What about my son? And how do you know his name?"

"I know a lot about him, and about you. Including the fact that Todd is not your husband's son."

The color drained from Jenna's face, leaving her a sickly gray. "How...? Who told...?"

Rachel laced her fingers together on her lap. "I'm working for Gabriel Rodriguez."

Jenna sank back in the chair, her shoulders slumped, her face turning from gray to white. "Wh-what does he want? It's been so long! What does he want with us now?"

"He wants to know about his son."

Jenna agitatedly shook her head. "No... No, Todd thinks Chuck is his father! You can't tell him it's not true! You can't bring in this man he's never seen and tell him, 'Sorry, Todd, but your parents lied to you all along. You don't take after your grandfather—you look like your real father.' You just can't do that!"

"Mrs. White... Jenna, I'm not suggesting that you tell Todd the truth. Gabriel wanted to know if he was a father, or if you'd had an abortion. If he had a child, he wanted to know whether it was a boy or a girl, if he was all right, if he needed anything."

"He doesn't!" Jenna cried. "He's got a father and a mother, and he doesn't need anyone else! You saw him yourself. Does he look like a kid who needs another father?" She jumped to her feet and paced the room, stopping in front of the family portrait. "Miss..."

"Martinez. Call me Rachel, if you'd like."

"I've been married to my husand for twenty years last month. It wasn't always the best marriage—we probably spent half of the first ten years fighting or separated. But I love Chuck, and these last years..." Her voice grew soft, and Rachel could see the hint of a smile touch her face. "For the first time in my life I'm truly happy. I love my husband, and he loves me, and we have a beautiful son. It doesn't matter to Chuck that Todd isn't *his* son. He couldn't love him any more if he were."

It was a familiar line that struck a painful chord in Rachel. How many times had her own mother told her that Ernesto loved her every bit as much as his own three children? How many times had she tried desperately to believe it?

Jenna turned, her expression suddenly hopeful. "You don't have to tell him where we are. You could tell him that you couldn't find us, convince him to give up looking. I'll pay you—"

Rachel gently interrupted. "He's in Denver with me now. He knows where you live."

Jenna seemed to collapse inside. Her steps heavy, she returned to the chair and sat down. "What does he want?"

"I don't know, exactly." She had been too afraid to ask, too afraid to say the time was "right." "I'd like to arrange a meeting between you. Talk to him. Tell him about Todd. Tell him how much your husband loves Todd, how much Todd loves his father." She made the suggestion hesitantly. It was cruel to ask the woman to deliberately hurt Gabriel, but, if he was considering claiming his son, it might get the message across that Todd didn't need him.

Jenna shook her head. "I don't want to see him," she whispered.

"One meeting. Is that so much to ask after what you did to him?"

She was still shaking her head. "God, I thought I'd never have to hear his name again!"

Rachel was startled by the vehemence in her voice. "I thought you were in love with him. You had agreed to marry him."

"Gabriel was a dream," she said softly, closing her eyes. "He was everything that Chuck wasn't at that time—kind, considerate, loving, easygoing...gentle." Opening her eyes, she looked sharply at Rachel. "I'm not saying that Chuck was a bad person—he wasn't. It was just a very rough period in our lives. I treated him poorly, and he treated me the same way. But Gabriel... I guess I did love him. He was so...perfect."

Rachel fought the desire to get up and walk out. No woman should be forced to listen to another woman talk this way about *her* lover. But loving Gabriel was personal, and this was business, so she remained where she was, her hands clenched into tight fists.

"I guess I loved what he *was*. I mean, here was this gorgeous man, the kind we've dreamed about since we were kids, you know? And he was absolutely the nicest man I've ever known. He respected me. He *liked* me. He treated me as if I had some purpose in life outside the bedroom and the kitchen."

"Why did you leave him?" Rachel heard the tremor in her voice and winced. "You were carrying his baby, and you had agreed to marry him. Why did you leave that way?"

Jenna twisted her wedding ring in slow circles for a long time before looking up. "I wasn't sure that the baby was his," she admitted. "You see...I had called Chuck one day, to talk, to see if we could salvage anything from our marriage. He wanted to see me, and I agreed to meet him in Phoenix. I spent the weekend with him, then went back to San Diego. Six weeks later I found out I was pregnant. I had been with both Chuck and Gabriel."

"Gabriel assumed that the baby was his."

Jenna nodded. "He was a great believer in fidelity. He never guessed that I'd been unfaithful to him with Chuck, or to Chuck with him. He didn't even know I was married. So, you see, I couldn't marry him—I already had a husband. Since I knew that the chances were good that the baby was Chuck's, and since I did still love him, I went back to him. I told him all about Gabriel, told him that I was pregnant, and he wanted me anyway. Our marriage has been stronger and happier ever since then."

"Will you see him?"

Jenna shook her head. "I can't."

"When I leave here, I'm going to meet Gabriel at the hotel. I'll tell him everything that you've told me, but it won't be enough to satisfy him. He's waited twelve years and spent a fortune to find out about his child. If you refuse to talk to him, he might come here to see for himself." She hated making threats, hated turning this woman's life upside down, but she said what she had to say. "You can lie to Todd, Jenna. You can lie to everyone. But you know your son, and you know Gabriel. Anyone who sees the two of them together is going to know that Chuck isn't Todd's father." She paused to let that sink in, then asked again, "Will you see him?"

Jenna's nod came slowly, her agreement grudging. "When?"

"This afternoon?"

Again she nodded. "Where?"

Rachel gave her the name of the hotel where they were staying. "Is the restaurant all right?"

Jenna nodded a third time. "In two hours. That will give me time to make arrangements for Zeke's mother to keep an eye on Todd and to..."

And to get ready to face her former lover, the father of her son, Rachel silently finished. She thanked Jenna, said goodbye and drove back to the hotel.

Gabriel was lying on the bed, the television switched to a cable movie channel. As soon as Rachel walked in, he turned it off with the remote control and got to his feet. "Well?"

"She's meeting you in the restaurant at one-thirty." She shrugged out of her jacket, draping it over the back of the closest chair.

"Did you see him?"

She was still for so long that finally he laid his hands on her shoulders and turned her to face him. Her eyes were closed, her lips compressed in a white line. "Rachel, honey?"

She exhaled, then breathed in deeply. "Yes, I saw him. He's handsome, happy and healthy."

He waited, and at last she finished, saying the thing that he wanted to hear. "And he looks very much like you."

Gabriel pulled her into his embrace, pulling the pins from her hair when he stroked through it. The search was finally over, and he had a handsome, happy, healthy son. He should be elated. He now knew what he had set out to learn so many weeks ago. But there was only a vague dissatisfaction, edged with jealousy that Rachel had seen his son, while he had been denied that privilege. "What did you think of Jenna?"

"My visit upset her very badly. She loves her son and her husband, and she's afraid of what you're going to do." She leaned back against his arms so she could see his face. "I all but promised her that you wouldn't do *anything*. I told her that you only wanted to know about him—nothing else." Her dark eyes were troubled, anxious, as she studied him. "Gabriel, that's true, isn't it? You're not going to do anything else, are you?"

He released her and walked to the window. There he stared out over the city and gave his standard answer. "I don't know."

"When are you going to decide?" she demanded. "We're here, Gabriel. We've found them. In less than two hours you're going to see Jenna again. Just when do you intend to make up your mind about it?"

"I don't know!" Was he going to accept that he had a happy, healthy eleven-year-old son who looked like him, then forget him? Or was he going to insist on his parental rights, on seeing his son for himself, talking to him, being with him, loving him?

He didn't know. He had put off making this decision, half believing that the time would never come when it would be necessary. Then, when he had realized that it *would* be necessary, that Rachel would find Jenna, he had still avoided it. Torn between what was right and what he wanted, he couldn't choose anything at all.

He turned around to face Rachel again, his arms folded across his chest. "What else did you discuss?" he asked grimly.

Sighing softly, she told him everything.

Chapter 11

Jenna was a few minutes early for their meeting. Rachel saw her walking across the dining room and slowly withdrew her hand from Gabriel's. He knew, without turning, the reason. She stopped beside their table, both hands clutched around the flat purse she carried, and spoke softly, "Hello, Gabriel."

"Jenna." His voice was blank, empty of emotion. He might have been greeting an old acquaintance instead of a former lover. "Sit down, please."

She pulled out the empty chair and sat primly, ankles crossed, hands folded in her lap. "Miss..." She forgot the last name again. "Rachel said I should talk to you."

"I appreciate it."

Rachel scooted her chair back and stood up. "I'll leave you alone—"

"No." Both Gabriel and Jenna spoke at the same time. His voice was commanding, hers pleading. Mutely Rachel sat down again.

They were all silent for several minutes, Jenna staring at her hands, Rachel choosing the view out the window, Gabriel watching Rachel. Finally Jenna broke the silence in a painfully awkward voice. "I thought you just worked for him, but you're friends."

"We're getting married soon," Gabriel replied, his dark eyes daring Rachel to argue.

"Oh. Congratulations."

When the uncomfortable quiet settled again, Rachel leaned forward. "This is ridiculous. You want to know about Todd," she said to Gabriel, then to Jenna, "And you can tell him. You'll both be more comfortable if I'm not here. Why don't you talk, and I'll wait in the lobby?"

Jenna started to protest, but Gabriel overruled her. "Thank you, Rachel." He stood up when she did, kissing her cheek before she walked away.

She found an empty sofa in the lobby beneath a painting of the Colorado mountains and sank weakly onto it.

Gabriel didn't love Jenna. A few days ago she had made the decision to believe him, but there had been that small insecure part inside her that hadn't been convinced. Now it was. He had shown little interest in her beyond the fact that she was his key to his son.

For a moment Rachel let the warmth of that knowledge seep through her. For so many years she had dreamed of his love, and now she had it. But Jenna wasn't the last hurdle. Gabriel's decision regarding Todd was the final obstacle. She suspected that he wanted to meet the boy, wanted to let the whole world know that Todd White was *his* son. That was why he was being so evasive, why his answer to questions about Todd was repeatedly, "I don't know." If he forced his way into Todd's life that way, her newly born faith in him would be sorely shaken. She wasn't certain that she could handle such a disappointment.

Maybe she wouldn't have to find out. Maybe this conversation with Jenna would satisfy his curiosity. Maybe he would be willing to let the children that *they* would have together satisfy his longing to be a father. Closing her eyes, she whispered a soundless prayer to that effect.

* * *

It was nearly two hours later when Gabriel and Jenna joined Rachel in the lobby. She looked from one to the other, her curious eyes seeking answers. Jenna looked weary, emotionally drained. Gabriel simply looked grim.

"Rachel." Jenna offered her hand, and Rachel stood up, taking it. "I wish I could say I enjoyed meeting you, but..."

"I know."

Jenna turned to Gabriel then. "I'm sorry," she said simply.

He didn't say a word. After a moment, she shrugged and turned to go. Gabriel stopped her with his quiet words. "I want to meet him."

Jenna whirled around, her purse sliding from nerveless fingers. "No!"

Her heart breaking, Rachel turned and walked away, heading toward the elevators. Gabriel watched her go, but made no move to stop her. "I know where you live. If you don't introduce me to him, I'll do it myself." His stance was aggressive, his eyes hard, his manner implacable. "He's my son, Jenna. I have a right to know him."

"He doesn't know you exist!"

"He will. Either you'll tell him, or I will. I want to meet him, Jenna. Tomorrow."

She blinked at the tears that were stinging her eyes. "Surely you don't expect me to tell him who you are!"

"Do you think I want to pretend to be somebody else, while your husband pretends to be his father?" he countered in an ugly, low voice.

"I could take him tonight and run so far that you would never find us!"

"You tried that before, and here I am." Suddenly his temper flared, and he let it. "Damn it, Jenna, he's *my son*! You've already cheated me out of eleven years of his life! You're not going to make me miss the rest of it!"

She picked up her purse and pulled a tissue from it. "Rachel said you only wanted to know about him," she whispered in an anguished tone. "She said—"

"She didn't know. It isn't her fault." He tilted his head back and stared at the ceiling thirty feet above them. "I didn't know myself until just now. Where can we meet?"

"We can't—"

"When we came in last night, we passed a park about six blocks from here. Do you know where it is?"

She nodded tearfully.

"Meet me there tomorrow at ten o'clock. Bring him with you."

"Gabriel, please—"

"If you don't, Jenna, I'll come to you. I'll find you, and I'll make damn sure he knows everything."

She stared at him, her blue eyes dark with an emotion that he was certain was hatred. "I hope you burn in hell, Gabriel," she whispered.

He smiled mockingly. "It won't be the first time. Tomorrow morning. Ten o'clock."

She nodded once, then left.

Gabriel took the elevator to their floor, then knocked at the room. When there was no answer, he fished the key from his pocket and let himself in. Rachel was sitting in one of the armchairs, her hands folded. She had changed from the rose-colored suit into white shorts and a fire-engine red top. Her hair was held back by a red and white striped clip; her socks were red, and her tennis shoes were white. Such a bright, cheery outfit, and such a grim, forbidding expression.

He knew that she was disappointed in him, and probably mad as hell, too. He closed the door behind him, dropping his key on the dresser as he passed. He sat down on the bed, stretched his legs out, folded his hands behind his head and said flatly, "Let's get it over with."

She nodded once in agreement. "You told me in the office that day that you just wanted to know that he was all right. You said you wouldn't try to play father to him unless he needed a father." She heard the faint accusing tone in her voice and knew from his defensive expression that he

did, too. "Don't change your mind, Gabriel. He *has* a father in Chuck. He doesn't need you."

"Chuck White *isn't* his father," he said flatly.

"Providing the sperm that creates the child doesn't make
a father. Being there when he needs you, holding him,
teaching him, giving him help and advice and love—that's
a father." They were lovely sentiments that had sounded so
wonderful when her mother had told them to her, so wonderful...and so hollow. She had never quite been able to
believe them. She prayed that Todd White wouldn't be faced
with them, too.

"I wanted to do all those things," he snapped. "It's Jenna's fault that I didn't get to, not mine." His eyes turned
dark, and his jaw set in a stubborn line. "What's wrong,
Rachel? Does the idea of playing stepmother to my son disturb you that much?"

She shook her head. "No, it doesn't disturb me at all.
What disturbs me is that you could be so insensitive."

"Insensitive because I want to accept some of the responsibility for my son?" he asked in disbelief. "There are
thousands of men in this country who have to be threatened with jail before they'll take care of their kids, and you
call me insensitive?"

She knew he had a right to be confused and angry. He had
expected her support, and now he wasn't getting it. The only
way she could make him understand was by telling him her
last secret. If she could make him feel her pain, her sorrow,
her disillusion, maybe he would recognize the harm he could
cause his son.

"When I was twelve years old, Gabriel, a year older than
Todd, a man came to our house to see me. His name was
Hector Laremos. I'd never seen him before, never heard of
him, but I should have. You see, he was my father."

She paused for a moment, her eyes closed, remembering
the pleasure Laremos had taken in telling her the truth, in
breaking her heart. After a moment, she looked at Gabriel
and continued, her voice unsteady. "He had told my mother
he loved her, had promised her marriage and forever, but

when she found out she was pregnant, he disappeared. She married Ernesto Martinez a few months before I was born."

She felt pain in her palms and looked down, seeing that her hands were clenched into fists, her nails biting into the tender flesh. She forced them to unfold and laid them flat on her thighs. "Ernesto was a wonderful father. He loved me as much as he loved his own children, and I loved him, too, as if I were his own child. Then Hector came."

She stood up, paced across the room and back again. Gabriel was motionless, watching, waiting. He knew that the tale was difficult for her, knew that remembering was painful, but he didn't offer her support. He waited, and listened.

"He didn't want to be my father—he just wanted me to know who he was, to know that I was a Laremos, not a Martinez. To gratify his male ego at seeing the child he had produced, he destroyed my image of my family. I no longer belonged, because I was a Laremos. Do you have any idea what it did to a twelve-year-old child to learn that her mother had lied to her all her life, that the man she loved dearly as father wasn't her father, and that this total stranger she despised *was*? It's been twenty-one years, Gabriel, but it still hurts. I have never been able to fully accept myself as a member of the Martinez family. I have never been able to love Ernesto the way I did before, and I will *never* forgive Hector Laremos for doing that to me. I will hate him until the day I die."

The silence echoed in the room. Rachel was watching Gabriel, but he couldn't bring himself to meet her gaze. Her message was clear: by insisting on meeting his son, he could cause the same anguish, the same heartache, in Todd. "But it's not the same," he murmured.

"It *is* the same."

"Your father didn't want you! I *do* want Todd!"

"Are you going to quit your job and move to Denver?"

"I—" The idea had obviously never even occurred to him.

"What kind of father can you be eleven hundred miles away? How often would you be able to see him? Once a year? Twice? Maybe three times, if you're lucky? Do you think you're such a wonderful man that he'll think seeing you a few times a year is worth the destruction of his family?" She gave a shake of her head. "You are an incredibly arrogant bastard, Gabriel."

She had called him arrogant many times before, but he'd never felt the sting in it until now. It sliced through him like a hot knife. *"He's my son!"*

She shook her head again. "He doesn't know you from the man in the moon. You mean nothing to him."

"You haven't even tried to understand the way I feel," he angrily accused.

"No. But I understand the way Todd will feel, because I've been in his place. I've lived through it, but not without scars that, to this day, are still tender and raw." She sat down in the chair again. "If you go to that boy and tell him that Jenna has lied to him, that Chuck has lied, that you're his real father . . . he'll hate you, Gabriel. I promise, he will hate you."

He numbly shook his head. "You're wrong, Rachel. I'm going to meet him tomorrow, and you'll see how wrong you are."

"I wish I were. I wish I didn't have the experience to know." Leaning forward, she took his hands in hers. They were cold, limp. "I love you, Gabriel. I don't want to hurt you. But meeting Todd is only going to bring you, that boy and everyone else sorrow."

"How convenient," he said sarcastically, "that, when you want something from me, you suddenly love me."

She sat back, folding her arms over her chest. "That's not fair. You've known for a long time that I love you."

He rubbed his eyes wearily. "You're right. I'm sorry. I need your support in this, Rachel. Please."

Her response was a slow shake of her head. "I can't give it."

"You don't understand. He's my son."

"Are you so selfish that you'll claim him at the cost of everyone he loves? Will you destroy his happiness, his security, his innocence and faith and trust, just to show the world that you have a son?"

"You're wrong," he said flatly, stubbornly. "That won't happen."

"I hope not," she whispered. "Dear God, I hope not."

The sky was dark, the city lights twinkling, when Rachel closed the drapes, then turned on a bedside lamp. Her head ached, and the muscles in her neck were taut. She and Gabriel had passed the last four hours together in this room without speaking or touching or even looking at each other.

The "final obstacle" she had been expecting was a major one. The coldness was growing between them, fueled by his anger at her failure to support him and her sorrow at his failure to understand her fears. If he followed through on his demands to meet Todd, she was afraid that she would lose him. Selfishly hurting a child that he claimed to care about was something that she wouldn't be able to forgive.

Stifling a longing sigh, she went to the closet and took out her suitcase. She had unpacked only a few things the night before. Now she removed a set of clothing for the next day and repacked everything else. She separated the few things that belonged to Gabriel, items that had gotten shoved into her bag when they'd left Albuquerque, and left them on the dresser, then zipped the suitcase.

Gabriel turned to watch her. "What are you doing?" His voice sounded harsh and unforgiving in the emptiness between them.

"I'm going home in the morning."

"You won't even wait until I'm finished?"

She shook her head.

"Are you going to take next week off?"

Again she shook her head.

"I thought we were going to L.A., so I could meet your family."

She smiled the saddest smile he had ever seen. "There's no need for you to meet my family."

He jammed his hands into the pockets of his jeans. "I suppose the marriage is off, too." His voice trembled with the emotion he was trying so hard to hide.

She came across the room to him, reaching for his hands. "You never asked me, remember? And I never accepted. We were waiting for the right time."

"So...marry me, Rachel. I love you, and I want to spend the rest of my life with you."

Slowly she shook her head. "I don't think the time is ever going to be right, Gabriel."

With a surge of temper, he flung her hands away. "I don't like being threatened, Rachel."

"I'm not threatening you."

"You're saying that if I meet Todd tomorrow, you won't marry me. If that's not a threat, would you kindly explain what the hell it *is*?"

She locked her fingers together in front of her. "The story I told you about my father...it's affected every day of my life. And I can't spend the rest of my life with a man who would do the same thing to his child."

"You're so sure that he'll hate me," he whispered, raising his hand to her hair. "There's a chance—"

She shook her head. "It's not worth the risk to an innocent child to find out." She raised her hand to wipe a tear from the corner of her eye, then rose onto her toes to kiss first one cheek, then the other. "Do what you feel is right, Gabriel, but be prepared to accept the consequences, and the blame, and the sorrow."

And be prepared, he added silently, to live without Rachel. He could have his son, or he could have her, but not both. It was a hell of a choice. "When I get back to San Diego," he began softly, "can I see you?"

There was that sad smile again. "You can see me. I just can't promise that there will be any future in it." She slipped her arms around him, pressing her face to his chest. "I don't want to threaten or blackmail you, Gabriel, but I don't want to give you false encouragement, either. We'll just have to try it and see, all right?''

When he had murmured an appropriate response, she hugged him tighter. ''Now, Gabriel Rodriguez, I'm going to seduce you. What do you think of that?''

''Ask me when you're finished and I'll tell you.''

She kissed and stroked him, undressed and caressed him. He let her touch him intimately, teasingly, torturingly; then he took control and did the same things to her, making her breath catch, her heart race, her body throb. When she was shuddering, pleading, when every ragged breath he took was agony, he found his place, cradled deep within her, and settled into a pulsating, sensuous rhythm that made her cry out, that made her writhe with need, that wrenched a helpless groan from deep in his chest. And when the sensations that spiraled through them, passing from her into him and back again, were too strong to withstand, he filled her and felt her shattering response. Even then, his heart pounding, his blood rushing, his body slick and heavy and still joined with hers, he knew that this might be the last time he could hold her like this, the last time he could love her like this. How would he survive it? he wondered bleakly, then found a better question. *Would* he survive it?

Gabriel leaned against the dresser, his arms folded across his chest—to stop from reaching for Rachel. To stop the pain that filled his chest from escaping and consuming him. He watched her add the final items to the small leather tote bag—shampoo, toothbrush and toothpaste, a brush—and saw her zip it.

''Don't go, Rachel.''

''I have to.'' She hesitated only a moment. ''Come with me.''

''I can't.'' He wished that she could understand what it meant to have a child, a part of himself, that he had dreamed and imagined and wondered about for twelve years. He wasn't like Hector Laremos. He loved his son the way a father should love. "I'll be home tomorrow or the next day."

She nodded. "What time are you meeting them?"

"Ten." A glance at his watch showed that it was nine-thirty. "If you'll wait—"

"No," she said rapidly. "Do you want to keep the car? I can take a cab...."

"No, you take it." He didn't have far to go. He looked at her, away, then back again. "I can be a good father, Rachel."

"Do you want to be a good father to your son, Gabriel?" she asked, her voice soft and pleading. "Stay out of his life. Let him be happy. Prove that you love him by letting him go."

He shook his head. "I can't do that."

"Then I'd better go." She left her bags at the door, then came back, cupping his face in her hands. "I love you, Gabriel. I wish you well." She kissed him, hard, hungrily, then walked away. Out of the room, and out of his life.

There was no sign of Jenna when he reached the park. He took a seat at a concrete picnic table, checked his watch and waited. He wasn't nervous about this meeting. He was too numb inside to feel anything at all, just a curious tightening in his chest, as if his heart were threatening to explode into a million pieces.

How long had it been since he had cried? He tried to remember, but couldn't. He had been a child—a lifetime ago. But that was exactly what he felt like doing now, because Rachel was gone.

He couldn't believe that he had let her go. Damn it, he should have stopped her, should have made her stay, should have made her understand....

He should have gone with her.

He had promised her things—love, happiness, no hurt, forever. He hadn't put restrictions on them, hadn't promised to love her as long as his son remained lost, hadn't promised not to hurt her unless, of course, he chose to.

She was his life, his love, his future, and Todd . . . Todd was his past. Jenna had tried to tell him, and Rachel had confirmed it—Todd didn't need him. He had a father, a man he loved and respected. But Rachel did need him, and he needed her—her love, her respect. As long as there was breath in his body, he would need her.

He checked his watch. She'd been gone half an hour. She was at the airport by now, booking a flight back to San Diego. She hadn't called for reservations from the hotel, hadn't been able to bring herself to do it—in the hopes that he would change his mind and go with her, he was sure. If he left now . . .

Hearing the slam of a car door, he automatically looked up. In the parking lot, not more than twenty yards from him, was Jenna. He looked from her to the other side of the car, where Todd stood.

Handsome, happy and healthy. Rachel's description certainly seemed to fit. He looked a great deal like Gabriel had at that age. He was thin and lanky . . . and young. In all his arguments with Rachel and Jenna, Gabriel had never realized just how young eleven years was. He was a child, an innocent, impressionable child. A shock like the one Gabriel was prepared to unleash on him could affect the rest of his life.

Jenna spoke to Todd, then started across the grass. Switching his bleak gaze from the boy to the mother, Gabriel shook his head, stopping her in her tracks. He stood up, took one last look at his son—at Chuck's son—turned and walked away.

It was a long trip to the airport, and once he got there, Gabriel found no sign of Rachel. He had her paged, but there was no response. Finally, with the help of his badge and a considerable amount of charm, he was able to learn that she had left for San Diego, via Los Angeles, twenty minutes before he'd arrived.

"When is the next flight?" he asked the agent who had sold Rachel her ticket.

"It leaves in two hours." Impressed by the urgency in his manner, the woman glanced at her co-worker, then lowered her voice and added, "If you want to check at the airline on the end, they have a nonstop to San Diego leaving in about ten minutes. Because of her layover in Los Angeles, you should arrive half an hour before her."

Thanking her, he went to the airline she'd recommended and purchased a ticket for the next flight. It was ten minutes until takeoff, then two and a half hours flight time. That gave him less than three hours to find a way to salvage the rest of his life.

Rachel stared out the window of the plane but saw nothing. She shouldn't have left Denver this way. If things between Gabriel and Todd went as badly as she feared they would, he would need someone—no, she corrected fiercely. He would need *her*. But she wouldn't be there, because she had run away again.

She loved him. She owed him her support.

But how could she support what he had intended to do, after living through it herself?

She closed her eyes, tilting her head back. She had been arguing with herself since leaving Denver. Now, after a forty-five minute layover at Los Angeles International, she was on the final leg of her very long journey. And what had she accomplished?

She had successfully completed a job that she had once thought impossible. She had let go of her guilt and anger and sorrow over Jack's death and Gabriel's betrayal. She had learned to love Gabriel all over again—if, indeed, she had ever stopped loving him. She had allowed herself to hope and dream of a future...and she had lost it. That overshadowed all the good things.

God, how was she going to live alone again after these weeks with Gabriel? How was she going to cope with loving him again, with losing him again? She was pretending to be strong and capable on the outside, but inside she was falling apart.

Maybe he had been right about Todd. Maybe the boy had accepted the news better than she and Jenna had expected. Maybe he didn't mind knowing that his parents had lied to him. He was a kid—kids were resilient; they bounced back from surprises. Maybe he even liked knowing that this tall, dark, Indian police officer from California was his father.

She wished she could believe it... but she couldn't. *She* hadn't been resilient. *She* hadn't bounced back.

The pilot's welcome-to-San-Diego-and-thank-you-for-flying-with-us speech sounded over the intercom. Rachel focused her gaze outside as they came in over the eastern portion of the city. Soon they were descending at a steep angle over the interstate; then, an instant later, the plane touched down.

She reached beneath the seat for her briefcase, then joined the slow line of passengers that moved through the plane and into the jetway. She would go straight to the office, she decided. There was the final paperwork to do on the case—the concluding report, the expense reports. And if that didn't take long enough, there was sure to be some mail to answer, some errands to run, someone who needed a hand with their own work. She would work until she was tired; then she would go home and work there, too, until her mind was too exhausted to even think Gabriel's name. And if she kept it up long enough, she would either get over him or collapse from physical and mental fatigue.

She cleared the jetway and entered the terminal, carefully ignoring the emotional welcomes many of the other passengers were receiving. She was alone. She had lived alone for many years, and she would be alone a great many more. She could accept that—it would just take time.

She walked past the tall, slender man in jeans leaning against the wall, not noticing when he fell into step beside her.

"Need a ride?"

She stopped so suddenly that the young woman behind her plowed right into her, dropping her bag. Rachel didn't hear her muttered complaint, didn't apologize or offer to help pick up her belongings. She just stood absolutely motionless, staring up at Gabriel, who was smiling his angel's smile, as if he had appeared out of her dreams, conjured up by need. By love.

He waited a long moment for her to say something. When she didn't, he spoke. "I take it you're surprised speechless at seeing me here."

"How did you get here?" Her voice was little more than a croak, but her heart was singing. He was here! He had come back, had left his son in Denver and come back to her!

"You took the first flight to San Diego that you found. *I* found a nonstop." He didn't know what to do with his hands to stop them from reaching for her, so he slid them into the hip pockets of his jeans. "I think this is the place where you say, 'I'm glad to see you, Gabriel.' Or, if that sounds too formal, you could start with, 'I love you.'"

Still staring wide-eyed, she ignored his suggestions. "What about Todd?"

He breathed deeply. "Todd is handsome, happy and healthy, and he has a father, and he doesn't need me. You were right, Rachel. I was willing to destroy his family, his illusions, his innocence, all for the sake of my ego. It would have been a disaster, for him and his parents, for me, and for you."

"Did you see him?"

He nodded. "At a distance. I didn't meet him, didn't talk to him. Everything you said was right. Rachel..." He shifted uncomfortably from one foot to the other. Nearly three hours of thinking and planning hadn't given him the right words to repair the damage he'd done, but he was going to try. "I know I make a lot of mistakes, and I do some pretty stupid things. I'm conceited and impulsive and hot-tempered and—"

"Don't forget arrogant," she said with a tiny smile.

"And arrogant," he added ruefully. "I make promises that I always seem to break, and I end up hurting you even though it's the last thing in the world I want, and—"

She laid her fingers over his lips. "Remember when you took me to Christopher and Shelley's house, and I told you that he didn't like me?" At his nod, she continued. "You said that, as a rule, telling someone that I used to be nuts wasn't the best way to make him like me."

He nodded again.

"Well, sweetheart, as a rule, telling a woman all your faults isn't the best way to get her to marry you."

He kissed her fingers, then pushed them away from his mouth. "Who said I was going to ask you to marry me?" he asked indignantly. "Maybe I just wanted you to know that I might not be quite as perfect as I appear to be."

"Oh." Wisely she hid the smile that tried to escape. "What happened this morning with Jenna and Todd?"

"When I got to the park where I was supposed to meet them, all I could think about was that you'd left...and I had let you. I let you walk out of my life once before—"

"You threw me out," she corrected.

He scowled at her. "I'm trying to be honest and open about my feelings here, so would you kindly shut up and let me grovel?"

She tried to look properly chastened, but the corners of her lips twitched with a smile anyway.

He laid his hand against her hair, soft and silky, so lightly that she barely felt it. "I lost you once before, Rachel, and it took five years and a lot of heartache to get you back. I'm not going to let that happen again. I don't think I could survive it again."

"What about Jenna?"

He gestured impatiently. "Jenna means nothing to me."

"What about your son?"

"He's Chuck's son, not mine. The only way I'm going to have a son, sweetheart, is if you quit talking, agree to marry me, go home with me and start working on it."

"You haven't asked me yet," she reminded him.

He guided her to the side of the corridor and pulled her close. His hand brushed gently across her cheek, her mouth, and settled on her jaw. "I love you, Rachel. I want to spend the rest of my life with you. I want to have beautiful babies with you. I want to grow old beside you. Will you marry me?"

She wrapped her arms around his neck, seeking his mouth with hers. "I love you, Gabriel," she murmured between kisses, "and I would love to marry you."

What else could she say? It was the right man, the right question, and, after a lifetime of waiting, it was the right time.

*   *   *   *   *

NORA ROBERTS
brings you the first
Award of Excellence title
Gabriel's Angel
coming in August from
Silhouette Intimate Moments

They were on a collision course with love....

Laura Malone was alone, scared—and pregnant. She was running for the sake of her child. Gabriel Bradley had his own problems. He had neither the need nor the inclination to get involved in someone else's.

But Laura was like no other woman... and she needed him. Soon Gabe was willing to risk all for the heaven of her arms.

The Award of Excellence is given to one specially selected title per month. Look for the second Award of Excellence title, coming out in September from Silhouette Romance—**SUTTON'S WAY by Diana Palmer**

Im 300-1

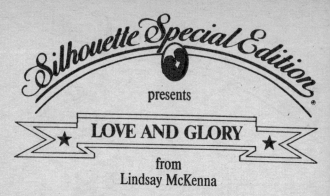

Silhouette Special Edition

presents

★ LOVE AND GLORY ★

from
Lindsay McKenna

Introducing a gripping new series celebrating our men—and women—in uniform. Meet the Trayherns, a military family as proud and colorful as the American flag, a family fighting the shadow of dishonor, a family determined to triumph—with **LOVE AND GLORY!**

June: **A QUESTION OF HONOR** (SE #529) leads the fast-paced excitement. When Coast Guard officer Noah Trayhern offers Kit Anderson a safe house, he unwittingly endangers his own guarded emotions.

July: **NO SURRENDER** (SE #535) Navy pilot Alyssa Trayhern's assignment with arrogant jet jockey Clay Cantrell threatens her career—and her heart—with a crash landing!

August: **RETURN OF A HERO** (SE #541) Strike up the band to welcome home a man whose top-secret reappearance will make headline news . . . with a delicate, daring woman by his side.

Coming in July from

Silhouette Desire®

ODD MAN OUT #505
by Lass Small

Roberta Lambert is too busy with her job to notice that her new apartment-mate is a strong, desirable man. But Graham Rawlins has ways of getting her undivided attention....

Roberta is one of five fascinating Lambert sisters. She is as enticing as each one of her three sisters, whose stories you have already enjoyed or will want to read:

- Hillary in GOLDILOCKS AND THE BEHR (Desire #437)
- Tate in HIDE AND SEEK (Desire #453)
- Georgina in RED ROVER (Desire #491)

Watch for Book IV of Lass Small's terrific miniseries and read Fredricka's story in TAGGED (Desire #528) coming in October.

You'll flip . . . your pages won't!
Read paperbacks *hands-free* with

Book Mate · I

The perfect "mate" for all your romance paperbacks

Traveling • Vacationing • At Work • In Bed • Studying • Cooking • Eating

Perfect size for all standard paperbacks, this wonderful invention makes reading a pure pleasure! Ingenious design holds paperback books OPEN and FLAT so even wind can't ruffle pages— leaves your hands free to do other things. Reinforced, wipe-clean vinyl-covered holder flexes to let you turn pages without undoing the strap . . . supports paperbacks so well, they have the strength of hardcovers!

Pages turn WITHOUT opening the strap

SEE-THROUGH STRAP

Reinforced back stays flat

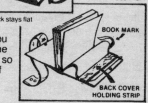

Built in bookmark

BOOK MARK

BACK COVER HOLDING STRIP

10 x 7'₄ opened
Snaps closed for easy carrying, too

Silhouette Desire®

1989
IS THE YEAR
OF THE MAN!

What makes a romance? A special man, of course, and Silhouette Desire celebrates that fact with *twelve* of them! From Mr. January to Mr. December, every month has a tribute to the Silhouette Desire hero—our **MAN OF THE MONTH!**

Sexy, macho, charming, irritating . . . irresistible! Nothing can stop these men from sweeping you away. Created by some of your favorite authors, each man is custom-made for pleasure—*reading* pleasure—so don't miss a single one.

Mr. July is Graham Rawlins in ODD MAN OUT by Lass Small
Mr. August is Jeremy Kincaid in MOUNTAIN MAN by Joyce Thies
Mr. September is Clement Cornelius Barto in BEGINNER'S LUCK by Dixie Browning
Mr. October is James Branigan in BRANIGAN'S TOUCH by Leslie Davis Guccione
Mr. November is Shiloh Butler in SHILOH'S PROMISE by BJ James
Mr. December is Tad Jackson in WILDERNESS CHILD by Ann Major

So get out there and find your man!

Silhouette Desire's

MAN OF THE MONTH . . .

MOM-1R